Praise for
Black Widow's Wardrobe

and for Lucha Corpi's
Gloria Damasco Mysteries

"Eighteen years ago, Licia Román Lecuona went to prison for killing her husband . . . Now that she's served her time, though, the woman called Black Widow seems to be more victim than aggressor— or at least that's how it seems to Oakland shamus Gloria Damasco . . . Gloria's third [adventure] is part mystery, part history, part travelogue, part spiritual speculation—a busy, many-layered invention stuffed within an inch of its many lives."

—*Kirkus Reviews*

"Dark family secrets emerge and passionate sexual intrigues abound as the story builds with a complexity worthy of a Ross MacDonald novel. Woven through the narrative is the grim legacy of pesticide poisoning suffered by farmworkers in the [California] Central Valley . . . A shattering conclusion, complete with the requisite gunplay, leaves the reader eager for the next episode of this excellent homage to detective fiction."

—*San Francisco Chronicle-Examiner Book Review*
on *Cactus Blood*

(please turn the page for more rave reviews)

"Gloria Damasco made her first appearance in Corpi's *Eulogy for a Brown Angel,* a mystery enshrouded in the Mexican-American communities of California . . . A tense plot laced with believable characters and historical facts." —Copley News Service

"Corpi weaves haunting dreams with real-life nightmares to create a compelling vision." —Linda Grant, author of *Blind Trust* and other Catherine Sayler mysteries

"The second installment of a detective-mystery series featuring Gloria Damasco . . . *[Cactus Blood]* is dark and mysterious, with old Indian haunts and visions of blood and death . . . Hard to put down . . . An excellent mystery." —*The El Paso Herald-Post*

"Gloria Damasco is one of the most original characters in today's mystery fiction. She's tough, vulnerable, smart, and possessed of distinctive skills, not the least of which is her spiritual ability to *see*." —Manuel Ramos, author of *Blues for the Buffalo* and other Luis Montez mysteries

"Corpi writes excellently." —*Hispanic* magazine

DEATH AT SOLSTICE

A Gloria Damasco Mystery

Books by Lucha Corpi

Crimson Moon: A Brown Angel Mystery

Palabras de mediodía / Noon Words

Featuring Gloria Damasco

Black Widow's Wardrobe

Cactus Blood

Death at Solstice

Eulogy for a Brown Angel

DEATH AT SOLSTICE

A Gloria Damasco Mystery

LUCHA CORPI

Arte Público Press
Houston, Texas

Death at Solstice is made possible through grants from the City of Houston through the Houston Arts Alliance and the Exemplar Program, a program of Americans for the Arts in collaboration with the LarsonAllen Public Services Group, funded by the Ford Foundation.

Recovering the past, creating the future

Arte Público Press
University of Houston
452 Cullen Performance Hall
Houston, Texas 77204-2004

Cover design by Pilar Espino

Corpi, Lucha, 1945-
    Death at solstice : a Gloria Damasco mystery / by Lucha Corpi.
    p.   cm.
    ISBN 978-1-55885-547-2 (pbk. : alk. paper)
    1. Mexican American women—Fiction. 2. Women private investigators—Fiction. 3. Extrasensory perception—Fiction. 4. California—Fiction. I. Title.
    PS3553.O693D37 2009
    813'.54—dc22
                                  2009036687
                                          CIP

∞ The paper used in this publication meets the requirements of the American National Standard for Information Sciences—Permanence of Paper for Printed Library Materials, ANSI Z39.48-1984.

9 0 1 2 3 4 5 6 7 8   10 9 8 7 6 5 4 3 2 1

AUTHOR'S NOTE

This novel is a work of fiction and it is not intended to reflect negatively on the reputation of any of the civil or religious institutions herewith mentioned.

PREMONITORY PREDISPOSITIONS

Neon light spilled from the kitchen into the hall. Sylvia Salvatierra and I hid in the office at the end of the hall. I took a place by the door. She crouched next to the desk behind me and called 911. Between short breaths, she blurted out her address. Her ex-husband was in the house. She had a restraining order against him. She pressed the "Off" button but kept the receiver in her hand.

Her rapid breathing made mine want to keep rhythm with hers. Soon I was hyperventilating. The buzz in my ears deafened every other sound. I gulped air and held it, then swallowed hard a few times. My ears popped just as I saw the shadow on the wall. I pointed my gun to the left of it and waited for Carl Salvatierra to come into my line of vision. A door creaked as it opened—the bathroom door since it was next to the kitchen. I signaled for Sylvia to be quiet. She crawled deeper under the desk.

Carl's shadow loomed just outside the office door. I could hear his intense breathing and the soft clearing of his throat. I saw his gun first as he stepped into the room. Fear traveled up my spine to the back of my neck. I held my breath in. If he heard me, turned, and we both fired on sight, one or both of us would end up on a slab at the morgue.

A creaking noise made Carl glimpse the area around the desk. He stood in place, his head cocked in that direction. A couple of feet behind him, I still had the element of surprise. I blew air out of my mouth with every quick stride. Carl sensed my presence too late. Right behind him, I pressed my .9mm against his back, just below his left shoulder blade.

"Put the gun down!" When he didn't, I repeated my command.

Carl's head turned rapidly from side to side, looking for a way out of his predicament. "Don't even try it! Drop it or I'll drop you!"

I heard the sirens of the patrol cars approaching the Salvatierra residence. So did Carl. He put his weapon on the floor close to my foot. I shoved it away. I stepped aside with my gun still pressed to his side.

"Get down on the floor! Keep your hands up!" I pushed against him until he went down. "Spread. Arms and legs. Do it!"

Carl spewed a stream of expletives between alcohol breaths, some aimed at his wife but most at me. I pushed harder on his back until he was lying face down on the floor, his arms stretched out above his head. I brought every ounce of my weight down on his upper back, pressing my knees against his shoulder blades. I holstered my gun and then reached behind me for my handcuffs. The police sirens blared closer.

I called out to Sylvia to turn on the ceiling light and let the cops in. She crawled out from under the desk and stood up slowly. She stared at Carl and me in shock.

"C'mon, Syl, turn on the light."

She didn't. I had Carl already handcuffed when I glanced at Sylvia again. The gun in her hand was pointed directly at her ex-husband's head.

Carl gasped and struggled to turn over onto his back. I felt as if my soul had suddenly flown out of my mouth with my breath.

"Give me the gun, Syl. You don't have to do this. He can't hurt you anymore."

"Don't try to stop me, Gloria," she said coldly. But her hand was shaking. "I'll never be free of him, not as long as he's alive!" She waved the gun at him. "*Cabrón, a ver. ¿Cómo la ves ahora, gran chingón?* How do you like it now, son of a bitch!"

The screeching of tires on the pavement signaled the untimely arrival of the cops.

Carl finally managed to roll over. His eyes moved as if in slow motion from me to Sylvia. His spit gurgled noisily in his throat. His neck muscles bulged as he tried to cough it up. In a raspy voice, he finally managed a plea for his life. "I'm so sorry. I just want you back. I won't hurt you ever again. I swear! I love you!"

Sylvia's eyes narrowed, and she threw her head back. She took her finger off the trigger but didn't lower the gun. Perhaps she was just enjoying for once that powerful feeling of being in control and had no intention of shooting him. But I couldn't take a chance, not with the cops about to break down the front door.

"Look at me, Sylvia. Syl, Syl, give me the gun. Don't throw away your good life. Don't trade it for his. He's not worth it."

A crashing noise told me the cops were in the house. If the cops saw the gun in her hand, if she made the slightest move, with all the adrenaline pumping in them, they might just shoot first and ask who, what and why later.

"Damn! C'mon, Syl, the gun."

Tears streamed down her cheeks. I slowly reached out until my hand was resting on hers. She let me take the gun without a struggle. I laid it on the floor away from Carl and set my .9mm next to it.

I reached out to raise Sylvia's arms myself, but she pushed me aside. Suddenly, she kicked Carl's face with all her might. He groaned.

I pulled her away and shook her. "Listen to me and listen good, if you don't put your arms up, we're dead. Do you understand me? Dead!"

I let go of her and raised my arms. She mimicked me.

"Over here," I called out to the cops. "We're okay. We have the suspect handcuffed."

Flashlights. Footfalls. Guns pointing and ready, the cops rushed in. I turned my head to the side to avoid being totally blinded by the lights. Someone flipped the ceiling lamps on.

"Move away from the weapons!" an officer commanded.

Sylvia and I did as told. Carl was very quiet, still lying on his side.

The officer came closer. I saw his badge, Sgt. M. Maciel.

"Who are you?" a second cop asked me.

"Gloria Damasco, private investigator. My license is in my jacket's pocket. This is my client, Sylvia Salvatierra."

The cop holstered his weapon, reached into my pocket and took out my wallet. "She's who she says she is, Sarge."

"There's a restraining order against this man, Carl Salvatierra." With my chin, I pointed at the guns on the floor. "He came after his wife with the Colt .38. The S & W .9mm is mine. My permit is also in my wallet."

The sergeant asked Sylvia to show him the restraining order. Sylvia looked around as if trying to remember where she had put it.

"Get it. Quickly," I prompted her.

She walked to her desk.

Sergeant Maciel slid his right hand into a latex glove and helped Carl up. He held Carl's chin between his index finger and thumb and looked closely at his bleeding nose and lips and his bruised forehead.

"Who did the damage?" he asked.

I shrugged my shoulders.

"That bitch! My wife! She did it! I want her arrested!"

"She got you good, eh? We'll get it all straightened out soon."

Sylvia pursed her lips and shook her head, as she handed the sergeant the restraining order.

Maciel looked at the document. "Take him in," he told the other cop, who immediately asked for my key to the cuffs. After restraining Carl with flex cuffs, he handed me mine, then walked Carl out while reciting his rights.

From the door, a woman officer reported there was no one else in the house.

"Mrs. Salvatierra, I want you to tell me what happened before your husband showed up and what happened here tonight. Can you do that?"

Sylvia began to talk about the circumstances that forced her to divorce her husband. She was crying hard. Amid hiccups, sobs and sniffles, her speech was often unintelligible. Maciel asked the woman officer to stay with her.

I walked the sergeant through the scene, trying to be as accurate as my distressed memory allowed me.

Back in Sylvia's office, the sergeant walked to the desk, leaned on it and proceeded to review his notes.

My body was as stressed as my mind, but I didn't feel the pain yet. I was sure I would be aching when the adrenalin level in my blood stabilized. "I'm getting too old for this," I said under my breath, thinking the sergeant couldn't possibly hear me.

"Maybe it's time to quit." Maciel gave me an unexpectedly sympathetic look when my eyes met his.

"Not ready," I said.

"Not enough punishment yet, eh?"

"No other passion to take its place."

Maciel gave me a complicit grin.

Sylvia was in no condition to be by herself, so I called her brother and mother. She held tightly onto my arm until they showed up.

"We owe you. Big," Sylvia's brother said.

"I hope not," I joked.

"Not to worry. We're good. Check in the mail next week." He led Sylvia out.

I drove to the Oakland Police Department to sign my deposition and pick up my gun and ID. During a break, I called my partner and husband Justin Escobar, who atypically insisted on coming to the station. I told him I'd parked in the Convention Center garage and would call and meet him outside the OPD.

Two hours later, I walked out of the Oakland Police Department exhausted. All my muscles ached but I was hungry.

Justin arrived on foot. He didn't ask for a report. He just held me in his arms, then massaged my neck and shoulders. I breathed in the familiar odor of his skin. Comfort and then desire replaced the pain.

"I have a surprise for you. It isn't far from here," he said.

We walked to the Downtown Marriot Hotel a few blocks from the OPD and next to the Convention Center on Broadway. Justin took a room key out of his pocket as we entered the hotel.

When the door to Room 1045 opened, I saw a table draped with a white tablecloth, two covered metal platters, two crystal wine-glasses and a bottle of wine already uncorked. "How did you manage all this?"

"I can be very persuasive. Plus it pays to have a cousin working as a chef here. Hey, I wasn't going to let my *chiles en nogada* masterpiece go to waste. And until we can get away for a honeymoon, this'll have to do."

My mouth was watering even before I took the lid off the platter. Justin was a great cook. But more than that, he was a lovely man and a great lover, though he probably would object to the "lovely" qualifier.

After we finished our meal, he called Dora, our partner at Brown Angel Security and Investigations, to let her know where we were. He laughed, handed me the phone and began to take off his clothes. I was unsuccessfully trying to keep my eyes off him. I barely paid attention to what Dora was saying.

"Who called?"

"Your sister-in-law—remember?"

I perked up. "Is something wrong?"

"No, everyone's okay. First thing I asked. She just wants you to call her ASAP. She wants you to look into a matter for a friend of hers, and yours, too."

"Did she say who?"

"A Lula Marie Ariz . . . tegui. It didn't sound urgent so I told sis-in-law that you probably won't return her call till tomorrow morning."

"That's good. *Gracias.*"

"*De nada.* And, hey, about tonight, I'll give you the same advice I just gave Justin. Do the blackberries and French cream thing!"

I could still hear Dora's wicked laughter when I hung up. But my attention had shifted to the flickering candlelight and the sound of water in the bathroom. I stripped, walked in and into the wet arms of love.

Justin and I checked out of the Marriot as the sun was barely visible above the Oakland hills. At the Convention Center garage, we got into our respective cars but took off in different directions. Instead of taking the Downtown Loop and I-580 home, I drove down Harrison, then around Lake Merritt. The rosy golden morning light of that Friday, June 17, 2005, was so beautiful. My mind drifted for awhile. I gradually focused on my vision of Carl Salvatierra's inert body lying on the pavement in a pool of his own blood. Only problem was that Carl was alive, facing arraignment that morning, a trial or a deal with a district attorney, and perhaps some jail time down the line.

Had I been able to avert the tragedy forecast in my prophetic dreams this time? Prior to the night before, I had never been able to save anyone whose life, in my visions, was fated to end. It bothered me no end to see what fatal blow destiny had in store for someone yet be unable to prevent it. But that was the nature of this dark gift, this extrasensory prescience in me—*la otra*.

Most people did not understand what clairvoyance was. My visions weren't a tidied bunch of related scenes laid out, like a classic story, in a linear narrative. They varied from images to smells and sounds that bombarded my dreams. My subconscious somehow sorted them out and stored them until, if ever, I worked on a related case.

Talking with some of my poet friends over the years, I realized that poets, without being aware of it, also went through a similar process as mine. All the incongruent elements of a poem were already present at various levels of consciousness or the subconscious. In the poet's case, the outcome was the poem. In mine, the results were not so easily discernible, not even for me.

Although at times I still doubted the legitimacy of my dark gift, I seldom allowed myself not to act on a vision. I pushed myself to do the necessary legwork to solve its cryptic warnings, regardless of its outcome. It was the only way to keep my twin psyches in check, my split spirit in harmony.

What would happen when I entered the darkness of another recurring vision plaguing my dreams more and more often? Two pairs of black eyes watching me in the night; a phantom horse and the horseman on him; the redolence of gardenia and rose and candle wax in the night air; the black curls and sweet face of a boy toddler searching for his mother; an animal's growl; a place of worship by the water's edge, steeped in the suffering of people; the voice of a woman saying, "Find this place and you'll find me." Would I survive being trapped in a body of water unable to free myself before my breath bubbled totally out of me?

I shuddered and tried to concentrate on the dawning of a new day, one more day out of a watery grave, I prayed.

At home, Justin was in the breakfast nook that was filled with the smell of oatmeal and cinnamon and the aroma of fresh-brewed coffee. He skimmed through the newspaper and circled headings and subheadings of articles he wanted to give a serious reading later. He was passionate about criminal investigations, global warming and related ecological issues, and about jazz and photography.

"Another mountain lion in Morgan Hill found resting on a tree branch in someone's backyard. We invade and upset the ecology of their habitat, but the big cats are the ones who get killed. And then we put them in a compound to protect them. With the *Bushits* in power, we'll soon have no clean habitat for humans either."

"Yep. The Bush way of dying," I said as I glanced at the headlines about the war in Iraq and the imprisoned so-called terrorists in Guantanamo Bay. I wasn't feeling very hungry. I sipped my coffee, then went into the shower.

"Not much to do at the office. Why don't you take the day off?" Justin piped in through the slit in the bathroom door before leaving.

"Maybe, after I finish my errands."

"Later, then."

I slid into a pair of tan Levis, a striped brown shirt and brown joggers. I looked up my brother Ernesto's phone number. He and his family had relocated from Sutter Creek to Stockton, and I didn't know their new phone number by heart yet. Until recently, my brother had worked for Lula Marie Blanco Aríztegui, managing her Oro Blanco winery in the California Shenandoah Valley.

My mother, my daughter and I had met Lula Marie a few times. She took a liking to us, and we reciprocated. She was well-read, and she and I shared a passion for literature. About five-feet-four, light-skinned with tiny freckles on her nose, she was always the perfect picture of petite elegance; her wavy strawberry-blonde hair, always smartly cut, complemented the hazel of her eyes. Witty, she laughed at her own foibles and contradictions as much as anyone else's, but she never crossed the line between good fun and sarcasm or contempt for anyone. Yet underneath her gentle wit and nature lay a very capable business mind.

Lula Marie and her sister, whom I'd never met, also co-owned the Oro Viejo winery near the city of Sonora. My brother still did the Blanco sisters' taxes and took care of other matters for them, but he no longer managed the wineries.

After a brief chat on the phone, my sister-in-law got down to her reason for calling me. "Something is going on with Lula Marie. She sounded strange, *muy preocupada*, when we spoke yesterday. I asked her about it, but she wouldn't tell me what exactly is bothering her. She talked only about some missing jewelry, family heirlooms."

"Why not call the local cops or sheriffs?"

"Exactly. *Lo mismo que le dije,* but she says that she called the cops. Apparently they haven't done much about it. So I suggested that perhaps you could look into it for her. I know you're very busy . . . and this is an unusual request."

"Yes, it is, but not because you're asking. I wouldn't want you to be caught in the middle of misunderstandings . . . of a mess. In my business it's better to deal directly with the client. I wouldn't know in this case who my client is."

"Lula Marie, *claro que sí.* As a matter of fact, she agreed and asked me to call you on her behalf. I wouldn't ask you to share your findings with me."

"I know. I'm just curious. Why do you think she didn't just call me directly?"

"My question also, and I'm not sure what the answer is. Lula Marie is so friendly and open, but she has a problem asking for help. She's done so much for us and never once asked for anything in return. To tell you the truth, Gloria, I'm really worried about her. We saw her last week. You know she drinks a couple of glasses of wine with dinner at most. But she was drinking a lot. Then she told me about this . . . jewelry theft. I have the feeling that there's more. I know it's a lot to ask, but could you at least go see her, talk to her?"

I sighed, knowing that I could not disregard my sister-in-law's plea. She was family, and her concern for Lula Marie was genuine. "Tell you what. I'll drive up to her place today. I can be there sometime between three and four. Would you mind letting her know since you already talked this over with her?"

"Happy to. *Gracias, cuñada.*"

I called Justin to tell him about the new developments, although I knew that he, as always, would want me to decide whether or not to take the case.

"Are you taking any hardware?" he promptly asked.

"Yes. 9," I answered, giving as little information as possible.

"Good. Take good care, *amorcito*."

Justin was a bit too cautious on the phone, whether mobile or land line. Although our behaving like Maxwell Smart and Agent 99 tickled my funny bone, I well understood his reason for being wary of someone listening in. Our van and office had been bugged before by a fed. But after the 9-11 terrorist attack and with the re-enactment of the Patriot Act, no person of color was safe from suspicion or surveillance.

At the Oakland airport on his way to Carson City, Nevada, for a client, Justin had already been discreetly questioned by a U.S. marshall posing as a fellow traveler, simply because of Justin's dark skin, curly hair, black eyebrows and black mustache. An armed national guardsman had kept watch over him until he boarded the plane with the marshall in his wake. Still, anyone listening on the phone would easily guess what our coded chat was all about.

I turned my attention back to my list of errands and checked off those that required immediate attention. The trip to the California Shenandoah Valley, where Lula Marie Aríztegui lived, would take me a couple of hours with good traffic. I was looking at a return trip home very late that night. It made sense to come back to Oakland the next day instead. So I packed a bag with some toiletries, black and blue jeans, a nightshirt, plenty of cotton socks and undergarments and a pair each of black soft-soled sneakers and hiking boots.

I grabbed my outdoors light jacket, which had plenty of pockets, although I was sure I wasn't going to need it. The summer solstice was only a few days away, and the temperature in the Shenandoah Wine Country was at least fifteen degrees above the mild sixty-eight in Oakland. I changed into a linen skirt, a sleeveless shirt and my wedge sandals.

Copies of Brown Angel Security and Investigations standard contract landed in my briefcase. Extra clips for the .9 mm, a pair of additional cells for the dry–wet flashlight, my compass and night and day vision binoculars went into the "hardware" bag.

All this attention to detail before a business trip always made me feel emotionally spent. Like traveling again with a baby, I thought, during a minute's rest. I filled a thermos bottle with the remaining coffee in the pot. I called my mother and my daughter and left messages telling them I was on a case and not to call me on my cell phone unless it was urgent.

Preparations completed, I loaded everything into the Volvo's trunk. After taking care of postal and bank errands and an in-and-out trip to the courthouse, I stopped to have lunch at Merritt Restaurant and Bakery.

At ten past one, I was on I-80 East to Sacramento. Past the state capital, I took Highway 16 heading east toward Plymouth and the Sierra Nevada foothills. I had no idea what trouble awaited me at my destination, but I was determined to enjoy what I could of the trip to California's legendary Gold Country.

ONE
IMPERFECT PICTURES

Lula Marie Blanco Aríztegui sat cross-legged in a lemon-colored rattan chair on the front porch of her Chilean *estancia*-type home behind the Oro Blanco Winery in California's Shenandoah Valley. She wore a white sleeveless dress with a wide mid-length skirt, on which delicate clusters of white and purple grapes had been silk-screened. Matching straw hat and espadrille sandals laced up to just below the calf completed her outfit.

A slim cigar smoldered in a gold-rimmed ashtray on the rattan table. A steady plume of blue smoke rose and filtered through the blue blossoms of the wisteria that provided the porch with shade. A tall stemmed crystal glass was half-filled with a dark red wine and stood next to its empty twin and a half full bottle of wine.

In front of me, fields of lavender, mustard, golden and red poppies and baby's breath spread upon golden slopes. Sparse groves of live and black oaks punctuated the hills. Behind me, perfect rows of grapevines. Their fruit, come September, would turn furiously sweet and be harvested, crushed, their juice drained into fermenting tanks, casks, then oak barrels. And the transformation into wine would be complete. This was the perfect picture of bucolic California—a California, I, living in the midst of the metropolitan San Francisco Bay Area, often forgot still existed.

Lula Marie smiled at me, showing a row of bright teeth, surely kept clean of nicotine stains by a zealous, highly paid dentist. She stood up as I climbed up the steps to the porch and opened her arms to hug me. We kissed on both cheeks.

"Gloria Inez Damasco, or should I say Escobar? I'm sorry I missed your wedding. I was in Chile visiting my parents. But I heard all about it. What a shindig! A mariachi and Dr. Loco's Rockin' Jalapeño Band, all that dancing even before the ceremony started, and the 'Baker from Hell' running away with your wedding cake." She laughed.

Justin and I had replayed that scene many times and laughed just as hard as on that afternoon when I ended on my back, on top of the *guitarrón* and the mariachi playing it, my neck, shoulders, chest and champagne-colored wedding gown smeared by crushed blackberries and *crème patissiere.*

"Come. Tell," Lula Marie said.

"Well, let me see. There's this Sam Cardona's Bakery on International Boulevard in Oakland. A week before the wedding, my mother goes to Cardona's Bakery looking to order my wedding cake. But she doesn't like any of the cakes there. So she walks to Carmen's Bakery across the street. She has no idea Sam and Carmen had recently gone through a bitter divorce. At Carmen's, she chooses my favorite: a white cake filled with fresh blackberries and preserves and *crème patissiere.* When Sam finds out my mother ordered the cake from Carmen's shop, he swears he'll get his revenge on his ex-wife for stealing his customers. But he doesn't get a chance to do it until everyone is seated for the ceremony. There I am, the blushing if middle-aged bride, ready to walk down the path on my brother's arm, and what do I see? My wedding cake has grown a pair of legs and feet and is running away."

"Sam the Baker?"

"Yep. At any rate, many of the guests stand up but freeze in place. I look at Justin, jaw dropped in disbelief. And hey, I am not about to let my cake get kidnapped. Not that day of all days. I rush after the running cake. The mariachi playing the *guitarrón* is right behind me. But I only have eyes for Sam the Baker. He's a very short but very strong man. He's getting away. I run faster, catch up to him, grab the tray and pull. Sam lets go of it. I reel back and . . . and the rest is history."

"*¡Es que es genial!* Just precious." Lula Marie was laughing so hard she had to sit down again. She regained her composure after awhile, raised the wine bottle and offered me some. I accepted.

"Most weddings are perfectly organized messes. But yours was a wedding worthy of a couple of private eyes, if you ask me."

I nodded and wiped the sweat off my forehead, still tickled at the recollection, but more excited at the memory of Justin's tongue licking the blackberry and cream off my face, neck and nipples that night.

"How are you doing? Is your divorce finally over?" I asked.

"It's already been over for six months. But you know how it is. My ex will never be out of my life completely. Well, we have a son together. That's that. He'll always find an excuse to make my life miserable."

"I'm sorry to hear that."

She sighed and raised her index finger and thumb to her right ear lobe first, then across to the left, as if to make sure she hadn't lost the diamond and alexandrite studs she wore. Then she reached for her cigar and took a drag. She let the smoke out slowly through her open mouth.

All sorts of questions ran through my mind, mostly having to do with the theft of her jewelry and the possible reason for her hiring my services. But I sensed Lula Marie wasn't ready to get down to the nitty-gritty.

"Seeing anyone?" I asked.

"Well, if you must know, yes."

She straightened her skirt, then pushed a renegade strand of strawberry-blonde hair over and behind her ear. I could see the concern in her hazel eyes.

"So, who is he?"

"I met him—Paladin Valenzuela—about three months ago . . . actually I knew of him before. He's very active in community affairs in the Gold Country. But, for some reason, our paths hadn't crossed before."

"Paladin. That's an unusual name."

"It sure is. But he's smart, wealthy and handsome . . . in a rugged kind of way. He wears mostly gray or brown tailor-made western garb, though I saw a picture of him in the Sunday paper, donning a tuxedo like he's always belonged in it."

"He sounds so unlike your ex. What does he look like? I mean, besides being a dark and handsome western man, born to wear tuxedos while rounding up the cattle."

"Sounded that funny, no? But he is attractive, an air of . . . how can I say it . . . secrecy about him. You'd think gray eyes like his would be dull, but there's *una chispa*, a spark in them. But his real plus is in knowing how to make a woman . . . you know what

I mean!" Lula Marie blushed, laughed. "Whew!" She fanned her neck.

"Pheromones, hormones or love?"

"I do find him very attractive—I can't deny that."

"What's his background?"

"He's the great-grandchild of one of the old Californios. Apparently, his family tree dates back to the time before the Gold Rush, before the Sutters, Fremonts and Stanfords ever dreamed of making their fortunes or rewriting history in California."

"And single and available?"

"Of course. A widower. No children. And he seems to be taken with me. But . . ."

"But you don't trust him."

"To be honest, I don't trust men in general. Am I being unreasonable, you think?"

"Not really. Not after what you've been through. And you haven't known the man that long. Give it time."

Lula Marie was lost in thought for awhile. What was I supposed to do for her? Find out what this Paladin's intentions for her were? Did she suspect him or her ex-husband of taking her jewelry? I added those questions to the mental list I had already begun to compile about the case. In the many years I'd dealt with clients, I sometimes felt it was better to ramble down the paths they took and make mental notes of everything they said until the objective of my search on their behalf became clear.

"Are you hungry?" Lula Marie asked suddenly.

When I replied with a "famished," she went into the house. I followed her in and took the opportunity to freshen up, then I went out to the porch again. I called Justin to let him know I had arrived safely.

A moment later, keys in hand, Lula Marie came out wearing a light purple silk and wool scarf around her shoulders. She secured the front door.

"I didn't know we were going out. Perhaps I should change . . ." Change into what, I wondered, remembering what I had packed for the trip.

"You look fine," she said as she walked to her pickup truck and I to my car.

I wasn't so sure. But my outfit, including my red blouse, sweaty under the arms, would have to do. As soon as I'd entered the Shenandoah wine country, I'd driven with the windows down, and my hair was a mess. But I couldn't have enough of the smell of hot, dry grass mixed with the fragrance of flowers and herbs, the smell of late spring in the valley. At the moment, I was as fragrant as a wet hot summer weed.

I took my .9mm out of my handbag and put it in my briefcase. With a digital lock, it provided better security. I grabbed both items to take with me and got in her pickup.

"Did you lock your car?" she asked.

"Yes. Why?"

"There have been some robberies along the highway. And some of the ranchers have also been missing horses and cattle. We've had no break-ins around here, but I'd rather be safe than sorry."

Confusion quickly nestled between my temporal lobes. No burglaries in this particular area. Were her jewels kept in a safe deposit box at a bank?

Unaware of my mental disarray, Lula Marie continued, "I think it's best if you spend the night. I have cosmetics, toiletries and a nightshirt you can use. And washer and dryer."

"My overnight bag is in my car. I came prepared."

"Good thinking. We'll get your luggage out and get you settled in when we get back." She sighed. "I just don't know what this world is coming to. Tcch. I guess people in Oakland are used to the high crime rate, but around here most people are decent."

Decent! Her comment about my hometown and all of us Oaklanders cut deep into my soul, but I held back my tongue.

Lula Marie sensed my discomfort and blushed, but she didn't offer an apology. Instead, she said, "At any rate, we're meeting my sister—you know she's my twin sister."

"I knew of your sister. But I had no idea she is your twin. I'm afraid I've never met either her or your brother-in-law."

"That's right. They were in Santiago the last time you were here. You'll meet them tonight. We're having dinner with them at the Cantero Cross Ranch."

Jewelry thieves, bank robbers, rustlers, a twin sister, unexpected dinner invitations. I sighed and added those to the ever-growing list of queries. My mind was beginning to feel cluttered. I couldn't yet decide where every bit of information belonged. But I would have to play the waiting game a while longer.

Along the way, the conversation mostly concerned her twin sister, Estefanía Feliz, and her brother-in-law, Carlos Manuel Cantero. The twin sisters had a solid and profitable partnership in their viniculture enterprises. Separately, the Canteros also owned the Cantero Cross Ranch. Estefanía Feliz was passionate about horses and managed the ranch. Until recently, her husband had been a partner in a mining operation, but had sold his shares to his two partners at a profit.

I listened but my eyes were glued to the road. I had never ridden in a vehicle driven by Lula Marie. It was a hair-raising experience. Perhaps it was the influence of the alcohol, but behind a wheel, this otherwise poised woman threw caution to the wind, not slowing down but speeding as we approached a turn on the very narrow Shenandoah Road. Suddenly, *Doctora* Jekyll was transformed into *Señora* Hyde, and this *señora* held my life in her hands. I should have expected this turn of events immediately after I saw that half empty bottle of wine and the slim cigar's plume of blue smoke rising to Heaven. Or was it to Hell?

Closer to the end of Shenandoah Road, Lula Marie slowed down to enter Highway 49, the main artery that connected most of the towns in the Gold Country. I let out a sigh of relief, which didn't go unnoticed by my hostess. She chuckled.

"Nice scenery, isn't it? I've lived here most of my adult life. But I haven't gotten my fill of it yet."

"I can see why," I admitted.

The California Shenadoah Valley and the Gold Country were equally beautiful, but they had their own distinct personalities and ethnic mix. Along Highway 49, folks in other pickups or SUVs on the road were mostly of white European descent. I was sure those picking grapes in the vineyards or tending to guests' needs at restaurants and hotels were Mexicans and Latinos. I saw a few

Asians but hardly any African Americans. I was surprised at the number of people on motorcycles on the road.

Most amazing, however, was the change in the landscape as soon as we left the Shenandoah Valley and entered Highway 49. The higher sloping golden foothills of the Sierra Nevada were still visible in the distance. But even one hundred and sixty-six years after the discovery of gold at Sutter's Mill and the reforestation efforts of more recent eco-minded generations, great expanses of hilly land displayed fewer trees. The forests of old had paid the price for the lumber needed to fortify the deep shafts of quartz lodes inlaid with gold and for the Forty-Niners' homes and dreams of easy riches. The soil had been poisoned by the mercury needed to extract gold from quartz. Adding to the injury, fires scorched hundreds of forest acres every summer.

Lula Marie had also been lost in thought for the last few miles, and I wasn't sure she had seen the signpost for the private road to the Cantero Cross Ranch. She hadn't.

"You have to turn left . . . NOW," I said and braced myself for the very sharp last-minute left turn onto the driveway.

Able to avoid a collision with an incoming van, she had to brake hard not to hit the wrought-iron gate.

"WO-O-OH!" we both exclaimed.

Lula Marie laughed. I rubbed my neck muscles.

Two majestic black oaks flanked the gate. An intercom device was mounted on the side of the gate. Before Lula Marie pressed the intercom button, the gate began to open by itself. Someone somewhere in the house had to be aware of our presence and knew exactly who was in the truck.

I looked up and spotted a motion-sensitive surveillance camera nestled between a high branch and the trunk of one of the oaks, its sole eye focused on us. As we drove in, I also glimpsed another camera fastened to the other tree, facing a different direction. Why was there a need for such a security system at the Cantero Cross Ranch? Patience was still the operative word.

Hidden behind a row of live oaks, about two hundred feet from the gate was the main house: a large, one-story, early nineteenth-century Spanish-style adobe. It had been whitewashed and refurbished to its past splendid beauty. A wide portico ran the length of its front and extended from it as a wraparound covered breeze-way. Flanking the house were twin gardens with dahlias of every conceivable color and size, one variety of deep dark purple that it looked almost black.

I wanted to look more closely at the flowers, but the front door opened. We were ushered into a spacious living area with a beamed ceiling by the housekeeper, a middle-aged, dark-skinned woman with salt-and-pepper hair, displaying a dimpled smile and a beauty mark under her right eye. Her eyes brightened as she greeted Lula Marie. She pointed to the dining room on her right, where the Canteros awaited our arrival.

I immediately noticed the two approximately six-by-eight-inch monitors, now showing the gate and the grounds around the entrance to the ranch and the digital pad and intercom below them.

The housekeeper signaled for us to leave our belongings on the console table below the equipment. I felt uneasy to let my handbag, and especially my bag briefcase with my gun in it, out of my sight. But I talked myself out of my occupational paranoia and put both items next to each other, then strolled behind the two women.

Lula Marie inquired after the housekeeper's daughter in Spanish. The housekeeper was grateful to her and the *señores* for hiring a nurse to look after her ill daughter. I heard Lula Marie apologize for some unspoken travesty. The woman absolved Lula Marie with a "*No se mortifique, seño.*"

As we entered the dining room and then the adjacent family entertaining area where the Canteros sat, I was ready for a striking resemblance between Lula Marie and Estefanía Feliz. I wasn't quite prepared for Estefanía's piercing, almond-shaped, dark-brown eyes under arched eyebrows or her darker skin and straight brown hair pulled back and neatly gathered in a bun. She was taller than Lula Marie, who immediately kissed her sister on both cheeks, a greeting not reciprocated by her fraternal twin. Estefanía's middle name was Feliz, but little happiness showed in her countenance to honor that name. She wore brown linen slacks and a cream rayon shirt with wide long sleeves rolled up to her

elbows. Her clear complexion was free of makeup. She smelled of
Dove bath soap.

Estefanía turned to me and extended her hand to shake mine
but said nothing. She looked at me directly. I held her stare and
her strong handshake without blinking or taking my eyes or hand
away. Her upper lip curved up to the left, which I interpreted as a
smile, perhaps a gesture of welcome as well.

After hugging Lula Marie, a smiling Carlos Manuel Cantero
approached me, saying, "*Bienvenida a nuestra casa que es ya suya.*"
I smiled at the very formal my-house-is-your-house welcome. But
I didn't get a chance to extend my hand and introduce myself, for
he immediately held me by the shoulders and lightly pressed his
lips to both my cheeks. He let go of me right away but placed his
right hand gently between my shoulder blades. He steered me to
the sitting area, where the housekeeper had already poured an
amber wine into aperitif flutes on a silver tray. Next to the wine
tray were two porcelain platters of antipasto and cocktail-size
turnovers.

Carlos Manuel lifted two glasses off the silver tray and handed
me one and the other to Lula Marie. He offered the third to his
wife, who took the glass from him with her left hand, her fingers
gently sliding over his in a sensual caress. A glance of marital com-
plicity passed between them. Then, Estefanía turned her head
slightly to her left and glanced casually out the rear sliding door
that led to the back porch. I followed her gaze up to a stable and
a corral about one hundred feet from the main house. There, a
man in a blue shirt and jeans tended to a black stallion. I also
caught a glimpse of Lula Marie's forehead and the two deep furrows between her brows. She attempted a smile, then lifted her
glass and said, "*Salud.*" Everyone joined in the toast.

"Mrs. Damasco, try Emilia's wonderful *empanaditas,*" Carlos
Manuel Cantero said.

"Please call me Gloria."

"I will if you call me Cantero, like everyone else does."

The housekeeper handed me a plate with some of the cocktail-
size turnovers on it.

"These are delicious . . . Emilia?"

"*Muchas gracias, señora*"

She gave me a dimpled smile of appreciation and made sure everyone else was taken care of before she announced that dinner would be ready in an hour.

Comfortably seated on twin armless chaise lounges in the entertainment area, Lula Marie and Estefanía were engaged in conversation. It was obvious that Lula Marie was telling the story of my wedding cake to Estefanía. They threw a few amused glances in my direction. No matter how much I myself had laughed at the hilarious mishaps on my wedding day, I now felt a wave of red creeping up my cheeks.

"Those two can go on talking for hours. They're so different yet so alike," Cantero said in Spanish. "It seems you and I are on our own for the next hour. So why don't I give you the twenty-cent tour of the house and immediate grounds while there's still light."

"That'd be lovely."

In his seemingly habitual manner, Cantero placed his hand between my shoulder blades and gently guided me to the hall. He was older than his wife. Lula Marie and Estefanía Feliz were in their mid-forties, give or take. Cantero was approximately fifty-five. Of average build and height, with large brown eyes, a Roman nose and a pleasant smile, he wouldn't be considered a handsome man. But he exuded a kind of old-world charm, which, coupled with his self-confidence and abundant wit, made him attractive. He was passionate about his ranch and its history, sprinkling our tour of it with lore about the Castro family who had owned the adobe and the grounds around it long before the Gold Rush.

Trading bits of information about early California history, Cantero and I moved from room to room. Red oak floors with redwood inlaid borders ran through the whole house, except in the kitchen and hallways done in Saltillo red tile, as were the two fireplaces in the living and the family entertainment areas. Well-equipped and ample, the kitchen had Mexican tile countertops and red oak cabinetry and furniture.

Everything in the house reflected the good taste of its owners, from the delicate bronze and wrought-iron sun-shaped mirrors above the fireplaces, the Zapotec area rugs, tapestries and decorative pillows in rich Mexican colors in the bedrooms to the mission-style furniture, hand-crafted especially for them.

In the study and library, the large mahogany desk dominated the space closer to the French doors opening to the dahlia garden. Opposite the door was shelf after shelf of history books. Nicely displayed in two glass cases, some tomes and maps—surely collectors' items—were written in old Spanish, while others were in modern Spanish and English. A round mahogany table and padded chairs made reading a comfortable experience.

"Your California history collection is impressive," I said.

"It's my hobby—well, more like an addiction."

I admired the old sepia portraits of various individuals from the turn of the twentieth century that decorated the walls behind the desk. But most salient among them were a large framed reproduction of Charles Christian Nahl's painting of Joaquín Murrieta and a silk-screened poster of Tiburcio Vásquez by a Latino artist unfamiliar to me. I also noticed the small surveillance camera tucked in an upper corner of the room, its eye pointed somewhere between painting and poster.

"Do you know anything about Murrieta and Vásquez?" Cantero asked.

"Too little, I'm afraid. I tried to find books about them, especially after I saw Luis Valdez's *Bandido* performed by El Teatro Campesino many, many years ago."

"Quite a few books have been written about the Murrieta legend, in particular, as you can see. You might want to begin with Rollin, aka Yellow Bird's biography of the bandit-hero that made the Murrieta legend popular. But if you want a good study of this area's history and the process of collective memory about the Gold Rush, you might choose Susan Lee Johnson's *Roaring Camp*. If you're interested in a woman's point of view, you might find Sarah Royce's *A Frontier Lady* fascinating."

He pointed at a certain area where those books were shelved.

"Now, let me show you the gardens." He led the way through the French doors that opened to one of the dahlia gardens. We strolled among the flowers, admiring them and continued our tour.

"The household staff quarters and Estefanía's business office," he explained when he saw me looking at two large adobe cottages not far from the main house.

On one of the lower hills farther up, a chocolate-brown wooden barn rose in the midst of an oak grove next to another wood cottage. The barn was probably home to sheep grazing or resting under the trees now.

"Our self-powered lawn mowers," he said about the sheep. "The grass dries up pretty quickly after the winter rains let up. A forest fire here would be absolute hell."

I heard whinnying and neighing and turned around, looking for the horses.

"We have about thirteen horses, not as many yet as we'd like. But we're working on it, now that we have Diablo."

"Diablo?"

"The black stallion in the small corral. Horses are my wife's passion. I don't know of any man who knows more about horses than she. Come. Let's see how Diablo's doing; he's been a bit under the weather lately. *Susto*, I've been told."

Diablo was a victim of *susto*? Until then, I had never heard the word used to describe the psychological impact of extreme fright or stress—a kind of Post-Traumatic Stress Disorder—on animals. I had to admit it made sense and wondered what or who had spooked the stallion.

"Do you know how to ride?" he asked.

"I do, but I don't ride often."

I stopped a short distance from Diablo. I noticed the two short twin thin white stripes running from behind the stallion's left ear to just below the jaw.

The horse handler was the same man I had seen through the sliding door in the dining room when I first arrived. Taller than Cantero, he was much younger than I expected, perhaps in his late twenties. He was firm yet gentle with the horse. What struck me most at the moment was his straight hair, as black as the horse's mane. He wore it loose over his shoulders.

Cantero approached the horse. "How's 'Old Nick' doing?" he asked the handler.

"Diablo is restless—*muy inquieto*."

"Julio, Gloria. Gloria, Julio," Cantero introduced us.

"*Mucho gusto*," I said.

Julio said nothing but looked directly at me. I had to contain a gasp as I stared at him, mesmerized by two striking round eyes with irises as black as his hair, framed by straight brows. But it wasn't their physical beauty that struck me most. Those eyes were the portals to a premonitory dream. I had just entered my vision. My heart picked up its pace.

"Come closer, Gloria. This Diablo is really an angel." Cantero soothingly rubbed the stallion's forehead.

Diablo lowered his head but looked at Julio. The handler also lowered his head, then pinched his nose with thumb and index finger and tilted his head toward me. When Diablo took a few steps in my direction, I knew what the handler's gesture meant. I stood my ground as Diablo raised his head and gazed at me. I smiled and slowly stretched my arm and hand toward him. The horse moved closer until his neck was touching my arm. Lightly, I passed the back of my fingers over the soft hair on his mane. I let him smell my hand and rub my ear with his nose. When I lowered my hand, Diablo began to back away slowly and suddenly turned and trotted to the other end of the corral.

"He likes you. Diablo is usually shy and wary of strangers," Cantero said.

"Knows good people when he sees them." Julio smiled—a dimpled smile, pushing up a beauty mark on his right cheek.

I was about to ask him if he was related to Emilia when we heard Lula Marie's call to dinner. I waved at her. When I turned my head to say good-bye to Julio, he was already walking to the end of the corral to join Diablo.

Cantero and I began our walk back to the house. "It's been quite an experience."

"Your visit with me or your visit with Diablo?" Cantero asked, jokingly.

"Both. And I must say, I'm impressed with Julio and the way he handles Diablo. I knew about horse whisperers, but I never quite understood how close man and horse can be."

Cantero gave me an amused look. "Just don't say that in front of my wife. Estefanía thinks that Diablo is *her* horse."

One scrumptious dish of Chilean and Mexican cuisine followed after another. A rightly proud cook and housekeeper, Emilia enjoyed watching us consume her creations. A couple of glasses of Oro Blanco Pinot Grigio complemented the feast nicely. But I was ready to burst out of my linen skirt. Lula Marie, on the other hand, had eaten little and drunk a lot.

Guess who's driving home, I thought, but tried not to dwell on the trip back to her house. I turned my attention to Cantero, who at the moment was warning that Emilia's piece de resistance, *torta borracha,* a Mexican cake soaked in brandy and sprinkled with crushed walnuts and shredded coconut, was still to come.

Estefanía looked at her watch. After asking Emilia to have dessert, brandy and coffee ready in the study in twenty minutes, she walked across the living room, then down the hall. I wondered where she was headed.

Every so often, during dinner, I had caught her looking out past the back porch to the corral and the stables. She snuck a look at her watch each time. A tinge of red ran up from the hollow of her neck to her jawline. Afterward I asked myself whether her interest resided on her sick horse or the whisperer, Julio. Yet her husband seemed oblivious to her disquietude. A voice in me issued a warning.

After helping herself to another glass of the Pinot Grigio, Lula Marie tottered across the dining room, out of the sliding door and onto the back porch to smoke. Cantero watched her with concern, excused himself and joined her. In the soft glow of dusk, Julio's silhouette jumped over the corral fence and strolled to the back of the house.

My stomach wasn't the only part of my anatomy about to burst. I walked down the hall and stopped by the console table to get my handbag. My stomach and heart did a summersault. Sure that I had left my handbag next to my briefcase and not on top of it, I immediately checked the lock to my briefcase but saw no signs of tampering. I heard a door open and close somewhere in the back of the house. I couldn't see anyone. Perhaps it was Estefanía Feliz going out to meet Julio. But the Canteros' romantic or sexual escapades were none of my concern, unless they made it my business.

I grabbed my handbag and found the bathroom. When I reached in for my small cosmetic bag that was kept together with my cell phone in a smaller zippered compartment, I felt the texture of paper. Odd, I thought since I didn't keep any receipts in there. I took out the slip of paper. It was a note, unsigned and written in Spanish, asking that I meet the note writer at the Golden Nugget Taverna in Jackson, the next day at 2 p.m. "*¡Urgente!*"

Nothing was missing. My bag had been left unattended for more than two hours. I could only account for Cantero and Julio's whereabouts. Lula Marie and Estefanía Feliz had been alone in the dining room during my tour of the premises; I had no idea where Estefanía went after she left the dining room. The housekeeper Emilia tended to dinner. Unless there was someone else I hadn't met prowling through the house, any one of the three women could have put the note in my handbag. I couldn't think of any reason Lula Marie or Estefanía would need to see me alone when I was obviously there at their request. The housekeeper Emilia had mentioned a convalescing daughter who was beign looked after by a nurse. Was this daughter also staying at the cottage? Did the daughter's nurse live there, too? And who looked after the gardens, the sheep pens and the stables?

It was time for answers. Taking my handbag with me, I headed toward the study. Everyone was seated at the table when I went in. Cantero rose and motioned for me to sit on a leather chair next to him.

I managed to have a few bites of the *torta borracha* and a cup of coffee instead of the brandy. I complimented Emilia, who gave me her usual smile of thanks. I observed her as she moved through the room tending to everyone's needs. She was affable and considerate of others, but not obsequious. She appeared calm and in control. If Julio was indeed Emilia's son, he had inherited from Emilia more than her dimpled smile. I sensed, however, that neither of them was the note writer.

Cantero stood up and closed the door after Emilia walked out.

"You're probably wondering why we asked you here. But first we want you to know you're always welcome here, if you take up the case or not."

Estefanía nodded her agreement, but shifted focus when Lula Marie began to rearrange the wineglasses on the table. She walked over to Lula Marie and held her hand, perhaps simply to keep her fraternal twin from going on with an annoying task.

I took my notepad and pen out.

"I'm listening. You don't mind if I take some notes, then I might read not all but some of them back to you and your wife for accuracy."

"Fine with us," Cantero said and then added, "I believe you already know that some of my wife's jewelry is missing. But there is more."

"Excuse me, but before you go on, would you mind telling me where the jewelry was kept?"

"In our safe deposit box, here in the library. Lula Marie, my wife and I are the only ones who know the combination by heart."

"Okay. Please, go on. What's missing?"

"A pair of antique diamond and emerald earrings rumored to have belonged to Empress Carlota of Mexico."

Cantero retrieved a photo from a desk drawer and showed it to me. "The appraiser took it for insurance purposes."

I admired a pair of delicate tear-shaped emeralds surrounded by tiny diamonds set in white gold. On the white edge framing the snap, the appraiser had written, "Carlota's Tears."

"I'm not sure I understand. Did the earrings belong to the Empress Carlota?" I asked.

"Provenance is difficult to verify. There are no certificates of authenticity—not unusual in cases like this. However, the craftsmanship dates back to mid-nineteenth century. You're a student of history, so you probably know that Carlota went literally mad after Mexican President Benito Juárez had her husband, the Emperor Maximilian, executed."

"I'm familiar with the story. The Battle of Puebla during Mexico's war against the French occupation army is the reason Chicanos celebrate the Cinco de Mayo throughout the southwestern United States."

"Precisely. It's said that Carlota was wearing the emerald earrings when she heard of her husband's death. Overtaken by her grief, she pulled the earrings so hard she injured her earlobes, or so the story goes. She refused to wear the earrings again and gave them to one of her servant girls before leaving Mexico."

"I see. I'm assuming that you reported the theft to the local authorities and the insurance company."

"Yes, of course, we notified the sheriff's office and filed a claim with the insurance. Eventually they will pay. What is important, though, is that Lula Marie's life has been threatened. And we have no idea how these two and other unfortunate events are connected, or what to expect."

"Threatened in person or by phone?" I asked.

"No. Two anonymous notes. The first in the mail four weeks ago, postmarked in Sonora—California, of course. It said: 'You'll pay for what you're doing. Stay away. You have no right.' The second was left on Lula Marie's windshield two days after the first. 'Stay away or pay with your life.'"

"Stay away from what or whom?"

Cantero shook his head. "We immediately got in touch with the sheriff again. But Sheriff's Deputy John Marshall, who came to talk to us, told us that unless the sender was caught red-handed, blah, blah, blah. He gave us the usual cockamamie excuses. He dismissed the threats as probable pranks by some 'bored teenager out to no good' or perhaps a disgruntled employee, which wasn't the case at all. The notes were checked for fingerprints but none was found. The deputy increased their patrols around Oro Blanco and the ranch, and that was all."

"Did he also have the handwriting compared to that of the Oro Blanco winery staff?"

"That's what he said."

"I'm assuming the threats stopped."

"They did. But a few days later, Carlota's Tears disappeared from the safe."

Cantero seemed hesitant. He glanced at his wife, who reached for her sister's hand.

"What are you not telling me?" I asked.

He thought for a moment and began to tell me about Lula Marie and Estefanía's horseback riding habits. I wasn't sure where he was going with his story, so I just listened and wrote down everything important.

When he was finished, I read my notes back to him.

"Your wife and Lula Marie often ride in the evening when it's cooler. Sometimes, Emilia's daughter Virginia or Julio rides with them. On May 15, two weeks before the first life-threatening note, you and your wife were in San Francisco on business when Lula Marie called. Virginia had been thrown off her horse and rushed to the hospital in Sacramento. She had two broken ribs, trauma to the brain. She was in a coma. You rushed back to the ranch. Two days later, Virginia came out of her coma. But she had no recollection of her accident and the events leading up to it. Her doctors believed that her amnesia was temporary but couldn't tell how long it would last. Anything else you'd like to add?"

Again, Cantero looked at Lula Marie, then at Estefanía.

"I don't know exactly where you're going with this. But I can tell you this much. You suspect Virginia's fall from the horse wasn't really an accident, or I wouldn't be here, right?"

Almost in a whisper, he said, "Not exactly . . . I know what I'm about to tell you will sound incredible. I have my doubts. This is what Lula Marie told us. I wish she could tell you herself. But as you can see . . ."

"I'll ask her about it later. Please, go on."

For the next twenty minutes, I listened to Cantero describe the incident. Listening to him tell stories of old during our tour of the ranch, I knew he was a storyteller. So he guided the story, adding his own interpretation of the facts, embellishing or qualifying them. I was fascinated but wary of the accuracy of the events in question. So I tried my best to scrub the facts of the case clean. Again, I read my notes back to him.

"Now, you've told me that the night of the accident, the sun had just begun to set but there was still enough light for Lula Marie and Virginia to see where they were going. Both of them and their horses are very familiar with the terrain near the creek bordering the ranch. Suddenly, they saw a flash of light around that area. Lula Marie was certain she heard voices coming from behind the trees by the creek's edge. They also heard the roar of a motorcycle. Without a word, Virginia began to ride in that direction.

"Lula Marie feared for the young woman's safety and rode after her. When they got closer to the creek, a dark horse came out

of nowhere. The horse 'glowed' as if it were made of 'black neon
light,' and stood still not far from them. But their horses became
restless. Then suddenly, Virginia prompted her horse and foolishly rode not away from but toward the neon horse. Lula Marie tried
to take the reins from Virginia's hands to control her horse, but
the young woman resisted. In the struggle, Virginia lost her bal-
ance and fell off her horse. The dark neon horse reared on its hind
legs and took off down the path to the creek nearby. Virginia's
horse ran after him. Lula Marie quickly dismounted and checked
Virginia, who was unconscious. She had her cell phone with her
and immediately called Julio, then 911.

"Just before Julio arrived at the scene, Lula Marie heard the
whinnying of the black neon horse a second time. She didn't see
it, but her horse, like Virginia's, also took off and disappeared in
the brush by the creek. Although Julio looked for the horses that
night, he couldn't find them. The next morning he caught up
with a small herd of wild horses, but Lula Marie and Virginia's
horses weren't among them. They didn't return to the ranch on
their own either."

"Is that all?" I asked.

"No, not all. You have to understand, no one, including
Emilia, blamed Lula Marie for Virginia's accident. But she felt
guilty anyway. After the arrival of the threatening notes, she got
very depressed. She insisted that a nurse be hired to look after
Virginia during her convalescence. We agreed it was a good idea
for both Lula Marie and Virginia's sake. So we hired a nurse, Hilda
Gallardo."

"Do you two, or perhaps Emilia or Julio, have any idea what
made Virginia ride after the dark neon stallion?"

Cantero shook his head. He was pensive.

"What is it? What's still bothering you?" I asked.

He cleared his throat. "I don't know how to put this because
I personally do not believe in ghosts. But Julio, Diablo's handler,
remember?"

"I remember Julio and your wife's horse Diablo. Please go
on."

"Well, Julio told me that Mexican Americans in the area
believe this particular dark 'neon' horse is Joaquín Murrieta's

horse. The ghost horse has been sighted in many places up and down Highway 49. Sometimes, or so folks say, they've seen the Ghost of Sonora riding it as well . . . folktales, I suppose."

"Murrieta's ghost? My, my . . ."

"Unbelievable, isn't it?" Cantero smiled, probably at my befuddled expression.

Estefanía smiled too, but hers was a secretive smile. Did she know the identity of the man masquerading as the legendary bandit? Was Julio the Ghost of Sonora? I couldn't run freely down that trail at the moment.

"You might as well tell me the rest. And please don't leave anything out, no matter how ridiculous or trivial it seems." I urged.

"I really don't know if what's been happening to Virginia lately . . . let's just say that we believe her nurse, Hilda Gallardo, may be responsible for some strange goings-on in the staff quarters."

"So Emilia's daughter, Virginia, and her nurse, Hilda Gallardo, are both staying in the staff quarters."

"Virginia is. But Hilda comes in at six in the morning and leaves at five in the afternoon. Emilia, with the help of Julio and Milagros, takes care of Virginia at night . . ."

"Just a second, please. Who is Milagros?"

"I'm sorry. Milagros is our gardener. But she and Virginia have been friends since high school."

"And she lives in the staff cottage, too?"

Cantero nodded.

"Did you hire Nurse Gallardo through an employment agency?"

"No. Emilia's other daughter—she's married and doesn't live here—she recommended Hilda Gallardo to us. They know each other from church. We met with Hilda, her references checked out and we hired her. Whenever Emilia, Julio and Milagros are out for the evening, Hilda spends the night at the cottage. That was the case a week ago. Hilda said that she heard a strange noise and woke up . . . at about one in the morning, I believe. At first, she thought that perhaps Julio or Emilia had come back. But when she went to check, she didn't see them. She went into Virginia's room. And she found a dozen yellow roses around Virginia's head, like a halo. There was also some sort of testimonial note on the pillow, with only three words written on it, '*Gracias, Santísima Niña.*'"

"*Santísima Niña*. Are you saying that Virginia is a saint?"

"Apparently this grateful person believes she is."

"Did you find out who left the note or what Virginia was being thanked for?"

"I—we—don't know who. And how this individual managed not to be seen by anyone is beyond me. We're hoping you'll be able to find out about this and everything else happening around here. We're very concerned, as you can imagine."

"I can understand why. Do you still have that note? May I see it?"

Cantero took out a slip of paper from a desk drawer and showed it to me. I did not want to take out the note in my handbag to compare the handwriting on both.

I looked at it carefully, then handed it back to him. "I'd like a copy of it, when you get a chance."

Cantero returned the note to the desk drawer.

"Like you, I find all of these events very odd and disturbing. Also, I agree with you, they're not just a series of coincidences. But I need some time to digest it all. Let's meet again tomorrow morning. I may have some other questions for you then."

"That sounds reasonable," he said.

Lula Marie had dozed off in her chair.

"I think I'd better take this Sleeping Beauty home." I got up.

"Wouldn't it be better if you two spent the night here?" Estefanía asked.

"Thank you. But I left my car and my overnight bag that's in it at Oro Blanco."

"Will you be able to find your way back to Lula Marie's? It's really no trouble accommodating you both tonight," Cantero said.

"We'll be fine. I'm sure I can find my way back to Oro Blanco."

"Let's help you up," Cantero told Lula Marie.

She gave everyone a silly smile. With Cantero's help, she began her wobbly walk to the front door. Estefanía stayed by my side.

"Do you have an extra bottle of water? It'd help me stay awake," I explained.

"I'll get it for you." She left for the kitchen.

I retrieved the note from my bag and the one left on Virginia's pillow from Cantero's desk drawer. At a glance, it seemed each note had been written by a different individual. I put them back where each belonged. I waited outside the study door for Estefanía. I looked at my watch. It was 11:28. Barring a mischance, Lula Marie and I would be reaching Oro Blanco at the stroke of midnight.

Estefanía came back shortly with a cold bottle of water. She handed me a slip of paper with her and her husband's phone numbers. I gave her my business card, including my cell phone number. We said good night. She did not see me to the door.

Cantero waited by the truck until I adjusted the seat and mirrors. I waved goodbye. Just before I reached the gate, I stopped briefly, got my gun from my briefcase and put it in my handbag. I also checked Estefanía's handwriting against that of the note left in my bag earlier. No match.

I drove out the gate and turned onto Highway 49. Lula Marie, strapped to the passenger seat, was fast asleep. I was driving through the dark heart of the Gold Country, virtually alone with all sorts of unanswered questions on my mind.

TWO
FOREGROUND DIVINATIONS

I was on foot, running, pursued by someone. I ran faster, stopped and looked over my shoulder. He was still coming. I sprang up, covering a greater distance in leaps that took me higher and higher. I was totally airborne. I closed my eyes. I knew that if I looked down, I would hit the ground in no time. I couldn't help it and opened my eyes. I immediately began to spiral down. But my body never hit the ground. Instead, I was sucked into a spinning vortex as I heard the growl of an animal and a scream. I smelled fresh blood. I awoke with a start and immediately jumped out of bed.

The first part of my dream was familiar. I'd had it often during my childhood and in adulthood from time to time, especially when I was under great stress. Usually, no extra sensory visions accompanied it. Fearing events that seemed possible outside the parallel universe of extrasensory perception was a sort of psychological check, a means to confirm that my instinct for survival still worked as it should. But I didn't feel reassured this time. Instead of awakening just before my body hit the ground as I usually did, my psyche had crossed over into the realm of a vision.

Somewhere in the house, a clock chimed the sixth hour. Sunlight already streamed in through the cherrywood plantation shutters and the champagne-colored silk drape panels. On my first visit to the estancia house, Lula Marie had told me that her parents had chosen to combine the colors of table wines, and aperitif liqueurs, and liquors and use the unique palette to decorate and furnish every room in the house.

The living and adjacent dining areas were the port and cognac rooms. The guest room where I slept was the merlot and champagne room. It was next to the sherry and Cabernet Sauvignon room, Lula Marie's bedroom. But the bathrooms and the kitchen

34

were the exception, named after the world region where the marble and granite in them were from.

My color lyricism at home followed no particular hue or tone or period furniture themes, just the directives of my fancy: comfort, function and beauty, with Chicano-Chicana arts and crafts providing the piquancy.

I opened the cherry shutters. Outside, it looked like a morning perfect for an early hike. But leaving Lula Marie out of my sight was out of the question. At least that part of my obligation to her and the Canteros was clear.

I was intrigued by everything I'd heard the night before, which was already a strong enough reason to pursue the case. But more than that, my ever-present need to make sense of my visions, to prove them right or wrong, already compelled me to take it.

Then there was the stallion Diablo and his handler Julio, although I had no idea yet what role either of them played in my visions. Horses were a constant motif in my life. I was almost always aware of them wherever I happened to be. Perhaps I'd been a horse in a past life or a rancher or a warrior.

Lula Marie moaned in the next room, pulling my attention back to the present. I gathered my clothes and stopped in her room on my way to the guest bathroom. She was still fast asleep. The night before, I had noticed the silk-covered, beautifully embroidered album on her dresser. But I was too tired to admire it. My curiosity piqued now, I opened it to the first page. I looked at the twin sisters, wearing identical dresses, their differences and similarities frozen at age nine or so.

I flipped through the pages of names and birthdates of relatives in their family tree. On the last page, like the lines of a circular poem, Lula Marie had written number and letter sequences, each sequence separated from the next by a hyphen. The lines, written in purple ink, were cleverly used to form a cluster of grapes. I studied the sequences and soon was able to make out a Social Security number, a driver's license and a few other things that were most likely credit card numbers. A sequence beginning with the letters LRL followed by six digits stood out.

I strolled to the guest bathroom. A lone hand towel on a brushed-nickel ring hung next to the marble-topped vanity. I reached into the linen cabinet above the toilet tank and pulled a bath towel out. A bundle of dried lilacs tied with purple ribbon slid out and fell to the floor. I picked it up. I saw the small card laced in the ribbon. "To my Lilac, who colors my dreams purple" was hand-printed on a lavender-colored card, above the initials P.V.

Paladin Valenzuela wasn't much of a poet, I thought as I stepped under the shower. And surely he wasn't as important to Lula Marie as he hoped for, or she would have kept the lilac bundle and love note in the master not the guest bathroom.

The warm waterfall cadenced down my body as the names of all the people possibly involved in this case bobbed up to the surface of my mind and queued there. Estefanía Feliz Blanco and her husband Carlos Manuel Cantero were first in line, followed by Paladin Valenzuela, Lula Marie's lover-suitor, then by the house-keeper Emilia and her daughter Virginia and a second daughter, whose name I didn't yet know, the horse whisperer Julio, who might also be Emilia's son and maybe Estefanía Blanco Cantero's lover and finally the gardener Milagros, whom I hadn't met yet. Who did she belong to?

Except for the nurse, Hilda Gallardo, all the other domestic staff members had been introduced to me by their first names as if their family name—their pedigree, so to speak—was of little significance.

The multiethnic social fabric of present-day California had been woven during the gold rush era. The social struggle for equality among the races had had its inception then, too. And since then, it had been borne by every generation of immigrant and native Californians alike. But when it came to ethnicity and race, currency or gold nuggets was not a sure ticket into a white community's inner circle. I wondered how well the Blancos, Canteros, Valenzuelas and Arízteguis fared among the predominantly white European population of present-day California's Gold Country.

Showered and dressed, I made my way to the kitchen to make coffee. I was already into my second cup and ruminating on the subject of ethnicity and class during the gold rush era when the phone rang, first in the kitchen, its echo reaching me from someplace else in the house. After the third ring, the call was picked up by the answering machine next to the phone. An instant later, I heard Cantero's voice call Lula Marie's and then my name. "Gloria, if you can hear me, please pick up," he said a second time.

I greeted him while I walked down the hall to check on Lula Marie, still asleep.

Cantero did not return my good morning. Instead he said, "Please come quickly. Don't worry about Lula Marie. Her housekeeper will be there shortly. She can look after her."

"What's the matter?" I asked, already knowing in my heart I wasn't going to like the news.

"Hilda Gallardo was found dead early this morning. Virginia is missing." He hung up before I could ask where and how.

Carrying my handbag and briefcase, I was ready to walk out of the house when someone pushed the door open. A woman I assumed was Lula Marie's housekeeper stepped in. Her face was down as she tied her unruly, curly auburn hair with a band but using only three fingers and her thumb. Her index finger was covered by a large bandage. She gasped and took a step back when she saw me.

"I'm sorry. I didn't mean to scare you," I said.

"It's okay. You must be Mrs. Damasco. Miss Lula said you're going to be staying here a few days. Are you leaving? Let me cook you some breakfast."

The two dark circles under her eyes belied the cheerfulness in her voice.

"Thank you, but I can't stay. Would you mind telling Miss Lula that I'll be at the Cantero Cross Ranch if she needs me? She's still asleep."

"I heard the bad news on the radio," the housekeeper said unexpectedly.

"Bad news? About what?"

"About that nurse that was found dead at the Cantero Cross Ranch." She made the sign of the cross.

"A nurse?"

"Mrs. Hilda Gallardo."

Lula Marie's housekeeper squinted, then rubbed the tip of her short wide nose and sniffled a few times.

"Sorry to hear that. Was she your friend?"

"No. I didn't know her well. I talked to her a couple of times when I was at the ranch with Miss Lula. She is—was a very nice woman. She took care of Virginia Moreno. Sweet Jesus, who would want to hurt La Santísima Niña, too?"

Moreno, at last I had a last name, a fact insignificant in the shadow of what Lula Marie's housekeeper had just said.

"A girl saint? Who is she?"

"Virginia, Virginia Moreno. Hilda Gallardo, the nurse, took care of her."

"I see. Why is Virginia Moreno considered a saint?"

"Oh, she is, believe me. She grants miracles with the help of the Lord and His Blessed Mother. Thank the Lord Jesus, I'm in good health. But people swear all she has to do is look at them or touch them and they're cured. My neighbor, Mrs. Mendoza, she was very ill. Her kidneys, you know. Her son Diego, he doesn't live with his mother. Her only son, you know. But at least he brought her the spoon La Niña uses to eat her tapioca pudding. She likes tapioca pudding. Isn't that adorable?" the housekeeper's face glowed.

Mrs. Mendoza or her son Diego could have left the miracle testimony note and the roses on Virginia's pillow, a lead worth pursuing, so I said, "So La Niña cured Mrs. Mendoza?"

"She did. Diego taped the spoon to his mom's back, where it hurt. In a few days, she was walking around, eating well. She didn't have to have her blood cleaned up. You know, what's it called?"

"Dialysis?"

"Yes, that's it. Doctors just can't explain it."

"Do you know who gave this Diego Mendoza the spoon?"

"Hmm. I don't. No one told me."

"Where do you live?" I asked her.

"In Sonora. Have you ever been there?"

"Sonora, California, not Mexico? Yes. When I was a young girl, my family and I stopped there on our way to Yosemite every summer."

"Tell me, what radio station were you listening to?"

"1098 KAMR, Radio Amor in Lodi."

I thanked the housekeeper, got in my car and drove out.

I didn't tune in to Radio Amor right away. I needed silence to try to make some sense of all I had heard from Cantero and Lula Marie's housekeeper. Hilda Gallardo's death and Virginia Moreno's disappearance were disturbing enough. Young Virginia was considered a saint, able to perform miracles. Her sainthood status was well known among the Spanish-speaking communities from the California Shenandoah Valley all the way to Sonora at the south end of Highway 49. And in only a few weeks after her accident. Odd.

Who had determined that these were miracles? The Catholic Church of late was extremely reluctant to acknowledge, let alone give its stamp of approval, miracles, demonic possessions and exorcisms. Even when the Vatican determined some cases to be worthy of study, the process of vesting a human being with sainthood was long and tediously thorough. But no one became a saint during his or her lifetime. I shivered at what that fact might mean in Virginia Moreno's case.

Miracles and saints, angels and demons walking among us, not to mention ghosts of legendary and historical figures—people believed what they wanted. They acted on those beliefs, even to the point of fanaticism in some cases, depending on their psychological needs for reassurance or their ill-informed consciences. All of us Americans had become so painfully aware of what blind, misguided faith had done on September 11, 2001. And before then, in 2000, when the Christian Right elected a president to rule, along the lines of a single western religion, in the most ethnically and religiously diverse country in the world.

My questions at the moment, however, had more to do with basic human actions than atrocities committed in the name of God or Allah. I stopped briefly at the winery's gate and wrote the Moreno name after Emilia, Julio and Virginia in my notebook. I wondered who had given the spoon to Diego Mendoza. Had he gotten it himself without being seen by anyone at the ranch? Had he left that note on Virginia's pillow? Or had money changed hands? Who paid whom?

Hilda Gallardo topped that list since she spent most of her time by Virginia Moreno's side. But the miracle-hawker could be any of the housekeeper's children or the gardener Milagros. I also added Lily Mendoza and her son Diego to my list of suspects in the miracle-hawking business.

This case was already beginning to drive me crazy. I felt like I was in the middle of a García Márquez novel: All those names, all those miracles and miraculous coincidences. Or were they? I found the fact that Lula Marie's housekeeper—whose name, thank God, I hadn't asked for—knew who I was and what I was doing there more unsettling yet. Someone close to the ranch was keeping tabs on what was happening there, and not just about me, and passing the information to others.

I assumed that, like any other radio or television station, Radio Amor monitored police communications. Technology had transformed both the way the news was gathered and disseminated. So it didn't seem out of the ordinary for the radio station to get word of anything newsworthy as soon as the cops were called. But when I tuned in to Radio Amor, hoping to get a few more details about the tragedy, the program being aired was a prerecorded religious program in Spanish, with no news breaks or flashes, except for the brief station identification.

I turned the radio off when I arrived at the Cantero Cross Ranch. I pressed the intercom button. Although no one answered, a few seconds later the gate opened. I made a mental note to ask the Canteros about the security system and personnel at the first opportunity.

I parked next to a red-striped black Harley Davidson. Two helmets were perched on its seat. A somber Julio was already waiting for me.

"I'm so sorry to hear about your sister and about Mrs. Gallardo."

He didn't correct me regarding his blood relation to Virginia and accepted my expression of sympathy with a nod of his head.

"*El don* y *la doña* asked me to take you to them. Hope you don't mind," he said, pointing with his chin to the Harley Davidson.

He handed me a helmet, puts his on, then helped me with mine.

"It's a beautiful bike."

"It's okay. It takes me where I need to go."

"Where do we need to go now?"

"Over the hill to the sheep pens and barn, then down to the creek area. From there, we'll have to hike up to where Hilda's body was found."

With my handbag slung across my chest, I mounted the Harley Davidson. He cranked it, and we took off with a roar.

A legendary ghost on a motorcycle—I remembered my suspicion the night before that this young man could be riding around the countryside in Joaquín Murrieta's garb on a horse similar to Diablo. I didn't dismiss the thought altogether, especially since it would explain why his sister Virginia rode toward the neon ghost horse the night of her accident.

Fifteen bumpy minutes later we arrived at a knoll bordered by a tall barbed wire fence marking the end of the Canteros' property. We got off the motorcycle. An oak grove on the other side of the fence served as a natural barrier between properties. Some of the trees had been cut down, but the lumber hadn't been removed.

"Who owns the property on the other side?" I asked while I stretched my stressed thighs.

"No one. It's part of a local park. There's a gate a short way down the slope."

He began to walk alongside the fence. I followed.

"Is this where your sister had her accident?"

"Not here, but close enough."

"Why do you think she rode toward the ghost horse and not away from it?"

Julio kept on walking. But I wasn't about to give up.

"Who do you think might have kidnapped your sister and why? Do you know?"

He turned around to face me. "No, I don't. Sure hope I find him first, though."

"You must know your sister is considered a saint—La Santísima Niña."

He shook his head, turned again and began to walk away from me.

I sprinted to catch up to him. "Do you think some religious fanatics might have kidnapped her?"

No reaction from him. I touched his elbow. Julio stopped but didn't turn around. I stepped around to face him.

"I'm really sorry, but we have to talk about this. Trust me. We might not get another chance."

"Look. I know you've been hired to find out who's responsible for all the things that have been happening at Cross, my sister's accident and now . . . all this."

"I've been hired to look into a jewelry theft and the threats on Lula Marie's life. I . . . no one expected this to happen."

His eyes watered, and he threw his head back, perhaps to force the tears down into their wells. "Okay, I'll answer your questions. But we have to keep moving."

"When was the last time you saw Hilda Gallardo?"

"She was with my sister all day yesterday and Thursday. My mom says she left at about six both days. I didn't see her leave."

"What can you tell me about her?"

"Not much, really. She lives in Jackson, about twenty minutes from Cross. I've never been to her house. She's married. Has a young daughter, I think. I don't . . . I never trusted . . . that's all I know about her."

"Why didn't you trust Hilda?"

"She loves—loved—my sister, but started bringing strangers into the house without asking us first."

"Yes. I know about the rose halo incident and the miracle testimonial note. Do you know what made Hilda think your sister could heal the sick?"

He shook his head. "Don't know why Benita sent us the woman. Nothing but trouble."

"Is Benita your other sister?"

"Yeah. My oldest sister."

"Does your sister Benita live in Jackson, too?"

"She does."

"Was she at the ranch yesterday?"

"I'm sure she wasn't. Why do you ask?"

"How does she get along with Virginia?"

He squinted. "Benita has nothing to do with this. You're wrong!"

"Calm down. I'm not accusing anyone. Not yet, anyway. I'm just eliminating possibilities. Believe me, my questions are just the beginning. Look at them as rehearsal for the real deal when the sheriff and his men start with their questions."

"Benita almost never comes to Cross. Never asked her why. I guess 'cause my mom always goes to see her in Jackson."

"Where was Virginia last night? I didn't get to meet her."

"At home, our home. My sister doesn't go out much. She had her bath. She and Milagros talked and watched TV together."

"I understand Virginia and Milagros are good friends. Milagros is the gardener, isn't she?"

"Yep. She and my sister went to high school together. They've been best friends since."

"Does Milagros live at the ranch, too?"

"Yeah. She and Virginia share a room."

"So what else happened last night?"

"Not much more to tell. I went in. We all watched TV. Milagros went to bed a while later. Estefanía—*la doña*—she came in to say good night. She left. Virginia went to bed. Went to bed myself."

"What time was that?"

"About nine-thirty."

"Did you hear your mom come in?"

"I didn't. I hit the sack and was gone. But my mom always checks on Virginia before going to bed."

Give or take a few minutes, Emilia had probably finished her chores at about the time Lula Marie and I had started back to Oro Blanco.

Julio and I came to a gate in the fence, went through it, then down a path leading from it. I could hear voices in the distance and the sound of streaming water closer to us. A distinctly deeper voice rose above the others.

"Hmm. Who's the loud guy with the deep voice? Do you know?" I asked.

"Sounds like Sheriff's Deputy John Marshall. He thinks Hilda's death might be nothing more than an accident. At least that's what he told *el don y la doña* this morning." Julio looked at me.

"But you don't believe that's true."

He shrugged his shoulders. "Deputy Marshall couldn't find a black cow in a herd of whites if he tried. An accident? Pff."

"Was Hilda in the habit of walking around this area?"

"Never. She always stayed pretty close to the house, and today was her day off, anyway."

"Who found her body?"

"One of the forest rangers. Must've been around five-thirty, maybe earlier. He usually comes by before sunup. Trying to catch whoever is stealing horses and cattle around here."

"I understand two horses from the ranch also disappeared. Any idea what happened to them?"

"Nope."

"Have you ever seen the ghost—the neon horse? I've been told people around here think it's Joaquín Murrieta's horse. Do you know who Murrieta was?" I asked and watched for any tell-tale gesture that he, dressed as Murrieta, had been riding around the countryside on Diablo.

Julio tilted his head and gave me a single-dimple smile. "I know about Murrieta and about his horse Tornado. This horse is not Tornado's ghost, believe me."

"So you've seen the black stallion. Do you think the rustlers are using it to lure the other horses and steal them?"

"Could be. But he is a very dark gray mustang, not black, free and frisky, like the wind. And yes, his mane and tail glow in the dark"

"Why is it that no one has tried to rope the mustang? A horse like that . . ."

"I've seen him around an old boarded up house. People say the house is haunted. Maybe that's why people think the gray mustang is a ghost horse, too."

"But you don't believe in ghost mustangs or haunted houses?"

"Ghosts are part of the old Mexico, my mom's world, not mine. But there's something weird about that house. I've also seen mountain lion and dog tracks close to it. Must be something in it the lion wants."

"Maybe the mustang? But I wonder if a mountain lion might have attacked Nurse Gallardo."

"Mountain lions usually drag their kill to a safe place to hide it. The place where she was found? Too out in the open. And the cat would have to be totally starved or sick to go after the mustang. That horse would be too much for the cat. But . . . it happens."

"You know a lot about horses. I really admire the way you handle Diablo. He's absolutely magnificent. But more than that, he's like . . . he's got an old soul in him."

Without meaning to I giggled at my comment. Julio too found it amusing.

"What has Diablo spooked? The lion?"

"Could be. I found his tracks by the creek area, too. He's getting closer."

My heart flipped in my chest, and I shuddered. "Closer to the ranch?"

"It won't be long before he shows up at Cross. The sheep pens, plenty of food there."

"And you think Diablo senses the danger even though it's not immediate."

"Oh, yes. He does."

I tried not to think about the mountain lion. Encounters with wild animals, other than with birds and butterflies, were not my idea of fun in the wilderness. Now it seemed I'd have to be looking over my shoulder for yet another kind of predator.

We resumed our walk down to the water's edge, to a place where large stones made it possible for us to get across the stream. Julio was ahead of me. Golden dragonflies swooped down to the water and hovered over it. Small fish in search of their daily morning meal swam up fast, trying to snatch the dragonflies, but went back down empty-mouthed. The morning sunlight trickled through the trees, making the streaming water sparkle and the sandy edge of the creek glitter. "Specks of gold," I said under my breath. "Gold" echoed in my mind.

Several metallic and cloth items were half buried in the sandy edge. From where I stood, it was difficult to tell if they'd been there a long time. Since Lula Marie and Virginia had heard voices coming from the creek area the evening of Virginia's accident, I asked Julio if people still panned for gold around there.

"Tourists still try their hand at it." Pointing at the slope, he said, "Up again. You first."

A path lined with rocks on both sides wound its way up to the top of the slope. Yellow police tape cordoned the area off there. A green and white van was parked just outside the crime scene. Horses whinnied, but at the moment I couldn't see them.

I clambered up ahead, grabbing onto the rocks on both sides. When I got to the top, I looked for Julio. The dragonflies still hovered in mid-air, but he was no longer behind me.

Cantero waved me on to the paved road that divided the large grassy area where he and Estefanía waited. Farther down, a man in uniform was talking to two other men. His hair flared redder in the morning sunlight. The other two men were wearing coveralls, and I assumed they were the crime scene crew.

The redhead, in uniform, was probably the Sheriff's Deputy John Marshall that Julio had mentioned. He towered a head over the other two men who were between five-ten and six feet tall. The deputy walked over to a green and white patrol car parked opposite the place where the Canteros stood. He got into his vehicle and drove off.

A dense forest, sprawling uphill, began almost immediately past the picnic tables and benches beyond the crime scene yellow tape. Two red plastic markers had been placed on the paved road, about four feet across from each other, to identify a wide vehicle's tire tracks. The tracks stopped about a foot short of a silhouette drawn with chalk on the pavement. The position of the body caught my attention instantly. But I would have to wait for a better opportunity to see it closely.

I stopped briefly to look at a long single tire imprint overlaid by a second tire track. I was sure they were motorcycle tire tracks. Had Julio been lying to me? Could I be that wrong about him? On the other hand, the motorcycle seemed to be a favored mode of transportation up and down Highway 49.

"Shall we? I want you to meet Gerald Finley—Finn. He's an Amador County forensics specialist," Cantero said.

He waved at a third gray-haired man in coveralls, who held a camera in one hand and numbered markers in the other. He had already placed some of them on several spots. To reach him, we had to walk on the grass.

"Where are we?" I asked Estefanía.

"Shadow Creek Recreation Area."

"Is that the only road leading to this place?"

"Uh-huh."

"Hey, Finn, how's it going? I want you to meet Gloria Damasco. As I mentioned before, she'll be looking into the jewelry theft at the ranch for us, maybe into Mrs. Gallardo's death and Virginia Moreno's disappearance, too. I hope," Cantero explained.

I greeted Finn with a head nod since he was wearing his latex gloves.

He flashed a wide smile, his best attribute and a contrast to his soulful blue eyes. "We always welcome all the help we can get. Do you need gloves?" he asked me.

"I have my own, thank you," I replied.

I was delightfully surprised at the invitation to view the crime scene with him. But I couldn't help wondering why I was the recipient of such a privilege, especially since Finn's generous gesture might cost him his job.

"Let's get on with it then," Finn said, unaware of my mental query.

"We leave you in good hands. Julio will come by to pick you up in about forty-five minutes."

"No need. I'll take her. I still have to process your staff quarters. We'll see you at the ranch," Finn said.

The Canteros walked back to their horses while Finn showed me the plaster impression he had just made of the motorcycle tracks. A jagged line zigzagged across the tire imprint.

"The rear tire seems to have been slashed, then repaired and not replaced," I said and made a mental note to check Julio's motorcycle tire tracks later.

Other prints were visible on the bare ground around the grassy area. "Are all of these dog tracks?"

"Dog and mountain lion tracks," Finn said perfunctorily.

I could only pray that the animal's growl in my vision was of the canine not the feline kind, although some dogs could be as equally predatory as lions.

Finn called my attention to another set of tire tracks made by a four-wheel vehicle this time. He scooped small amounts of a reddish soil material in the grooves and poured it into a small evidence bag.

"Dry clay?" I asked.

"Yes, but not from around here."

"So she was killed someplace else and her body was transported here. Do you think whoever brought her here counted on a mountain lion dragging the body away?" I asked.

"Not likely. She's been here too long. Mountain lions like fresh kill. And there are no telltale signs that the body was dragged here. She was brought here in a large vehicle."

"And to a spot where local residents walk their dogs."

My remark got Finn's attention. "What's your take on it?"

"I'm not sure. But it would have been just as easy to bury her in those woods. Assuming this was no accident, whoever dumped the body wanted someone to find her, perhaps give her a proper burial. That means remorse, up close and personal."

"Possible."

"But if her body was transported here, where do you think she was killed?" I asked.

"Maybe Tuolomne County."

"I understood she lived in Jackson."

"Yes, but my guess is that whoever did this probably lives in Sonora or thereabouts. That's where you see clay of this particular color and consistency. And Sonora is in Tuolomne County."

I was already having a hard time remembering so many people's names, how was I going to keep the names of counties straight, too, I wondered. "Time of death?" I asked instead.

"The M.E. estimated it sometime between four and five in the morning. As I said, Mrs. Gallardo had been dead two hours when the park ranger found her."

"Would the killer have enough time to travel from wherever to here, dump the body and get away without being seen by the rangers?"

"Oh, yes, plenty of time."

"And the cause of death?"

"Pending the final findings, of course, the cause of death is a stab to the heart. Come and look here. Tell me what you see." Finn's blue eyes fixed on mine. He tilted his head slightly and waited for my answer.

Was I being tested? I took my time looking over the taped silhouette, then finally said, "I'm almost sure whoever dumped the body here wasn't in any hurry. Nurse Gallardo's legs are together, laid side by side, but her arms extend straight out from her body at about a forty-five degree angle each. The odds of a hurriedly disposed body landing in that particular position are a million to one. The two rather small blood stains on the pavement more or less correspond to the middle of each hand, and the third stain to her chest, perhaps just below her heart. No blood spills or spatters anywhere else. Her body forms a cross," I said.

Finn confirmed with an "Uh-huh."

"Someone went to a lot of trouble to pose her body. Was she lying face up or down?"

"Face down."

Feeling like a "Jeopardy" contestant, I asked, "What about her feet, forehead or back? Any wounds there?"

He raised both his graying eyebrows and gave me a smile of approval. "Except for some postmortem bruises to her legs and feet, there were none other than the punctures in her hands and the fatal stab to her heart."

"What about the weapon?"

"Not found so far. A sharp, slim, pointed object, not a knife." He looked at me again. "Curious, isn't it?"

Head tilted, he waited again.

"A case of stigmata," I offered, keeping my fingers crossed behind my back.

"Looks like it, doesn't it? I've heard of people whose hands and feet bleed for no apparent reason, resembling Christ's wounds during the crucifixion, though I've never before seen those marks on a body, dead or alive. Maybe you're more familiar with cases of stigmata than I am. I apologize if mistaken, but I'm assuming you're Catholic."

"Yes, I was raised Catholic. As a child, I remember reading about Saint Catherine of Siena, who was a mystic and a stigmatic. But I guess it could happen to anyone. Like you said, a huge dose of religious fervor mixed with an equally powerful desire to identify with Christ's suffering on the cross manifests itself in the person's body as stigmata. But, did the medical examiner say anything about Hilda's hand wounds? Had they begun to heal?"

"They had."

"Hmm. So those were inflicted before the stab to her heart. Could they have been self-inflicted?"

"There's always that possibility, but it's not backed up by the evidence so far. The autopsy should confirm it or rule it out, though."

"So it might not be a *true* case of stigmata. Were there any signs of sexual abuse?"

"None that the M.E. could clearly see."

I watched while Finn methodically collected and bagged more samples of materials from the tire tracks. He took photos, using either a Polaroid or a more sophisticated camera, and in some instances, both. He then made plaster impressions of the tracks and labeled all the evidence bags.

"We're almost done here. We'll see what we find at the ranch," he said.

"Do you know that Virginia Moreno is considered a saint by some people?"

"Not really, but it doesn't surprise me. I was at the ranch to gather evidence, both after the jewelry theft and again when they found a halo of yellow roses around the young woman's head."

"Did you find any fingerprints on the safe at the time of the theft?"

"None other than Estefanía Cantero's. She said she had last worn the emerald earrings when she and her husband attended a social affair in Stockton. Cantero said an envelope with about five hundred dollars was in the safe. But the cash wasn't taken."

"That's odd. Any strange prints in the staff cottage after the roses were left on Virginia's pillow?"

"We found a large number of prints in the staff quarters and in the main house. But all of them turned out to be the staff's, including Mrs. Gallardo and Estefanía's, none of Cantero's in the cottage. Mrs. Gallardo's partial prints were found on some of the rose stems, but it seems she had unwittingly handled them."

"What about on the note?" I asked.

"On the notes threatening Mrs. Aríztegui's life? None."

Oops! I had almost put my foot in my mouth as I had meant to inquire about the miracle testimonial note left on Virginia's pillow together with the roses. It seemed Finn had no idea that the note existed, and I couldn't help wondering why the Canteros hadn't turned it in to him or the sheriff's deputy.

I took out the note that had been left in my handbag the night before. Finn was a forensics specialist, and I would not have a better opportunity to identify the person who had so vehemently asked for my help. Having to turn in the note to Finn as evidence was worth the trade. I handed him the slip.

"It was left in my handbag last night while I was at the ranch. I wonder if Hilda Gallardo's prints are on it."

"Let's find out. I have her fingerprint card and a kit in the van. I'm assuming you handled it. So I need your prints, too, just for comparison."

As a private investigator, my prints were already in the system. I took off my latex gloves, as we walked to his van. He took out his fingerprint identification kit. I extended my right palm.

He dusted the note on both sides gently and thoroughly. One partial print and four other clear prints were visible. He took photos of the prints. He compared my prints to those found on the note using a photography magnifying glass. He did the same with Hilda's fingerprint card.

"You might be right. You understand I need more time to be sure. But yes, as far as I can tell, Mrs. Gallardo handled this note. I'll send it to Sacramento for analysis after we get a sample of her handwriting."

Finn lifted the prints from the notepaper, meticulously labeled every item and bagged it. He returned his equipment to his kit and locked all the items in a large metal box labeled "Evidence."

"I think we're done here." He took off his coveralls and put them in the van.

I shouldn't have been surprised when I saw his shoulder-holstered gun. Forensic personnel in general were trained in the use of firearms, just like any other cop. But the gun clashed with my image of Finn as a gentle, soft-spoken man. I couldn't imagine him ever using that weapon. The same thought about me had probably crossed his mind, too.

When we were already settled in the van, he said, "I assume you're not going to keep that appointment in Jackson."

"I thought about not showing up. But what if?"

"What if what?"

"What if Mrs. Gallardo told someone else about her reason for wanting to talk with me? What if that person decides to show up?"

"You leave nothing to chance, do you? I wish you were working for us."

I blushed at his unexpected compliment. We came to a crossroads and I remembered what Julio had said about a haunted house somewhere around there. I told Finn about it.

"I think I've heard about a haunted house around these parts. Part of the Gold Country's lore," he said.

"Have you ever been there?"

"No, but I think I know where it is."

"I'd like to take a look at it after we finish at the ranch. Can you tell me how to get there?"

"Sure. But what does it have to do with Mrs. Gallardo's murder?"

"I'm not sure. I'm thinking more of Virginia Moreno's disappearance. Whoever abducted her might have taken her there. Abandoned, out of the way and haunted. It sounds like an ideal place to stash the young woman without someone being the wiser. I'd like to take a look at it and eliminate the possibility."

"It won't take long to get to the place from here. And now I'm curious myself."

Finn made a left turn onto a dirt road. I memorized every turn in case I needed to find my way back there. I noticed the large number of tire tracks on the road.

"I guess lots of people take this road. Where does it go?"

"It's one of the back roads to Sutter Creek and Jackson."

Fifteen minutes later, he turned again onto another unpaved road and drove for about two hundred feet to the house at the end of it, hidden behind huge oak trees.

As I stepped out I noticed the single tire tracks on it, especially the one showing a jagged slash across the tread. Finn took out his camera and snapped a few shots of the tracks, then went back to the van to get his crime scene equipment.

I surveyed the façade that still showed the fading, smoky reminders of a fire. Two large Chinese wind chimes hung from the porch. Ruffled by the breeze, the large metal tubes still chimed and echoed in the wind. Dried ivy covered most of the outside walls.

Finn and I looked through some of the small holes in the wood boards covering the windows and front entrance.

We circled around to the barren dry, barren back yard. The stench of animal waste was almost unbearable. Swarms of flies hovered over or landed on the piles at one end of the yard. I cupped my hand over my nose and mouth while I fanned the flies away from my face with the other.

"Dog crap," I said.

"Lots of it."

Finn took out a pair of fresh latex gloves and I reached in my bag for mine. He began to snap pictures while I tried the knob of the black wrought-iron door covering the back door. It was locked. I noticed two small plastic containers, the aluminum brand seal still attached to them, next to a large drum full of water. I picked them up. Kozy Shack tapioca pudding. Virginia had been there. Was she still here, tied up and gagged?

"What've you got there?" Finn asked.

"Tapioca containers. I understand Virginia Moreno loves tapioca pudding. I'd like to check the place. Do you have a crowbar in your van by any chance?"

"Matter of fact, I do." Both his eyebrows went up. "But I have something better. Master keys." Finn hurried back to his van.

Strewn all over the yard were cigarette and cigar butts. Some looked fresher than others. I noticed some dark stains on the thin plastic bags covering the piles of dog crap. I pointed them out to

Finn when he returned. He bagged the tapioca containers, some of the butts and took samples of the stuff on the plastic coverings.

"A colleague in ACU—Animal Control Unit—said something about dog fights somewhere around the hills. Maybe this is the place. I'll have ACU look into it."

"But if they have dog fights here, where are the animal cages or the large bloodstains? What do they do with the dead dogs? Maybe inside the house?"

He immediately got to work on the locks.

"I'm going in first." Finn reached for his gun. I took mine out, too. We rushed in.

No one was there. The place was cleaner than I had expected. Large plastic bags piled up in one of the rooms. Next to them lay several thick plastic cylinders and a large bag that contained plastic hangers.

In a second room, six bunk beds were covered with old sheets and blankets. Human odor still clung to them. Several long and short hairs were caught in the weave of the blankets. Finn lifted the hairs and put each in a separate small manila envelope.

The air seemed oppressively thicker in that room than in the rest of the house. Being there made me feel anxious. I attributed my distress to a short bout of claustrophobia. But when I reached under one of the thin mattresses and my hand came in contact with an oval metallic object, static electricity zapped my fingers. The image of a woman wrapped in a blue shimmering cape and sitting in a rowboat flashed through my mind. I knew there was more to my feeling.

"Damn!"

"Are you okay?" Finn asked.

"Oh, yeah. Just a shock. Lots of static electricity in this room." I lifted the thin mattress but I didn't reach for the silver Virgin of Guadalupe medal and chain under it.

"Let me get that for you." Finn held the chain up and looked closely at the medal. "Looks like I might be able to lift that print on it." He snapped photos and bagged it. Sacred Heart religious card with the Lord's Prayer printed on the back was found under another mattress.

Finn took pictures of everything he felt was important, he bagged and labeled two bottles of shampoo and the soap bars in the bathroom. I tried both the toilet and the faucets. There was no tap water anywhere in the house. It was probably brought in from the water drum outside. A bucket in a corner of the bathroom was used as a toilet, probably recently, judging by the strong lingering odor.

In the living room, we found five clothes racks on wheels with many hangers still on them. But other than the tapioca pudding containers, I could not find anything that would tell me where to search for *Santísima* Virginia Moreno next.

"Who lived here before the fire?" I asked.

"I don't know, but someone has been sleeping here. Homeless people maybe, or maybe the men who run the dog fights."

My arms felt cold and I shivered. I started out the back door, surprising Finn.

"You don't really believe the house is haunted, do you?"

"Nah, I just want to get going. Virginia's out there, someplace, hopefully still alive."

On the way to the Cantero Cross Ranch, I finally got the nerve to ask Finn about his friendship with Cantero.

Finn gave me a quizzical look followed by a wide smile.

"We met in college and became good friends. After college we went our separate ways. I got a Ph.D. in criminology and forensic science. Carlos got graduate degrees in geology and agricultural sciences. We kept in touch for awhile, but eventually lost track of each other. Then I went to work for the coroner's office in L.A."

"That must've been something."

"It was. Brutal work. Long hours. Lots of stress. The job pressures finally got to me. After our two kids went off to college, my wife and I decided to get out of L.A. Three years ago, I applied for this job and got it."

"How did you and Cantero reconnect?"

"When we moved to the area, my wife and I went around doing the tourist thing, you know, visiting mines, caves, museums, wineries—lots to see here. We met Lula Marie when we visited the Oro Blanco winery. We got to talking with her. She liked us, and we liked her, too. We exchanged business cards. And one day, she called to invite us to a party at the winery. Low and behold, Cantero was there with Estefanía, who of course we hadn't met before. So Cantero and I picked up where we had left off. How did you know he and I were old friends?"

"You strike me as a smart, fair-minded and honest person. So you had to care a lot for the person asking you to bend the rules especially when your job is on the line. Coercion didn't seem to be the case, so longtime friendship had to be."

"Right on."

When we arrived at the ranch, the front door opened immediately. The Canteros, followed by Julio and Emilia, stepped out on the portico. Compelled by the same disquieting feelings, both Finn and I stood still beside the van for a few seconds. We didn't know what kind of evidence we would find there, but we were both certain grief awaited us.

Finn followed Emilia to the staff quarters. Julio headed for the stables. I went into the main house to discuss matters with Cantero and Estefanía. In light of the developments, we had to redefine my role and objectives in the latest investigation. After a lengthy conversation, we all agreed that these seemingly unrelated events were pieces of the same puzzle. I stressed the need for their honesty and straightforwardness. I also reassured them that anything they wanted to be kept confidential would remain so. I gave Cantero a copy of our agency's standard contract.

"What I just said is outlined in more detail there. I'm assuming that Lula Marie and both of you are my clients. But who, in particular, would I report my findings to?" I asked.

"I know you'll be asking Lula Marie for information from time to time, but please don't disclose all your findings to her. As you saw last night, she is in no emotional condition to deal with all of this. My wife and I keep nothing from each other. So you would report to me directly," Cantero said.

"I didn't mention this to Finn, but I'd like to know why you didn't turn over the note that was left on Virginia's pillow."

"Estefanía and I discussed precisely that on our way back here. We decided to give the note to Finn as soon as he's finished at the cottage. But at the time it happened, we believed it was the thing to do . . . for selfish reasons, yes. We didn't want all kinds of religious fanatics trespassing at all hours or invading anyone's privacy, especially after the jewelry theft. But we also wanted to protect Virginia and her family."

"Who do you think might have started the rumor that Virginia could grant miracles?" I asked.

"We suspect that Mrs. Gallardo herself did. We're just glad we were able to contain it before it got out of hand," he replied.

"Not so. I just had a very interesting conversation with Lula Marie's housekeeper earlier this morning."

"With Aster?" Estefanía asked.

"Yes, if that's her name. I'm sorry I didn't ask her for it," I explained.

"A woman about five-feet-four, mid-twenties, dark olive skin, curly auburn hair, green eyes, rather thin?" she asked.

"That's her."

"What did Aster say?" Cantero asked.

"Among other things, she had already heard about Hilda Gallardo's murder, apparently while she listened to Radio Amor on her way to Lula Marie's. I gathered from what she said that a lot of people up and down Highway 49 know about Virginia's miracle-granting powers. So I have the feeling that it won't be long before the press shows up around here, especially after the bizarre details of Nurse Gallardo's death get out."

Estefanía gasped. For the first time, I saw Cantero lose his composure and curse under his breath.

To help them keep their eyes on the ball, I asked them to tell me about everyone who worked for them, beginning with the gardener Milagros, since I knew very little about her. I took out my pad and pen.

"You don't think that she has anything to do with this. Not Milagros," Estefanía exclaimed.

"I need to look into everyone's background. It helps me in the process of elimination."

Estefanía deferred to Cantero, who said, "Milagros and Virginia are good friends. They went to school together. When Milagros came to visit during high school, she used to help

Virginia with the gardening and never asked for anything in return, not even a meal. It soon was obvious to us that Milagros has a special talent for growing flowers and vegetables. You've seen what she's done with the gardens. So we offered her a job and room and board. She came to work for us about four years ago, right after high school."

"Where does her family live?"

"As far as we know, Milagros lived with an older sister who owns a restaurant in Plymouth," he said.

"What is Milagros's last name?"

"Velásquez," Estefanía answered.

"Does her sister ever visit here?"

"Never."

"How about the shepherds? Who are they?"

Just a short while back, I was complaining about so many names to remember. Now I was asking for two more.

"Anastasio and Zenón are brothers. They tend to the sheep but also help feed and groom the horses. They've been with us for five years. They're good people. No police records. We trust them completely. As for other workers, we hire day laborers when need-ed, but we've had no need for extra hands for awhile," Cantero said.

"Were the shepherd brothers here last night?"

"They were already gone before you and Lula Marie arrived."

"Where do they live?"

"In Amador City," Estefanía said.

"Goodness! So many people's names to remember, as well as many counties and cities, it seems. Where exactly is Amador City?"

Cantero grinned. "Not too far from here."

"We'd better get some maps of the region for you. I have some in the office," Estefanía offered.

"I'd appreciate that. What about the security system?" I asked Cantero.

"We had it installed right after the jewelry theft. Cameras 1 and 2 cover the gate and surrounding area; cameras 3 and 4 are on the roof of the staff cottage. Camera 3 covers the area between the staff quarters and Estefanía's office. The other, the triangle between the quarters, the main house and the stables. All the cameras are motion sensitive and are connected to motion-sensitive lights. There are blind areas, of course: the back of the staff quarters and the area between the stables and corrals and the sheep pens."

"I noticed there's also a surveillance camera opposite the safe in the study."

"Unfortunately, we had it installed after Carlota's Tears were stolen."

"Is the alarm system on during the day or only at night?"

"No, not during the day. Too many people are going in and out of the house. The 'stay in' feature is armed only at night before we go to bed."

"Who monitors your security system?"

"Electronic Protection and Security Services in Jackson. They have a list of names and photos of everyone who works and lives here. They also have personnel who can be deployed in a matter of minutes to check any suspicious activity. EPSS also monitors our security system at Oro Viejo, our winery near Sonora."

"Not at Oro Blanco?" I asked Cantero.

"My sister-in-law objected. Lula Marie values her safety but her privacy is more important to her. Given her emotional state, we didn't insist on it. But that can be remedied if you think it should."

"Not necessarily, but it might be a good idea to have someone stay with her at night. Obviously, right now I can't be that someone."

"We're going to insist that she stays with us, here at the ranch, for as long as necessary."

"Good. Have you been in contact with EPSS about any unusual happenings?"

"Yes, I have. They had nothing out of the ordinary to report—except for the presence of a mountain lion in the area around the barn where the sheep are kept, a couple of nights ago. They'll be checking the tapes for last night and report back to me," Cantero said.

"I'd like to review those tapes. Could you ask EPSS to send you copies?"

"Glad to. I also want to see them."

"I'd appreciate it if the two of you watch them with me. You could help me identify buildings and people."

Cantero got on the phone to the security company immediately.

A pained look in her eyes, Estefanía seemed ensnared in some mental brier patch since hearing my request for the security tapes.

Was it really possible for husband and wife—for any two people for that matter—to keep things from each other? A disturbing question since I had come to like Estefanía, perhaps because I sensed her vulnerability, hidden so well behind the mask of indifference and self-assuredness. But I also liked Cantero.

"I have a couple of questions for you," I said to her.

Estefanía snapped out of her reverie and took a deep breath. "What about?"

"Finn and I checked a house, off an old road to Sutter Creek and Jackson. I believe the kidnapper held Virginia there for awhile before moving her to another location. Do you know the place?"

"I do."

"People seem to think it's haunted. What do you think?"

"I've heard the rumors—dogs baying for the people who died there. People swear they see strange lights and hear things very late at night. I don't believe in ghosts, haunts or anything of the sort."

"Who died in that house?"

"A man and his two daughters lived there a long time ago. He was a very good tailor, but I understand he never left the house. His daughters did alterations, but also delivered garments, etc. I don't think I ever knew their names. I heard that all three died in a fire there."

"The house was never rebuilt. Who owns it now?"

"Probably the county, if no one has come forward to claim it."

"Do you have any idea what really goes on in that house?"

"I don't, but I suspect it's being used to raise dogs or maybe for illegal dog fights."

"That's what Finn said."

Cantero walked back in. "EPSS will send the tapes by messenger this evening."

"Great. If there's nothing else right now, I'd like to see what Finn's up to."

I picked up the copies of the contract signed by Cantero and me, and I gave him his. He handed me a retainer check. We shook hands.

"By the way, thanks for asking Finn to share his findings with me. It makes things easier. I hope he doesn't have to pay an exorbitant price for his generosity."

"He'll be okay. I'm sure he appreciates your concern, and so do we."

Cantero was himself again, charming, pleasant and in control.

Outside, I checked Julio's motorcycle tire track. It showed no jagged tread marks like those at the crime scene. I looked at my watch. It was quarter to eleven. I jotted down the time next to the information about the bike tracks. Then I called Justin.

After a rather tepid good morning, he said, "I'm afraid I have bad news. Carl Salvatierra made bail yesterday. This morning he was found dead, stabbed just outside his apartment house."

The image of Carl lying in a pool of his own blood flashed in my mind. I felt dizzy and had to lean on the Volvo. My vision had just become tragically real.

"Do they know who did it? Was it Sylvia?"

"No. Actually, Sylvia has a solid alibi. She was at work when it happened. The cops are looking for a home boy, a member of the Sureños gang. His street name is Pulga. Apparently a neighbor heard this Pulga guy and Carl arguing. Pulga left, but the police think he went back later and killed Carl. Everyone knows about Carl's addiction to gambling and drugs. I'm not sure what the Sureños are into, probably both sharking and selling."

"I'm glad Sylvia was cleared. Damn! I should have asked the cops to keep Carl in jail longer."

"You know the cops couldn't do that. Even if you had explained why, they wouldn't have believed you, anyway. It isn't your fault."

Julio stepped out of the dahlia garden on the other side of the main house. He signaled for me to join him.

"Gotta go. It looks like I'm going to be here for awhile. I'll call you this evening and explain."

"Be careful. And remember. You did save Sylvia's life, and hers was the life worth saving."

Justin was right. The choice had been clear. I would have been the hand of fate had Carl not given up when he did. But Justin had no idea how it felt to be myself and *la otra,* to have this prescient self in me. I could see in ways most people can't. And this simple fact compelled me to act on events beyond my control, to walk the fine line between reason and insanity.

By the time I joined Julio, I was commiserating with schizophrenics and tightrope artists.

"Dr. Finley would like to see you," Julio said.

We walked toward the cottage. The warm fragrance of sun-bathed dahlias reached my nostrils.

"Is the gardener Milagros around?"

"She's in the house, the main house, helping my mom."

Julio opened the door to the staff cottage for me and headed to the stables.

Putting a fresh pair of latex gloves on, I took a brief look in each of the rooms as I walked the length of the hall from the living area to the back door. Four medium-sized bedrooms, a kitchenette, a full bathroom and a sitting room made up the staff quarters at the ranch.

The bedrooms were scantily furnished but, with the exception of Emilia's, which had a double bed, all the other rooms had two or three single beds in them, perhaps to allow for any addition to the staff.

On her dresser, Emilia had assembled a number of tall votive candles, all lit now, before statuettes of the Virgin of Guadalupe, the Sacred Heart and Saint Francis of Assisi. On the walls were her family photos. Although younger, I immediately recognized Julio. He had mentioned that Benita was his oldest sister. Virginia had to be the youngest but the most popular as there were photos of her with another young woman, who I assumed was the gardener Milagros, and with a woman in a nurse's uniform. I pulled that photo out of its frame.

Virginia and Milagros shared a room. Framed images of the Virgin of Guadalupe hung above each bed. I was lured by an assortment of trophies on a shelf and medals in a Mexican stained-glass box. Virginia had won several local and state swimming and diving competitions while in high school.

Posters of horses and motorcycles decorated the walls in Julio's room. Most prominent among them were two large photos of Diablo ridden by Estefanía and Julio on different occasions. Books, mostly adventure stories, were stacked up on his dresser. Unlikely books to find in his collection were Isabel Allende's *Daughter of Fortune,* next to a stapled chapbook of Corky Gonzales's "I am Joaquín" and two anthologies of cowboy poetry. I opened the Isabel Allende's novel to the title page and wasn't surprised to see Estefanía's name on it under a single word, "Enjoy!"

When I joined him, Finn was dusting the rear screen door and lifting prints from it. He immediately handed me a small brown envelope.

"Take a look in there."

A green gem surrounded by ten small diamonds slid out of it and onto my hand. "Carlota's Tear."

"Right."

"Where did you find it? And where's the other earring?" I returned all the items to him.

"I found only one, on the ground, outside this door. I would have missed it, but those are real diamonds, as you can see—the light hit them just so. The shine caught my eye." Finn looked at his watch. "About a half hour ago—noon."

It was twelve-thirty. "May I borrow the two other items we found at the boarded-up house? The Virgin of Guadalupe medal and the Sacred Heart prayer card."

"I'll let you have the Polaroid snaps of them. Best I can do, you understand."

"Good enough. I'll get them back to you before you leave. How far is Jackson from here?" I asked.

"It's about twenty minutes, give or take, south on 49. You won't miss it."

"Good. I still have time to talk with Virginia's mother Emilia and her friend Milagros before I leave."

"I'm glad someone besides Marshall is going to. Cantero said the deputy already talked to Milagros while we were at the recreation area and scared the hell out of the poor girl. That fool threatened to have her deported unless she confessed. To what?"

Finn shook his head. I drew air in and let it out slowly to help me contain my anger. We exchanged business cards and cell phone numbers.

I walked around the cottage to the main house. I hated to see a cop or anyone else in authority immediately threaten a person of color, even those born in the United States, with deportation or harm. Ethnic rage was beginning to make my blood boil.

Emilia's hair seemed to have grayed considerably between midnight and noon. She held a rosary in her trembling hand and wrapped it around her wrist as I entered.

"Is it all right with you if I take this photo of Virginia and Mrs. Gallardo? I might need it. But I'll get it back to you soon."

"Okay."

"*Mucho gusto*, Milagros," I said and shook the young gardener's rough hand.

She pinched the tip of her thin long nose and sniffled. Her tears, caught at first in her dark thick eyelashes, were soon rolling down her freckled cheeks and collecting in the deep groove above her upper lip. She patted her eyes dry with a tissue.

Emilia immediately poured some coffee for me and warmed up some of the turnovers left from the night before. She reminded me of my mother, who, even in the most painful of life's circumstances, had always put the comfort of others before her own. She leaned back on the counter and waited.

I sat in front of Milagros. "I want to reassure you both that whatever you tell me will be kept in confidence. Even though others have already asked you similar or the same questions, I need to hear your answers myself. Is that all right with you two?"

Both women agreed with a half smile. Emilia rubbed the rosary's crucifix lightly.

"Did you see or hear anything strange last night?"

"The horses were restless, especially Diablo," Emilia answered.

"More than usual?"

"Yes. Diablo was quite restless."

"What time was that?" I looked at Milagros. "Do you remember?"

She shrugged her shoulders and gave me an apologetic glance.

"It was two-ten. I was ready to wake up Julio, but I heard him go out to check on Diablo. I went back to sleep," Emilia replied.

Julio hadn't mentioned the incident at all when we talked earlier.

"What time did Julio get back?"

Emilia rubbed her forehead with her fingers as if to help a recollection along, then shook her head. Milagros kept her eyes stubbornly fixed on the table, her lips tightly closed.

We all heard Cantero's voice somewhere outside the kitchen. Emilia went to the back door and opened it. Apologizing for the interruption, Cantero told the women they could go back to their quarters in about ten minutes.

"Is Dr. Finley staying for lunch?" Emilia asked right away.

"No. He has to get back to work. Estefanía and I are going to Lula Marie's house. We'll have lunch there. You two, try to get some rest."

Turning to me, Cantero said, "Keep me posted."

Emilia closed the door and sat at the table while I reviewed my notes.

"Milagros, you share a room with Virginia. Is she a sound sleeper?"

"Not really. She gets up to go to the bathroom sometimes. Most of the time I hear her but I go back to sleep." Trying to contain a tear, she hiccupped.

"Emilia, did you hear Virginia get up last night?"

"I did, but I heard the toilet flush, so I didn't get up to check on her. Now I know I should . . ."

Trying to draw her away from the edge of guilt, I asked, "Do you remember if Virginia got up before or after Julio left the house?"

"I'm almost sure it was after."

"It was after," Milagros confirmed.

"Has she ever wandered off—I mean—has she ever left the house, gone outside in the middle of the night?"

"No, she never did," Emilia said.

Out of the corner of my eye, I saw Milagros jerking her head slightly when she heard my question, but she remained quiet. She wasn't going to talk in front of Emilia.

"Is there anything else you can tell me?" I asked Emilia.

When she shook her head, I got up to leave.

"Let me help you with your things," she offered.

I squeezed her shoulder. "You go and get some rest. Milagros can help me."

Emilia walked out, her thumb already moving up to the first of her rosary beads.

"Let's talk a bit longer . . . outside," I said to Milagros.

She let out a sigh of resignation and followed me to the front door, then out to the portico.

"I know this is very hard on you, on everyone. But I need to ask you a few more questions. You and Virginia are best friends, and I'm sure she's told you things that she wouldn't want her mom to know. Look at me. I'm pretty old. And you wouldn't believe it, but I still keep secrets from my mom. And sometimes, so my mom won't worry, I have to lie to her too. But just tiny white lies."

For the first time, Milagros smiled. I shared with her what Lula Marie's housekeeper had told me about her neighbor's miraculous recovery from kidney disease. "Do you know how the Mendoza family got their hands on Virginia's spoon? Who gave it to Diego Mendoza?"

"I did. But Virginia said it was okay." Her tone was vehement.

"Are Diego and you . . . boyfriend and girlfriend?"

"No . . . Diego is . . . was Virginia's boyfriend, before the accident. Virginia changed after the accident. You know? She remembered Diego but it was like she wasn't hung up on him anymore. But she didn't know how to tell him."

"It's not easy to let someone down. Tell me about Virginia. Is she very religious? What does she like to do?"

"She likes old sit-coms. We watch them together every night. She never complains and never says anything bad about anybody. She always tries to help people."

"How does she help them?"

She thought for a moment, then said, "It's like she knows what to say to someone to make them feel good. Sometimes . . . I . . . you're going to laugh . . ." Her freckled cheeks turned red.

"I won't. Go on, tell me."

"It's like I could hear her in my head. You know? Like she would talk with me in my head, especially when I was thinking bad things . . . I dunno. Crazy, ¿*Qué no?*"

"Not really. Was she always like that or only after her accident?"

"Before and after. But she never said I was bad for thinking what I was thinking."

"The day of her accident, did she seem restless or upset about something?"

"No. She was happy, singing like a bird all day."

"So she wasn't happy all the time. Why not?"

"She always had terrible nightmares about some kinda bad creature with bright yellow eyes. The monster wanted her soul, she told me. When she had those dreams, she would pray aloud in her sleep. Sometimes, she cried like a baby but . . . like it wasn't her voice. I never tried to wake her up. I just waited until she did."

"Was that awful creature a horse?" I asked.

"You mean like Diablo? No. She loves Diablo, and he loves her, too. She calls him Dark Dancer because Diablo does a kinda cute dance when she's around. The day of her accident, she told me the monster in her dreams wasn't coming back. But that night, she ended up in the hospital."

"Has she ever talked to you about what happened that night?"

"I asked, but she never told me. I think maybe she remembered what happened, but she didn't wanna talk about it. She slept a lot and prayed a lot after she came home from the hospital. And sometimes she talked to herself out loud."

"Someone told me that she loves tapioca pudding. Is that right?"

Milagros smiled. "Yeah, she likes it, lots of it. And pecans and apple juice. But she eats mostly veggies. Sometimes she drank milk or ate something Hilda cooked for her, just to please her."

"How did Virginia and Hilda get along?"

"Okay. But, you know, Virginia gets along with everybody. Hilda . . . she told me that Virginia needed prayer. Prayer made her stronger."

"Do you believe that Virginia is a saint?"

"I dunno. Virginia's different than me, than all of us. Maybe she is a saint."

"Did you ever see her heal the sick or perform any other kind of miracle?"

"Not really. But three weeks after her accident, I caught a bird limping around just outside the back door. I took it in and showed it to Virginia. Hilda was reading aloud from the Bible. Hilda looked at it and said it had a broken leg. Virginia took it and covered it with both her hands. She closed her eyes and began to pray. Hilda also began to pray. I went to take a shower. Next I hear Hilda shouting, 'It's a miracle! *Mi Santísima Niña.*' I ran to the bedroom. I saw the bird on the floor. It wasn't limping any more. Then it flew out the window."

"Did Hilda Gallardo start the rumor that Virginia was a saint, that she could perform miracles?" I asked Milagros.

"Yeah, she did. It got weird for awhile."

"How?"

"When I trimmed Virginia's hair, Hilda took the trimmings to give to a woman who had cancer. Hilda said that the woman had been cured. Another time, she brought a woman we didn't know. Hilda said *la señora esa* was her cousin, who was going blind. *Las dos rezaron*—they prayed with Virginia. Hilda said her cousin began to see again. It *got* real weird."

"Did you tell Emilia and Julio about all this?"

"Not at first. I was afraid to tell them 'cause I thought they'd get mad at me. When someone left roses and the *testimonio,* the note, they were very upset. They thought I did it. I told them I didn't. I wasn't even here that night. So I had to tell them what Hilda had been doing. They talked to Hilda and told her to stop it or they would talk to the *señores*. She could kiss her job good-bye, Julio told her."

"What did Hilda do?"

"She stopped bringing people over. But Virginia's hairbrush, one of her T-shirts and other things went missing. Hilda brought lots of rosaries and had Virginia hold them. I never saw them again. I tried to tell Julio about it, but he said that Virginia was getting better. Hilda wasn't gonna be here for long."

"Did Hilda know she was about to lose her job?"

"No. They said they were gonna tell her in a few days. But now, she's . . . dead. You think Virginia's dead, too?" Tears streamed down over her freckles.

"I have to be honest with you. I don't know. But I will find out. I promise you. Now, please be straight with me. Did Virginia ever go out by herself? Did she ever leave the house? And why?"

Milagros combed her hair with her fingers. I reminded her I would keep her confidence. Finally, she said, "A few times, mostly at night to be with Dark . . . with Diablo. Sometimes she went to the stable and sat there telling him things. She used to do that before she had her accident, too. I'd go and get her before her mom missed her."

"Did Hilda know about Virginia's visits with Diablo?"

"She did. One time, when Hilda spent the night, Virginia went to the stable. I came home early. I went looking for them. Hilda was there with Virginia. But she never got near Diablo. Diablo didn't like her, she told me. I think she was right. Diablo got angry when she got closer to him."

I showed her the photos of the small silver medal and the prayer card. "Did these belong to Virginia? Or maybe to Hilda?"

"Maybe the medal. Virginia had one like it and never took it off. But Hilda had one like it, too."

"Did Virginia ever go out to meet with Diego Mendoza?"

"Not after her accident."

"But she asked you to give Diego the spoon. How did she know he needed it? Was he here?"

"He came to the ranch only once after Virginia's accident. He asked me if I would let him in the house. I told him I couldn't. His mom was very sick, he said. And Hilda told him to ask

Virginia to help her. He looked sick with worry, so I told him to wait outside our room by the window. Virginia agreed to talk with Diego through the window. He begged her to help him. He was crying. She was crying. And I was crying. Virginia gave me the spoon to give to him. I did, but I made him promise he would never come back to see her. I never wanted to see her cry like that again."

"Did she tell you why she decided not to see Diego anymore?"

"No. I guess she didn't wanna hurt him. Like I said, she didn't really love him, not the way he loved her."

"Was he okay with that?"

"I guess so."

"Where can I find him?"

"In Sonora, but I don't know his address."

"Okay. I'd also like to talk with Benita, Virginia's sister. I understand she recommended Hilda Gallardo for the job. How did Benita and Virginia get along?"

Milagros looked down at her flip-flops and wiggling toes.

"It's okay. You can tell me."

"I think Benita was jealous of Virginia. Everyone loved Virginia. And she was her mom's favorite because she was the baby. But Virginia loved Benita very much. Every time Benita was nasty to her, Virginia just took it."

She covered her mouth with her hand. "You don't think . . ."

"That Benita has something to do with Virginia's disappearance? She probably doesn't, but it's my job to look into everyone's relationship with Virginia. And also with Mrs. Gallardo, you understand? Please don't mention this to Emilia and Julio, not until I've had a chance to talk with Benita. I keep your secrets and you keep mine. Fair?"

Milagros grinned, and her eyes lit up. She gave me Benita's address and directions to her house. She walked with me past the garden outside Cantero's study.

"When this is over and Virginia is home again, you're going to have to show me how to grow dahlias like yours. They're absolutely gorgeous."

"I will," Milagros chirped.

I saw Finn putting things back in his van, and I gave him back the two Polaroid snaps. I headed for my car and got in. I called Lula Marie. She seemed to be feeling better.

"Estefanía and Cantero want us to stay with them," she said.

"It's a good idea. My bag is packed. Would you mind bringing it with you?"

"Happy to. Where are you now?"

"On my way to Jackson. Something I have to look into there."

"Will you be joining us for dinner at the ranch? I have to warn you, though, Estefanía is cooking tonight." She let out a nervous giggle. I assumed it was her way of coping with all the distressing news. But at least she sounded sober.

"What time?"

"Eight or thereabouts."

"I'll try. I'll call if I can't."

I still had about forty-five minutes before my appointment in Jackson. But I decided to take off anyway so I would have time to check the area around the Golden Nugget Taverna in Jackson before walking in. My heart sped up a little as I reached the gate. A heat wave crept up my thighs and then my belly, and soon, my whole body felt as if it were a grape in the hot summer sun.

Not now, I said to myself, knowing full well that this seething sensation was not related to the unknown waiting for me in Jackson. Estrogen and progesterone sparred in me. I wiped the sweat off my face and neck, turned the air conditioning up and took a left onto Highway 49.

THREE
SCOUNDRELS AND GRACES

Bed and breakfast inns, bistros, restaurants and antique and country stores lined up on both sides of Highway 49 as it crossed the city of Sutter Creek from one end to the other. I saw the visitors' office sign. I had begun to wonder how and when I was going to look into Joaquín Murrieta's life to track down his impersonator—purportedly his ghost. He might be Hilda's killer and Virginia's kidnapper, or he might know who was responsible. I was already up to my third eye in things to do. But I had about fifteen minutes to spare. And although I wasn't sure what good it'd do, I decided to pay a visit to the visitors' office.

An elderly woman, in a blue dress and pinafore greeted me as I walked in. She was friendly and just chatty enough. She immediately began to fill my hands with all kinds of brochures about Sutter Creek and many other cities along Highway 49, including Jackson, the seat of Amador County.

"Why is the county named Amador?" I asked, trying to find a way to ask her about Murrieta.

"You're Hispanic, dear."

I admitted my ethnic pedigree with a head nod.

"This whole area was owned by José María Amador before it became a U.S. territory. Señor Amador and his people were lovers of the land and took very good care of it. Not of the Ind . . . Native Americans, mind you. Everyone exploited them, sorry to say. But not as much as those roughnecks, gold diggers, soldiers and adventurers who had little respect for the land, the Native Americans or each other, for that matter. Thievery, lynching, murder, rape, drunken brawls, they sure were a wild bunch." She looked at me, then cupped her hand over her mouth to cover a giggle. "Sorry. Not everyone was that despicable."

"How about Joaquín Murrieta? Was he one of those despicable characters?"

"I'm afraid I know very little about his life, dear. Some people seem to think he was a good man who witnessed his brother's murder and decided to avenge him. And that's how he got caught up in some criminal activities. Others will tell you he was just a heartless murderer. If you want to learn more about him, you can check the museum in Murphys or the Amador County archives. Now, if you're interested, you can get guided tours of the mines around here. There are quite a few natural caverns, too."

She slid more brochures among the other pamphlets already in my hand.

"What can you tell me about Jackson?"

"It's the largest city around and the county seat with about thirty-eight hundred people. The whole town burned down in 1862 and had to be rebuilt. Nice shops and stores there, and a casino if you like gambling. It's owned by the Mi-Wuk tribe. The Native Americans are finally getting their fair share of the gold."

Two other visitors walked in, and she excused herself. I thanked her and went back to my car. I thumbed through the brochure on Jackson, then went on my way.

Closer to Jackson I saw the signs for two mines, the richest of the Mother Lode, according to the pamphlet. After the fire that took the lives of forty-seven miners, the Argonaut Mine had been permanently closed. But I could see the Kennedy Mine's main head frame crowning the shaft and rising over the top of the trees. Farther down, the steeple of a church on a hill kept watch over the mines and a cemetery where the Argonaut miners were laid to rest.

A left turn onto Highway 88, then down Main Street, led me to the Golden Nugget Taverna in a one-story wood building, sandwiched between an inn and a bistro. I found parking across from the inn, but a row of motorcycles parked alongside one another, and the bikers on them obstructed my view of the tavern's front door. Luckily, the bikers soon climbed onto their motorcycles and rode out. Three men went into the tavern as a couple was coming out.

I reached for my handbag, now a pound heavier, and took out all the tourist booklets, leaving in it only the two regional maps Cantero had given me.

I had just opened my car door when I noticed a man wearing dark-brown western slacks, a cream-colored long-sleeved shirt and a brown hat. He was walking at a good clip and soon was stepping into the Golden Nugget. Since I had no idea who I was meeting, he was as good a prospect as anyone else in there.

It was exactly two o'clock when I walked into the Golden Nugget. A bronze plaque with the year 1864 engraved in it attested to the antiquity of the building. Walking into the tavern and looking at the furniture in it was like stepping back to that distant past. Since there were no stools around the solid oak bar, anyone at the counter had to drink standing up. The three middle-aged men who had walked in a while before, leaned on the bar counter, beer mug in hand. They eyed the two younger fair-skinned brunettes, probably tourists, now looking at the photos on the walls and sipping white wine. Two other customers drank their beers while they played a game of checkers at a corner table.

I looked for the man who had entered the bar ahead of me. But he was either in the restroom or had gone in and left immediately through a rear exit. I located the back door on the left of the oak bar counter, next to an enclosed stage area, which could clearly be seen by anyone in the bar. To the left of the stage, a door bore a plaque that said "Private," which I assumed led to the tavern's office. Next to it were the restrooms.

I walked to the counter. The white-haired bartender greeted me with a "Hi, there." He looked rather tired, perhaps the effect of staying up late every night.

I ordered a glass of draft lager, locally brewed if available. He tilted his head as if surprised by my request.

"Best in the house. Anything to go with that?" He put a bar menu on the counter. I ordered some nachos and paid. I took a seat at the table farthest from the counter so I could clearly see anyone walking into the bar. A few minutes later, the bartender put a basket of nachos on my table.

I had already drunk half the beer and eaten most of the snack when a man walked in. He was brown-skinned and sported an Emiliano Zapata thick mustache, which made it difficult to guess his age. He had a white shirt, black pants and black walking shoes, and he carried a bucket with bunches of flowers in it. He greeted the bartender who gave him the okay to sell the flowers in his establishment.

The flower vendor offered a bouquet to the men at the counter, and one of them paid for the flowers. He then asked the vendor to take the bouquet to the brunettes. The women giggled, then raised their glasses to thank them. The men took their gesture as a come-join-us and ordered another round of drinks for everyone.

The flower vendor threw a glance at the bartender, then approached me. "*¿Rosas o dalias, señorita?*" he asked.

"*¿De dónde son las dalias?*" I asked, intrigued since street vendors rarely sell them.

He pulled out a bouquet of them, set it on the table and answered in a soft voice, "*Son de las que crece Milagros. Preciosas. ¿No cree usted?*" He glanced at the bartender, then at the door to the office.

Switching to English but keeping my tone low, I said, "Not so beautiful as Milagros herself. Who are you?"

Louder, in Spanish, I asked for a bouquet.

"My name is Diego Mendoza. I understand you're looking into Virginia's disappearance. You probably already know about Hilda," he whispered.

"I am and I do," I said.

Diego Mendoza! All sorts of questions came to mind, but the Golden Nugget wasn't the place to be asking them from a flower vendor. I got a ten-dollar bill out of my wallet and gave it to him. He reached into his jeans pocket and took out a five and a slip of paper, then handed both to me. With a "Gracias" to me and waving the ten-dollar bill at the bartender, who answered with a head nod, Diego Mendoza walked out the front door.

I put the bill and the paper in my wallet and returned it to my handbag, waited a couple of minutes, grabbed the bouquet and my handbag, said good-bye to the bartender and walked out. Diego had vanished.

Back in my car, I took the note out and read it.

"Sorry. I didn't want Valenzuela or Deputy Marshall to see me. Go to the Jackson Rancheria Casino, fifteen minutes from here. Map on the back. Two front doors. Walk in through the door on your right and start playing any of the slots there. I'll find you. Four o'clock."

Was Valenzuela the man who'd walked into the tavern ahead of me? But why hadn't I seen him there? It occurred to me that Valenzuela might be the tavern's owner, and he had been in his office all that time. Was he also the same Valenzuela who had been so obsequiously courting Lula Marie? And what did Deputy Marshall have to do with him? I would have to wait another hour and fifteen minutes to find out.

All the mental activity and the beer were beginning to have their effect on my mind and body. I could feed the parking meter and take a nap there. But I'd probably attract the attention of the Jackson city cops. So I decided to go directly to the casino, park and take my nap in the parking lot, hopefully undisturbed by the Mi-Wuk tribal police.

I looked at the map and read the directions: "Left on Highway 88, left on Court Street, right on New York Ranch Road and straight down that road to the casino."

I started down the street but slowed down at the next corner as a sheriff's white and green patrol car came to the stop sign. The window on the driver's side was rolled down. By the way the sheriff sat in the car, I gathered he was a very tall man. He had red hair, a ruddy complexion and the scars left by a bad case of acne. He had to be the Deputy Marshall who Diego mentioned in his note, the same deputy I had seen leaving the crime scene at the recreation area. I stopped and let him make the turn.

At the intersection with the very busy Highway 88, the deputy turned on his siren and lights to gain immediate access to the highway. I had to wait until it was safe to make the turn. The patrol car turned left again a short distance ahead. When I got to that intersection, I realized it was Court Street. But I didn't see his patrol car as I followed the street for a few blocks.

The steeples of two churches loomed a short distance ahead. One of them was Saint Patrick's Catholic Church. A short block from St. Patrick's, a more modern building housed the county courthouse. The Amador County Sheriff's office was straight across from it.

Sure that I had missed my turn, I circled around until I found
Court Street again. I followed it back to the intersection with New
York Ranch Road and made the turn. About four miles down, a
sign warned I was entering the Jackson Rancheria tribal grounds.

Fifty feet ahead, two buildings came into view, a large one-
story building next to a six-level parking structure and another
four-story building on a hill. A sign welcomed visitors to the
Jackson Rancheria Resort and Casino. I was pleasantly surprised
not to see any neon signs. I followed the signs to the parking
garage and found a spot on the fourth floor, near the elevator.

A warm but comfortable breeze was blowing and I lowered all
the windows a little to let the air circulate. I set my cell phone
alarm for twenty minutes. Slowly, my mind began to drift. Soon,
I was walking down a road, able to see only a few feet ahead of
me. I could hear the babbling of flowing water somewhere near
me and the sound of tambourines and triangles. It was night. A
man and a woman were in a rowboat. Then suddenly, a dark horse
came out of nowhere and reared on his hind legs. His front hooves
beat the air. Then he was gone. I followed a path, guided by the
sound of lapping water. I stretched my arms in front of me and let
my ear guide me to the water's edge. I breathed in the fragrance
of gardenias and roses. Pain shot from my elbow to the back of my
neck and across my upper chest. I saw a long tall counter. On its
center, a single candle flame flickered. The flame flared larger and
stronger. It illuminated a carving on the trunk of a tree. A voice
whispered in my ear, "Find this place and you'll find me."

I opened my eyes just before my phone alarm went off.

The Native Americans were finally getting their fair share of the
gold, the volunteer at the Sutter Creek's visitors' bureau said. She
was right. It was only three-thirty in the afternoon, and although
the casino was only half full, enough gamblers were there to make
the Mi-Wuk Native Americans richer.

Once I located the row of slot machines where I was supposed
to meet Diego, I strolled around the casino. It was much smaller
than some of the Nevada casinos but it replicated their style
—carpets, chandeliers, a pool fountain, plenty of places to eat, a

gift shop, row after row of slot machines around the card gaming areas, fake plants and no clocks anywhere. Unlike the Nevada casinos, however, no alcoholic beverages were served. Gamblers at the Jackson Rancheria had to take their losses sober.

No other establishment could boast of being an equal opportunity employer more than a Nevada casino or of having the most ethnically diverse population. Everyone—or rather their green gold—was welcomed regardless of race, age, religion or gender. But at the Jackson Rancheria, most of the gaming patrons were of white European, Mexican/Latin American or Philippino descent, with a few African Americans and other Asians in the midst.

Anonymity was one of the attractions any casino offered its clientele. But I had read somewhere that at least fifteen hundred surveillance cameras watched the action at any casino. The Jackson Rancheria casino, I was sure, was no exception.

When I heard someone announce over the loudspeakers that the shuttle bus back to Stockton was leaving in ten minutes, I checked my watch and strolled back to the area where I was to meet Diego. I sat on the side of the island where most of the seats were empty so Diego and I could enjoy greater privacy. I just hoped that someone up there, in security camera heaven, didn't read lips.

I studied the buttons on the panel, pushed the menu icon on the screen and read all about the winning combinations, including the bonus round, which could give me as many as eight thousand quarters if I played the maximum—three quarters. Three quarters! I was already going over the explanation I'd have to give Cantero for that particular expense. I took out a twenty-dollar bill and fed the machine. I bet one coin and waited only to find out I had just lost my quarter. Playing conservatively, in ten minutes I had already spent three dollars.

I was trying to decide if I should switch to the machine on my right when a man sat there. I snuck a look. The man was wearing a matching gray long-sleeved shirt and slacks and black cowboy hat and boots. He smelled of soap and Aramis aftershave lotion. He took out a bill from his shirt pocket and put it into the machine.

"How're you doing? Any luck?" he asked.

"None. The flower vendor I presume," I said as I recognized Diego Mendoza's voice.

He didn't answer my question and pressed the "Maximum bet" button instead.

I looked at him directly. He was probably in his late twenties, a fact that surprised me, since the gardener Milagros hadn't mentioned that he was so much older than Virginia. He had a tan, but his skin was lighter below the hollow of his neck. His deep-set, honey-colored eyes seemed to light up at the slightest provocation—like any woman staring at him as I was at the moment. But, with the mustache gone, his best feature yet was his shapely mouth and winning smile, displaying a perfect row of white teeth.

He did not resemble the flower vendor at the Golden Nugget. He had done an excellent job at hiding his identity. No doubt I had a master of disguise sitting beside me, and I wondered if he was also a master of other kinds of deception and why.

"So, what did Hilda want to talk to me about?" I asked again.

"Hilda knew who you were and that you'd been hired by the Canteros," he said.

"News around here travels faster than the old Pony Express. But, again, you haven't answered my question. What exactly did she want to tell me?"

"Hilda was afraid that Valenzuela was going to have Virginia kidnapped, but she didn't know why. She thought that if she hired you, too, you would be able to stop Valenzuela."

"Why ask me to meet her at the tavern?"

"She wanted you to see Valenzuela in person before you two talked."

"Who's this Valenzuela guy?"

"He goes by the name of Paladin, but his real name is Jerónimo. Not a man to trust, though. No siree. And Sheriff's Deputy John Marshall? A pile of shit."

Diego pressed the maximum bet button. His machine made all kinds of noises and we both looked at the screen. He had won two hundred quarters. I looked at the amount left in my machine. I had only twenty plays before my one-armed bandit demanded to be fed again.

"I'm assuming Hilda found out about Valenzuela's plan before I even arrived at the ranch. How?" I asked.

"I can't tell you yet. I promised to keep this individual out of it. But, believe me, she got the information from a reliable source."

"I'm afraid that's not good enough. She paid with her life for it. If you knew her and had her in as high regard as you seem to, you'd want Valenzuela brought to justice, not to mention finding Virginia alive."

Diego raised his eyebrows but didn't look at me.

I weighed the pros and cons of just walking out. But too much was at stake.

"Look. This is hardly the place to talk about all this, not with at least two or three security cameras focused on us right now. So I'd like you to please stick to the facts as much as possible."

"Gee! What do you know? I had you pegged as a story lover."

"Just the facts, please. Go on."

"Facts, colon. Valenzuela and Marshall like to play poker and Monte, a very popular Mexican card game during the Gold Rush. But not here at the casino. They and their . . . associates have a weekly game going at the Golden Nugget after hours. Sometimes at Valenzuela's ranch near Sonora. They usually have someone else deal for them to keep the game 'honest.' It was this dealer who overheard the two men arguing about something after the game two nights ago. The dealer forgot his jacket and went back to the tavern to pick it up. The bartender had already left. Marshall and Valenzuela thought they were alone in the tavern's office. The dealer heard Valenzuela say at the top of his voice, 'Look. I don't care to know about the problems with the other women and how unhappy they are. If you think that Saint . . . Santísima Niña . . . can help, go ahead. Won't do you any good, I can tell you that. I'm only doing this for . . . It doesn't matter. I'll take care of that Santísima Niña. Bring her to me. You know where.'"

"Wo-oh! Backtrack. Whose idea was it to kidnap Virginia?"

"Not clear to me either. I'm just telling you what was told me."

"Who were the other women?"

"If I knew I would tell you," Diego said and gave me a don't-interrupt-me look.

"Okay, go on. What happened next?"

"Hilda was always talking to anyone willing to listen about Virginia's gift to grant miracles. She called Virginia the Santísima Niña. The dealer realized they were talking about Virginia Moreno. He snuck out without being seen. As late as it was, he called Hilda and told her about their plan."

"Why didn't Hilda just tell the Canteros?"

"Maybe she thought she could take Virginia to a safe place, before the deputy could get his hands on her. Maybe she thought she couldn't trust the Canteros. I really don't know."

"Look. I can understand your need to be discreet, but . . ."

Diego looked at me and pressed his finger to his lips. A young woman, dressed in a cocktail waitress outfit and carrying a tray with plastic tumblers and bottles of water, was walking toward us. She gave Diego a wide smile.

He asked for two bottles of water and laid two dollars on the tray. He had just pressed the bet button and his machine noisily announced he had won four hundred quarters.

"You bring me good luck," he said and winked at the waitress.

She walked on, but I knew she would soon be back. I took the bottle of water Diego offered me, uncapped it and drank from it.

My mind was spinning as fast as the wheels in both machines. I was sure Diego was the so-called dealer and just as certain he counted on my reaching that conclusion. He was obviously afraid of either Valenzuela or Marshall or both. Valenzuela hoped to gain something by helping Marshall abduct Virginia, but was he desperate for ransom or miracles? Every combination of answers was as incomplete and fruitless as the non-winning spins of the slot.

I finally said, "You really know a lot of people, including this dealer you're talking about. And it's obvious you don't want Valenzuela and Marshall to know what you're up to, or you'd have no need to hide your identity, like for our meeting at the tavern. So what exactly do you do?"

Diego grinned as if he were expecting me to grill him.

"If you must know, I have my own business. I'm a real estate broker."

"A real estate broker. That's interesting. I guess it explains how you know many people up and down Highway 49."

"You sound surprised. What did you think I did, sell flowers?"

"No. I had you pegged as an actor. Have you ever considered playing the role of Joaquín Murrieta or El Zorro, perhaps?"

He laughed but immediately turned his attention to his machine. He had just won the bonus round, ten free spins. He pressed a flashing button. Automatically, the reels began to spin, stopping to register the amount won every time.

"Your luck is changing, too." He pointed at the screen on my machine.

Caught in the more intriguing cat-and-mouse game with Diego, unwittingly I had pressed the maximum bet button and had just won four hundred coins—one hundred dollars. My heart began to race. I felt slightly nauseous. A voice inside me warned me to stay on track.

"You seem to know a lot about Valenzuela and his business ventures. Have you had any dealings with him?" I asked.

"I sure have. I made it possible for him to buy the tavern and the inn next to it and some other real estate."

I drank from my bottle. "What else do you know about him?"

"I believe he and Marshall are involved in some . . ."

"Criminal activities?"

"Let's just say shady business deals."

"Including Hilda Gallardo's death and Virginia's disappearance—two women close to you?"

He straightened up in his chair but did not look at me or answer.

"I know about you and Virginia. I had no idea you also knew Hilda till just now. You two can't be neighbors, since she lives in Jackson and you and your mother live in Sonora. I know your mother has or had kidney disease. How's she doing?"

"You've been busy. I like that." He didn't answer my last question. Neither did he ask how I had come across the information.

"So how did you happen to meet Hilda?" I insisted.

"Hilda and I grew up in the same neighborhood and were in high school together. After graduation, she got her nursing license at a junior college. Then she got married and moved to Jackson.

I got my real estate license and stayed in Sonora. We see each other every so often. Her mom and my mom were good friends, too. After her mother passed, I helped Hilda sell the house in Sonora. That's all there's to tell."

"Seriously. How's your mother doing?"

"My mother was doing well for awhile. Now . . . I guess . . . Virginia did what she could . . ."

"I'm sorry to hear that. You're much older than Virginia. How did you two meet?"

His Adam's apple jerked up and down as he swallowed hard a few times, then said, "At a restaurant in Plymouth."

"At Milagros's sister's restaurant?"

"Uh-huh."

"You do get around."

"So do you. Yessiree."

"Most people I've talked to say that Virginia is very special. What attracted you to her?"

"It's not so much that hers is a great beauty. But she has this uncanny ability to . . . read you, like she knows your problems even before you open your mouth. I can't explain it. But I did fall in love the minute I met her. She makes you feel like everything is all right with the world. You'll see what I mean when you meet her . . . I hope." He rubbed the back of his neck.

"I'm sure I will. Did the Morenos approve of her relationship with you?"

"Julio didn't at first, but I convinced him that my intentions are—were—honest. Besides, actions speak louder than words. I always treated her and her family with respect."

After checking his watch, he pressed the cash-out button. I knew our conversation was over, if for no other reason than the sound of eight hundred coins dropping into the well. I looked around for buckets but I couldn't find any. Shortly, I realized he wasn't going to need them as he stretched his hand, pulled a piece of paper sticking out of a yellow blinking slot and put it in his pocket without checking it.

"Gotta go. I'm . . . showing a property at six. I'm sure we'll meet again. And I'll answer any other questions you have. Call me

later, please. I do want to help," he said, took out a business card
from his shirt pocket and handed it to me.

I looked at the information on the card. I flipped it over, more
out of habit than curiosity. My eyebrows arched up. It said:
"Calaveras County Museum in Murphys, demo game, Mexican
Monte by Diego Mendoza, Sunday, 11 a.m."

So he was the dealer who had overheard Paladin Valenzuela and
Deputy John Marshall's plan. I was impressed. But handsome Diego
Mendoza, who planned everything down to the last detail, hadn't
once asked how he could get in touch with me. Perhaps he was sure
he could find me again if need be. By the time I raised my head, he
had already cashed his voucher and was on his way out.

I cashed out and redeemed my voucher. I was lucky to be
walking out with a hundred dollars in my pocket. But the reels in
my mind were still on a futile haywire spin.

I rummaged through my notes and the piles of information I had
collected about each person I'd interviewed so far. Diego Mendoza
had become the central figure. He'd met the gardener Milagros
first, then he'd became acquainted with Virginia Moreno and the
rest of the Moreno clan through her. A second thread tied Diego
to Hilda Gallardo. Hilda had eventually ended up nursing Virginia
back to health. Diego had told Hilda about the kidnapping. He
was intimately acquainted with Paladin Valenzuela and Deputy
John Marshall's "shady business deal." Valenzuela was directly
involved with Lula Marie. But many threads still hung loose.
Virginia's sister Benita seemed to hold the other end of one of
them. She had recommended Hilda to look after Virginia and
might know about Hilda's concerns the day before, as could Mr.
Gallardo, Hilda's husband, who surely knew about her activities
the night she died. It was time to have a chat with them.

I checked my watch, then called Cantero.

"I have to stay in Jackson a little longer, and I might not be
able to make it in time for dinner. But I'd still like to review the
security tapes with you and Estefanía, if you don't mind."

"I don't. But is it going to take you more than a couple of
hours to get here?" he asked.

"I hope not. But if it's more convenient, you can just leave the tapes for me to review when I get back."

"It isn't that. It's just that cooking isn't one of Estefanía's fortes. It might take a couple of hours before we eat. So you'll probably be able to make it. May I ask you what you still have to do in Jackson? I might be able to help."

"I'd like to talk to Emilia's daughter, Benita. I understand she lives in Jackson."

"I'll save you the trip to her house. She phoned earlier. The whole family has gone to Jackson. Lula Marie is with them. A rosary is being said for Virginia and Hilda. You'll find them at St. Patrick's Church on Court Street. Do you know how to get there?"

"As a matter of fact, I do. I'll see you in a couple of hours then."

I had no trouble locating the church again. The parking lot behind it was full, so I had to find parking on the street a few blocks away. The walk did me good.

St. Patrick's was a rather small wooden structure rebuilt in 1868. The original building had been destroyed by the fire that ravaged Jackson in 1862. Like the adjacent rectory building, the sanctuary was painted yellow. The building displayed the standard cross over a golden cupola over the bell tower, trademarks of most Catholic churches.

I sprinted up the steps. The recitation of the Lord's Prayer grew louder as I entered. I expected to see the Morenos and the Gallardos, but the large number of people praying for the eternal rest of Hilda's soul and the safe return of Virginia, La Santísima Niña, surprised me.

I breathed in the smell of candle wax and the fragrance of incense, which had suffused with sanctity the air of all of my childhood Sundays. I would have liked nothing better than to get lost in the recitation, let my mind and soul rest and pray to be delivered from evil. But evil deeds, or rather the millennial struggle between human good and evil, begun in Paradise had brought me to this sanctuary.

"Glory be to the Father," the male caller of the rosary announced as preface to the third mystery. In black cassock and surplice, he was probably a deacon or sub-deacon. I wondered how it would sit with the parish priest or the diocese to know that most of those congregated there believed Virginia Moreno had saintly powers.

Despite any true or false claims, both Virginia and Hilda deserved the prayers of the faithful gathered there. Mine included.

The third mystery of the rosary was ending when I decided to look for Lula Marie. I made my way slowly down one of the parallel aisles leading to the altar area.

"Pss," I heard someone call softly. I felt a warm hand touch my arm. I looked at the hand, then raised my eyes. Aster, Lula Marie's housekeeper pointed at a spot next to her and stood up to let me through. I knelt beside her.

"Third Mystery," she explained. "I'm praying for Miss Lula Marie, too. She's such a nice woman. She just told me I can have next week off, paid. I guess she's going to be staying at her sister's ranch. But she's here now, you know." Aster pointed at an indistinct place somewhere closer to the altar. The circles under her eyes were darker. She seemed more subdued than the first time we'd met.

"Will you also be staying at the ranch?" Aster asked.

A woman in front of us cautioned us to be quiet. I was grateful, since I didn't want to engage in conversation with Aster there. Talking with Virginia and Julio's sister Benita would have to wait until the rosary ended. After a few minutes, I began to feel restless again.

"Oops! I forgot I have to call my husband. Let's talk after the rosary," I said. I made the sign of the cross and got up.

A surprised Aster stood up to let me pass. I could feel her eyes following me as I walked back to the doors. I turned around and waved at her. She smiled.

I sat on the top step, held my handbag between my legs and rested my elbows on my thighs. A wave of loneliness mixed with disenchantment began to creep up my spine. It was so long ago that I'd firmly believed goodness always somehow prevailed and human justice was possible. I still believed in people's innate goodness, but now I knew that justice, like safety, were illusions. I stood up before the powerful feelings took root in my soul. I got my cell phone out and called Justin. I briefed him on the turn of events and my findings so far.

"Do you trust this Diego Mendoza guy?" he asked.

"I'm not sure. Maybe he's not even a real estate agent in Sonora. I think he's the card dealer who overheard Valenzuela and Marshall talking about kidnapping Virginia."

"Wait. I'm going to Google him."

I couldn't help but chuckle at the way language worked. Who would have ever heard of "Googling someone" even ten years ago? American English had to be the fastest-changing language on the globe. A small wonder we in the United States could still make sense of what we said to one another, let alone hope for the rest of the world to understand us.

"What d'ya know? He is a real estate agent after all," Justin said.

He gave me the agency address in Sonora. I checked it against the information on Diego's business card. It was the same. I gave Justin Marshall and Valenzuela's full names and the little information I'd gathered about them when he offered to "Google" them, too. Since it was going to take a while, I asked Justin to text me the information.

A sheriff's patrol car moved slowly up the street as Justin and I said good-bye. Deputy Marshall was at the wheel. He parked in front of the sheriff's office, about a block from the church, but immediately began to walk toward St. Patrick's Church. I went back in as the deacon announced the fifth and last mystery of the rosary. I stood at a spot farthest from the door.

The door opened. I expected to see Deputy Marshall. Instead an old man walked in, hat in hand. He combed his gray hair with his fingers. He wore black jeans and a blue shirt already a bit frayed around the cuffs. His sandals creaked with every step. He genuflected, made the sign of the cross and sat in the third pew from the back.

I took a seat behind him. The door opened again. I did not look, but the old man glanced indifferently at the newcomer. His neck crooked a bit more to catch a glimpse of me. Despite his salt-and-pepper mustache and eyebrows, he didn't look as old as I'd thought at first. Something about his eyes seemed familiar. He got down on his knees. I rested my head on my laced hands and joined in the praying.

Out of the corner of my eye, I saw Deputy Marshall walk slowly up the opposite aisle, elbows out, thumbs digging into his belt. People glanced in his direction, then quickly went back to their prayers. Perhaps Marshall just wanted to make the presence of the law known to all Mexicans in the church. Intimidation of the defenseless was the deputy's MO. Soon, however, I realized Marshall was there for another reason. He stopped at one of the pews and signaled for a man to follow him outside. I recognized the bartender at the Golden Nugget Taverna. Marshall whispered something in the bartender's ear, and both men strolled to the door.

I debated whether I should bid God farewell, postpone my talk with Virginia's sister Benita till the next morning and follow them. The old man made the sign of the cross, stood up, genuflected and took a few steps back. He glanced in my direction and winked at me. Lecherous old buzzard, I thought. His smile revealed a perfect row of gleaming white teeth.

"A master of disguise." The words ran through my head like a news trailer on CNN. I quickly headed for the door.

Deputy Marshall's patrol car, with the bartender in it, waited to turn at the corner. "Old man" Diego wheeled a bicycle out from the walkway between the rectory and sanctuary. He reached the street, mounted the bike and began to pedal fast. The patrol car began the turn. On his bike, Diego hung onto it like a remora to a shark's fin.

People were leaving when I walked back into the church. I made my way to the front row after I spotted Lula Marie and the Morenos talking with some other people there. Emilia had her arms around a woman who was crying inconsolably. I recognized Benita, the oldest of the Moreno siblings, from the photo on Emilia's dresser. The deacon who had led the rosary joined others to express his sympathy to both families; their concern seemed to exacerbate Benita's grief. Her wailing could be heard in every corner of the sanctuary. Lula Marie was the first to see me, and she waved me on while she patted her eyes dry.

"Is something the matter?" she asked, looking into my tearless eyes.

"Just trying to keep my eyes on the ball."

"I see. Okay. Could I hitch a ride back to the ranch with you? As you can see, Julio has his hands full and won't be going back till tomorrow."

"Sure," I said, knowing that it would be useless to try to talk with Benita at that point.

"I'm assuming you want to express your condolences . . . I will tell them you're a friend visiting the area—okay with you?"

"Perfect."

Lula Marie introduced me first to Benita, who resumed her bawling after a very brief intermission, then to Hilda's husband, Sal Gallardo.

Sal Gallardo's weak handshake belied his muscular physique, which he liked to flaunt with rolled up short sleeves and tight jeans. He had short cropped hair, a fuzz of a mustache and a goatee. He stood straight, placing his left hand behind his back while keeping his restless daughter close to him with the right. He barely looked at me as he politely listened to my words of condolence, and he expressed his gratitude with a simple "Gracias." He caught a sigh midway and sucked it in while his small, dark-brown eyes looked past me and skipped up and over the empty pews one at a time, as if he were counting the number of hurdles between him and the front exit. His thin lips pursed as he glanced at Benita, still torn up with emotion and being comforted by everyone.

No sympathy, sorrow or despondency, nor any other emotion expected under the circumstances showed in his calm gaze. Shock followed by denial, a need to make the Morenos responsible for his wife's death, misunderstood machismo or a desire to be strong for his child's sake—all possible reasons for his seemingly emotional detachment.

I knew that boring through this man's defenses was going to be hard. But no one else could provide details about Hilda's activities the day before her death and about her reasons for not notifying the Canteros about Virginia's possible abduction.

Lula Marie's housekeeper Aster approached the group and hugged Benita, Emilia and Julio.

"Your sister is all right. I know it in my heart. Have faith," she said.

She turned to Sal Gallardo and his mother and expressed her condolence, then said hi to Hilda's young daughter, who hid behind her grandmother's skirt.

Sal Gallardo turned away from those gathered around both families. Without a word, with his daughter and mother in tow, he began to walk to the front door.

"Are you ready?" I asked Lula Marie.

She wasn't ready to leave yet, so we agreed to meet outside. Lula Marie's housekeeper Aster walked with me to the door; outside a silver pickup truck was backing into a parking spot across from the church. The housekeeper said good-bye, ran down the stairs and heading to the parking lot behind the church.

All clad in black, a man stepped out of the truck. "There he is, one and the same Valenzuela," I said to myself. He was the man I had seen entering the Golden Nugget Taverna ahead of me that afternoon and Lula Marie's suitor. I didn't want him to see me, so I walked back into the church and stayed out of sight.

Paladin Valenzuela spotted Lula Marie and walked over to her. He put his arm around her shoulders and gently led her away from the people there. After a brief talk, Lula Marie began to walk toward the rear while Paladin shook hands with the Morenos, the deacon who had led the rosary and the many others gathered around him.

"Paladin will take me home. I'll see you there," Lula Marie said, looking in Valenzuela's direction. "Go, unless you want him to know who you are."

On the way to my car, I went over my conversation with Diego Mendoza at the casino. He could provide me with information about Deputy Marshall and Paladin Valenzuela, their habits, their activities and business ventures. Keeping close tabs on them might lead me to the place where they kept Virginia, hopefully still alive. But, to accomplish those goals, I had to keep under their radar. My identity and purpose there were already common knowledge. Staying at the ranch would make my job extremely difficult, an unnecessary risk for me and others.

A disappearing act was in order.

FOUR
DEATH'S REALITY SHOW

The golden glow of twilight remained on the western horizon, but night had already fallen over the Gold Country. It was still Saturday, the same day Hilda had been found murdered and Virginia had disappeared. But I felt as if I had circled the earth twice already. And I hadn't yet reviewed the security camera tapes, hopefully already in Cantero's hands.

Near Sutter Creek the traffic intensified as locals and weekend tourists rushed to bars and restaurants. A motorcyclist recklessly weaved through traffic behind me. When he almost hit a couple of jaywalkers, drivers honked their horns or flipped him off. He finally got the message to slow down.

The traffic into town was heavier, but only the biker and I remained in the lane out of Sutter Creek. He kept his distance for awhile. But he was soon right behind me. His yellow-striped black blazer flapped in the wind like the wings of a night-hawk. His dark helmet and visor made it impossible for me to see his face.

The traffic in the opposite lane eased off. Keeping as far to my right as possible, I gave the biker an opportunity to pass me. But he seemed more interested in having a road tease, accelerating as if to pass me but then slowing down to weave across both lanes.

"Thrill-seeking freak." I tolerated his shenanigans since I was only about five minutes from the Cantero Cross Ranch. The biker finally decided to make his move as a pickup traveling in the opposite lane got closer. I pulled my foot off the gas to slow down. The man had to be crazy or high on some drug of choice to run parallel to my car. But the daredevil held his course. The driver of the pickup honked at him but did not slow down either. With the truck virtually on his face, the biker from hell cut right in front of me. I swerved to avoid him and came within inches of slamming into the side of the hill. It took all my willpower not to hit the brakes hard. I finally regained control of the car but not my

91

breath. The biker disappeared behind a bend in the road. A bubble of fear caught in my throat dropped down my windpipe. I coughed it up, turned the hazard lights on and drove slowly.

"What now?" The biker was in the middle of the road ahead. He started out slowly again. I was less than a mile away from the ranch. I put my gun between my handbag and the back of the passenger seat. I turned off the hazard lights and rolled down my windows.

"Let's see who chickens out first, *cabrón*." I stepped hard on the gas. The Volvo zoomed ahead. The biker wasn't expecting such a reaction from me but in seconds it put enough distance between us. I took my foot off the gas and made a safe right turn onto the Cantero driveway. I pressed the intercom button at the gate. The loud revving of the bike's motor sounded closer again. And I was past doubt that this guy was only a thrill seeker.

The gate opened, I rushed in and parked behind the oak tree. The motorcycle's revs dropped to an idling hum just outside the gate, then roared off again. I listened until I could no longer hear the bike, holstered my gun and took out my flashlight.

Through the iron bars, I pressed the intercom button and asked Cantero to buzz the gate open and let me out then again back in. He did. One thing about Cantero, he never asked me why.

I checked the tire imprint on the loose ground. This was the same motorcycle tire tracks Finn and I had seen around both the Shadow Creek Recreation Area and the fire-gutted house. If I had any doubts about the pressing need to do a Houdini act, they were swiftly dispelled.

Cantero was waiting for me when I drove up to the house. "What happened? You look worried."

"I'm okay. But let's talk about it later."

I put my bags on the floor. He picked them up and started down the hall. We talked as we walked.

"Did you get the security tapes?" I asked.

"Yes, the DVD arrived about an hour ago."

"When can we see it? That is, if you're still willing to watch it with me and help me identify people and places."

"I went ahead and previewed the first track. But Estefanía needed my help in the kitchen, so I didn't get back to it. Offhand, nothing unusual happened between six and eight p.m. Nothing that we don't already know happened at the gate, our tour of the grounds before dinner, the staff's ins and outs and so on."

"That saves me some time. Thanks. How long will it take us to view the rest?"

"About forty minutes. But why don't we review it right after dinner? You're probably starved. So are we. You can give us your report, and we can talk while we eat," he said, already steering me to the hall with his hand between my shoulder blades.

"Where's Lula Marie? She said she was going to hitch a ride back with you," he said.

"Paladin Valenzuela showed up at the church when we were getting ready to leave. He's bringing her home. She didn't want the two of us to meet just yet. I appreciate it."

A grunt of disgust scraped his throat. "We won't wait for her, then."

We arrived at the room assigned me for the night. Always the gracious host, Cantero pointed to the set of towels on the bed, reminded me where the bathroom was, and set a key on the dresser before he closed the door behind him.

The clatter, which could be heard throughout the house, could have fooled anyone into believing they'd walked into a foundry, not the Cantero's kitchen. I too was a noisy cook, but Estefanía sure topped me. She was on the phone with Lula Marie, telling her dinner was ready, when I walked into the kitchen.

"Is that man staying for dinner?" Cantero asked.

"No. I made that clear to her."

"Smells good," I said.

"My wife is a very good cookbook cook. Not everyone has to be a composer, right?" Cantero said.

"I'm also a recipe artist when it comes to cooking. My husband is the virtuoso in our family."

Estefanía was pleased with my comment. She gave Cantero a disdainful shrug of the shoulder.

He laughed. "Let's eat. Lula Marie can eat when she gets here."

"What's the rush?" Estefanía asked.

"We're reviewing the security tape right after dinner. We want to get to it right away."

"Okay. So, please, help yourselves."

We ate in silence for a few minutes. Who could talk when every bite of the braised beef stew with onions simmered in beer, the risotto and the grilled vegetables was a perfect delight.

"You might be a cookbook artist, but this meal is as delicious as any Chez Panisse creation."

For the first time I saw Estefanía blush.

"Before I tell you what I found out today, I'd like to ask you a few more questions. Your answers might help me put things into perspective," I said.

"Ask away," Cantero replied.

"I need information about Paladin Valenzuela and Sheriff's Deputy John Marshall, anything you know about their activities, business ventures and so on. So far I've found out that Valenzuela is fifty-eight years old, was born in San José and his first name is Jerónimo."

"Ah, so those two hyenas are involved in this. It doesn't surprise me. Paladin claims to be a descendant of an early Californio family. That's a lot of hogwash. Both he and Deputy Marshall suffer from delusions of grandeur. No one knows exactly how Valenzuela amassed his fortune. Rumor has it that he's been involved in a number of shady activities, that he was already under criminal investigation by the authorities in the Santa Clara Valley—Silicon Valley—when he relocated to Jackson. But nothing so far has come of it. He seems to cover his tracks well.

"I'm sure if you ask Deputy Marshall, he'll tell you Valenzuela is an upstanding member of the community. We know both are scoundrels. But what *we* think of Paladin is beside the point. He is regarded as a benefactor and philanthropist in the community, especially after he began to donate large amounts of money to local charities for their community projects. He's gotten a few community service awards. His name and picture finally made front page after the opening of the Dry Creek Christian Community Center outside Jackson. He donated the land and the building, and he pays for the part-time director's salary. I don't know if he would be of help to you, but the director's name is Renato Fierro—people call him 'The Deacon.' Fierro isn't really a man of the cloth, but he just laps up the respect that goes with the surplice."

"But what exactly makes you two so suspicious of Valenzuela?"

This time Estefanía answered. "Paladin is no paladin. He's a rustler and a hustler. A lot of cattle and horses have disappeared since he moved into the area. But he targets mostly the small ranchers and farmers. As it is, making a profit from a farm isn't easy. The crops in many cases aren't enough to sustain them. So Paladin immediately moves in to purchase their land and homes for just a little more than most mortgage institutions offer. And he ends up as the good guy."

"A hyena," Cantero piped in. "I'm sure he's responsible for the fires, too."

"What fires?" I asked Estefanía.

"A couple of suspicious fires somewhere near Sonora. But to our surprise, the fire investigators couldn't find any proof of arson. The homeowners were low-income people, some uninsured or underinsured. They couldn't secure enough credit to rebuild."

"And let me guess: Paladin Valenzuela came to their rescue."

"He sure did. He wants to convince people he's a great man with a big heart. He sees himself as the hero of the people, the defender of the poor and downtrodden—the poor and downtrodden being mostly Mexican Americans."

"Lula Marie told me about the 'hostile' takeover of your quartz mining operation by Western Quartz. Is it possible that Valenzuela was behind it?" I asked Cantero.

"So you think there's a connection between him and the murder and kidnapping?"

"I know it sounds far-fetched. I'm only eliminating possibilities here. You see, I've been focusing on Hilda and Virginia as the targets, but maybe they weren't. Maybe you are. And the women just got in the way. So far I haven't a clue as to anyone's motive."

"Maybe it's not so far-fetched. I remember considering the possibility when I looked into Western Quartz. WQ is a private corporation. Only the names of the father and son appear as corporate owners. That doesn't mean there aren't other 'invisible' partners. He could be one of them. But it's all legal, as far as we know."

"So why would Valenzuela come after you?"

Cantero shook his head. "Our paths never crossed before, not until the man got interested in Lula Marie."

We heard the intercom buzz. Estefanía and I stayed put. Cantero took his time getting to the front door. He was courteous but curt.

"I'll call you tomorrow. Sleep well," we heard Valenzuela say to Lula Marie a few minutes later.

She came into the kitchen and sat down. Lula Marie immediately helped herself to the food but not the wine. Cantero stayed by the front door, monitoring Valenzuela's exit, then joined us.

"Cantero, when you said that both Deputy Marshall and Valenzuela suffer from delusions of grandeur, what exactly did you mean?"

"Valenzuela claims to be related to a Californio family. But Marshall claims to be a direct descendant of James W. Marshall."

"The man who discovered gold at Sutter's Mill in Coloma? Wow!"

"One and the same. The deputy apparently has the papers to prove it but hasn't made them available to anyone. Not long ago, the California Gold Rush Museum asked him if he would donate the historical documents to them. He wanted to sell them, but the museum could not match his price. They asked if he would let them at least authenticate the documents, free of charge. But he declined."

"So he might not really be who he says he is?"

"That's my take on it. He doesn't really have the documents. Otherwise, why ask for a lot of money, way over what the museum can afford? That egomaniac just wants to use the Marshall name for his aggrandizement."

"But maybe Deputy Marshall decided to join forces with Paladin to claim the land he believes he's entitled to," Lula Marie suggested.

"Tch. There's no land or property, just as there is no fortune in gold. James W. Marshall eventually lost his land and claim to squatters and gold diggers. He received a small pension from the government, and that's all. He invested first in a quartz mining operation and then in a small winery. He lost everything when the winery went bankrupt. He ended his days drunk and penniless in Kelsey, California, in 1876."

"Well, whatever it is, Marshall is up to something. I'm sure," Lula Marie said.

"What is he up to?" Estefanía asked.

"I'm not exactly sure what, but when we were walking out of St. Patrick's, Marshall was waiting for Paladin. I didn't quite understand what Marshall was saying, something about some unfinished business in Sonora. But he sounded pretty angry. He told Paladin, 'You know what they say, if you want it done well, do it yourself. I've done what I had to do. Now it's your turn.' Then he walked out on Paladin. I asked if everything was all right. Paladin said that the deputy was tired of being a cop. He wanted Paladin to invest in some land deal so he could retire from the force. But Paladin said it was a 'risky deal.' He didn't say why, and he changed the subject right away."

"Hallelujah!" The hyenas are fighting. Good." Cantero looked ecstatic.

"I don't share in your excitement. Virginia was apparently abducted by Marshall with Valenzuela's help," I said.

"What!"

"Who told you that? How do you know?" Lula Marie was obviously upset.

I told them about Hilda's note, my meetings with Diego Mendoza at the Golden Nugget and my conversation with him at the casino.

"You've told me about Paladin's underhanded methods to acquire land and other real estate. I know about the Golden Nugget and the adjoining inn. But what exactly are Valenzuela's other legitimate businesses?" I asked Lula Marie.

"I don't really know the extent of it. Let me see. He owns another bar and inn in Sonora, and lots of land he plans to turn into housing developments. The San Francisco Bay Area is 'busting at the seams,' he says. Home prices have gone through the roof there. So people will soon be looking for affordable housing in the San Joaquín Valley and the towns along Highway 49."

Cantero and Estefanía kept shaking their heads throughout Lula Marie's explanation.

"I understand he owns a ranch in Sonora."

"Yes, a cattle ranch, La Herradura, between Jamestown and Sonora."

"Have you been there?"

She glanced at her sister before she answered. "Only a couple of times, once for dinner when we first met, then again more recently. He lives in a lavishly decorated hacienda there. My style is different, but he's very proud of the velvet drapes and dark heavy oak antiques."

"I'll need directions to his ranch."

"Sure. I'll write them down for you and draw you a map." Lula Marie went to the study to get paper and pencil.

"Finn has probably told you that he believes Nurse Gallardo was killed in Tuolomne County, in Sonora. Hilda Gallardo and Diego Mendoza are childhood friends and their families lived next to each other in Sonora," I explained.

Their blinking eyes betrayed their ignorance of those relationships.

"But why is that so important?" Cantero asked.

"Because Diego and Virginia used to be sweethearts before her accident, and he asked Virginia to heal his dying mother."

"Wow! I didn't know that," Lula Marie said as she walked back into the kitchen.

"So he might have kidnapped her," Estefanía said.

"Maybe I'm wrong about him, but I don't think so. I think he's honestly interested in bringing her home safely. He was trying to help Hilda, who, as I told you, knew about the plans to kidnap Virginia. Hilda also knew about me and why I was here. As I said, she wanted to hire me so I could protect Virginia. Even before I arrived, many people up and down Highway 49 knew who I was and why I was here."

"Who do you think told them?" Lula Marie asked.

"That's up for grabs. But your housekeeper Aster told me this morning that she had heard the news of Hilda Gallardo's death and Virginia's disappearance while listening to a Spanish radio station. It was barely two hours after Hilda's body was found. That's how fast news travels around here. Given the bizarre circumstances surrounding Hilda's murder, I wouldn't be surprised if reporters show up at your door very soon. And to top it all off, someone—a biker—has been sent to deal with me. He tried to run me off the road just outside Sutter Creek. Finn and I found this same guy's motorcycle tire tracks at Shadow Creek Recreation Area and around the house where we believe Virginia was taken right after she was abducted."

"Who's the biker and who does he work for?" Lula Marie asked.

"Need Gloria say his name?" Estefanía remarked. Lula Marie was mortified at the implication that Paladin Valenzuela was behind the attempt on my life. But she didn't refute the possibility.

"I don't know yet. But I now find it nearly impossible to keep under their radar, not to mention out of their range. So I'll be leaving the ranch tomorrow morning. I have everyone's phone numbers. I'll be in touch daily with whoever is available from now on. I'll also keep in touch with Finn to follow up on the investigation at his end."

"Let us know how we can help," Estefanía said.

Cantero stood up. "Let's watch the security DVD now. It's all set up."

"Each DVD is a visual pastiche of activities recorded by the various cameras. They focus on the areas between the main house, the staff cottage and the office building, as well as the front gate. The cameras and lights are activated when someone triggers any of the motion sensors. The numbers here, at the bottom of the screen, show the camera number and the date and time," Cantero explained, then added, "And as you can see, the time span is between six p.m. Friday, June 17, and six a.m. Saturday, June 18 —all of last night. As I said, nothing out of the ordinary happened between six and eight p.m. But if you want to see that section, we can start at the beginning."

"No need. Let's go on from that point."

Camera 4: At eight o'clock, the gardener, Milagros, went to the staff cottage with a basket of clean and folded laundry resting on her hip. Emilia stepped out of the kitchen and called Milagros back. The young woman went back into the kitchen and out again also holding a shopping bag.

At eight thirty-five, keeping close to the wall of the staff quarters, someone—possibly a woman—moved slowly at first, then made a dash for the rear door of the house. The lights went on, but the woman moved out of the spot fast. I could barely make out her features.

Cantero rewound the tape and then played it again, frame by frame. Estefanía moved closer to the television set and looked carefully at each frozen image.

"Do you recognize her?" I asked.

"I think that's Hilda Gallardo."

"What was she doing here? Wasn't she off yesterday?" Lula Marie asked.

"And no one saw her," Cantero added.

"We were having dinner. And the rest were busy with their chores," Estefanía said.

"I think that's when she left the note in my handbag, asking me to meet her at the Golden Nugget Taverna. As I told you, the note wasn't signed. But Finn found her fingerprints on it. Do you two remember what she was wearing when she was found dead?"

"I believe she had on a white cotton shirt and navy-blue cotton sweater and pants," Estefanía said.

Cantero agreed. He pushed the forward button. Hilda became a shadow again, slipping away and disappearing behind the staff cottage.

At nine ten, camera 4 recorded Estefanía's after-dinner visit to the cottage. No one uttered a word, least of all me. Our silence must have been overwhelming for her.

"I was checking on Virginia. And I also wanted to talk to Julio about Diablo," she explained.

Lula Marie's mouth puckered. Cantero's eyes were fixed on the television screen, watching his wife come back home thirteen minutes later.

The cameras also recorded the usual ins and outs of the rest of the staff until eleven thirty, when Emilia went to bed.

At two ten in the morning, camera 3 was triggered and the light went on a second later. Dressed in a dark shirt and boot bottom pants, a hat and what seemed to be chaps, someone scurried across the corrals. The rider was out of camera range as soon as he entered the stables. At two twenty-five, a woman also ran toward the stable. She was wearing a long white nightgown. We could only see her back.

"That's Virginia. But who's the man? Not Julio. And dressed like that? What the hell went on here last night?" Lula Marie asked.

Cantero didn't answer but rewound the tape and replayed the scene.

For me, the events and times coincided with what Emilia and Milagros had told me earlier. The horses were restless, especially Diablo. Julio went out to check on them. Fifteen minutes later, Milagros heard the toilet flush and assumed Virginia had done it. But she didn't remember when or if Virginia had gone back to bed.

I waited for the Canteros to reconfirm the identity of the night visitor and the woman on the screen.

"It's Virginia, all right. When she can't sleep, she goes to the stable. I guess she gets comfort from being with Diablo. Sometimes Milagros but usually Julio goes to get her. She probably heard Julio leaving and followed him," Cantero said.

"How do you know Virginia does that?" Lula Marie asked.

"EPSS sends me a weekly written log of activities. I usually call them if I think there's something out of the ordinary. Then they send me the DVD. But EPSS hadn't sent this week's log yet." Cantero sounded matter-of-factly.

"Are you sure that was Julio? Did he often go riding at night, dressed like that?" I asked.

He replied with an "Uh-huh." But for someone who loved to talk, he was thoughtfully silent. Lula Marie watched him, a pained look in her eyes.

"He didn't come out of the cottage, though. The camera would have picked him up. It's like he suddenly appeared from behind the office building. Could I see that again?" I asked Cantero.

He rewound the tape and replayed the last scene.

I watched the man's silhouette. I was now sure Julio wasn't the individual running to the stable. But I kept my suspicions to myself for the time being.

"Let's look at the rest," I said.

We all hoped to see Virginia going back to the staff quarters. The fact was that she never did. None of the cameras had recorded the night rider's exit out of the stable either on foot or horseback. And at three in the morning Hilda was back, dressed in the same outfit she had worn to her death. She boldly stood in plain sight this time. She looked in the windows and tried unsuccessfully to open the cottage's front door.

"Freeze it!" Estefanía got very close to the screen. "Look at this," she told her husband and pointed at something on the screen.

We all moved closer.

Lula Marie raised her hand to her mouth and muffled a "No."

"Carlota's Tears," I said. "I can't tell if she's wearing both earrings. Can you?"

"No. When we saw her body, she didn't have them on either," Estefanía said.

"And Finn found only one of them near the staff cottage's back door, so . . ."

Cantero, who had said little, suddenly exploded. "This is unbelievable! How did she know the combination to the safe? Emilia and her children have a lot to explain."

"Don't jump to conclusions yet," Lula Marie warned. "There must be another explanation. Hilda was in and out of the house. She could have hidden and watched you or Estefanía open the safe and learned the combination."

"Hidden where? Under the desk? We would have seen her," he said.

"Maybe through the window or the doors to the garden."

Cantero stood up, paced up and down for awhile. He went into the kitchen. Estefanía followed him there. Lula Marie and I agreed that it was too early to pass judgment on Hilda or the Morenos.

I went into the kitchen. "Please wait until we have all the facts before you talk to the Morenos. We don't know what exactly happened. Not yet," I said.

Estefanía held Cantero's face between her hands. "Please, my love, listen to Gloria."

He finally agreed with a head nod.

I returned to the entertainment room. "Let's finish watching the tape."

Lula Marie and I sat on the floor in front of the set, our legs crossed, like young girls watching their favorite Sunday morning television program. But this was real-life television, and we watched Hilda Gallardo's last moments on earth. She tried the front door of the cottage, but it was locked. She hesitated for a second and then walked to the corner, turned and disappeared again in the darkness behind the staff cottage. The screen went gray and the tape commenced its short, silent run to the end of life's reality show.

I welcomed the warmth of Lula Marie's arm on my shoulders.

Although my body screamed for rest, my mind was still going at full speed. Closing my eyes, I tried the self-hypnosis techniques I knew, but none worked. I finally visualized my own bed, Justin and me in it, his arms around me, his body contouring mine, his warmth spreading like a second aura up from my toes to my scalp. Soon darkness grew inside me, and I conceived sleep.

I woke up three hours later. Even though the temperature in the room was comfortable, I was trembling, chilled to the bone. Estrogen and progesterone sparred within me, fighting for control of my body, and all my senses. I knew it well.

I thought of my mother, who, when faced with a sudden attack of night chills, promptly got out of bed, reached for broom, bucket and mop and furiously slapped the kitchen floor until it sparkled. For two years before her menstruation stopped altogether, her kitchen floor was the cleanest in Oakland, probably in the state and nation as well.

Floor-scrubbing wasn't the kind of activity I could undertake at the moment. But I was sure that it would take a while for my warring hormones to work up a truce. So I got up and put my socks and robe on. I wrapped myself in the soft and warm blanket draping the easy chair and walked to Cantero's library.

I turned the desk lamp on. Joaquín Murrieta stared at me from the wall. I doubted the wild-eyed man in the painting resembled the real Murrieta. The bandit-hero had presumably been photographed only once while alive, although innumerable prints of his alleged pickled, distorted, severed head were sold.

I hardly gave credence to people's belief that Murrieta's ghost—the Ghost of Sonora—was seeking justice for oppressed Mexican Americans, now as in old times, roaming the roads of the Gold Country. But, from what the Canteros said about Jerónimo Paladin Valenzuela, he saw himself as a defender of the poor and downtrodden, who were mostly Mexican Americans. To many of them, he had become some sort of hero. Perhaps Valenzuela aimed at fashioning himself after the legendary Murrieta. Just in case, I decided to read about the real bandit-hero.

Unlike my home library, where Linda Goodman's *Sun Signs,* Shakespeare's *The Tempest*, Rolando Hinojosa's *Ask a Policeman,* Manuel Ramos's *Ballad of Rocky Ruiz,* and Sarah Cortez and Wallace Stevens's poetry shared shelf intimacy, Cantero's library was thankfully well organized. But it contained mostly history volumes.

I looked for the Murrieta section. A laminated author and title list hung from a thumbtack. Some Latino scholars had written creative works or historical accounts of the legendary bandit-hero's life and exploits. My trembling fingers guided my eyes to the names familiar to me—Isabel Allende, Pablo Neruda, Luis Valdez, Humberto Garza, Irineo Paz, Luis Leal. María Herrera-Sobek, José Limón and Benjamín Alire Sáenz were among the authors who had written articles on Murrieta as well.

A handbound letter-sized volume displaying the title, "Murrieta Online," attracted my attention right away. I pulled it out. I was about to turn and sit at Cantero's desk to read, when another wave of cold lapped over my hips and lower back. I pulled the blanket around me, but a patch of skin just below my cervical vertebrae felt as hot as cinder. I glanced out the French door and at the dahlia garden beyond them, suddenly feeling that someone out there was staring at me at that very moment. I retreated to a darker area in the library and threw another look out the doors. The tall dahlias swayed as if someone pushed through them. I scanned the darkness. I saw no one. Looking at the tree tops, I was certain the invisible wing of the wind was the culprit.

My hands no longer shook, and my body felt warmer. I had just scared my hormones out of their wits. I chuckled, sat at the desk and began to read.

The handbound anthology contained essays and articles by historians, iconoclasts, journalists and other friends and foes of Murrieta. Several articles had been downloaded from tourism and real estate agency websites, but none of them from Diego Mendoza's company. They were intended to attract visitors and prospective clients to the Gold Country. Yet another article had been downloaded from Stormfront.com, a "White Pride World Wide" organization, which began by talking about Joaquín Murrieta as "Another murdering Mestizo . . . elevated to a 'Civil Rights' Hero." Oddly, it had an interview with one of Murrieta's descendants; they talked about an annual caravan of horsemen from Fresno to the site of Murrieta's grave to celebrate his life. I wondered if Joaquín's great-grandnephew knew who was using him and for what purpose.

The controversy over Murrieta's true identity was fascinating. But more intriguing was the claim that his life and deeds had eventually given birth to the legend of El Zorro—the fox. I found myself quickly ensnared in the debate.

By no means were we the only culture in the world to celebrate the lives of "good" outlaws. Mexicans and Latin Americans had a peculiarly soft cultural spot for the bandits-turned-revolutionaries and the guerrilla fighters. Our history was full of them, their exploits and the just causes they embraced on behalf of the poor. Chucho el Roto, Pancho Villa and Emiliano Zapata, Ché Guevara, Lucio Vásquez and Sub-Comandante Marcos, among many. And in California, Joaquín Murrieta and Tiburcio Vásquez. Epic songs, *corridos*, were written about many of them. Unfortunately, a lot more was known about the other men than Joaquín Murrieta. Journalists and historians alike cited few primary sources.

Despite some writers' claim that Murrieta was from Chile, most of the authors agreed that Murrieta had been born in the

Mexican state of Sonora, circa 1830. He was only eighteen when he and his sweetheart—perhaps his wife—Rosa Feliz, arrived in California, accompanied by Jesús Murrieta and three of the Feliz brothers.

The coincidence of Murrieta's sweetheart's last name and Estefanía's middle name didn't escape my attention. Maybe her parents had been fond of the Murrieta lore or Feliz was a girl's name favored by Chilean families. The fact was that the Murrietas and the Felizes, like hundreds of Mexicans and Chileans, began mining the precious metal near Sonora, California, a town where most of the Mexican and Chilean miners lived.

Since these "foreign" miners, an article mentioned, had already worked in their respective countries' silver and copper mines, they actually taught the California gold seekers how to mine for gold. Instead of gratitude for sharing their knowledge and mining skills with their U.S. counterparts, the newly instituted California legislature smacked them with a "foreign miners' tax" as high as a monthly 20 percent of their mined gold. True, the author claimed, that this tax applied also to other European foreigners, who were mostly German, French and Irish. But when the non-European gold miners complained, their claims and homes were taken, if they didn't comply. It wasn't until the European "foreigners" and taxpayers stormed the state capital to demand the repeal of the tax that the legislature lowered it to 16 percent, then finally to 4 percent.

No doubt injustices and atrocities were committed by the new Anglo American owners of the California territory, particularly against the old owners—the Californios and other Mexicans. Perhaps Murrieta and his band sought to even the scales by stealing from others what had been stolen from them. And maybe for that reason Mexicans referred to Murrieta as "El Patrio"—"The Patriot," offered him shelter and kept his identity secret. And he rewarded them handsomely, which earned him the reputation of "The Robin Hood of El Dorado."

Although history usually offered a myopic point of view, which in many instances was mostly the victors' interpretation of the facts, it had two sides. With that in mind, the author of one of the articles argued that two events of a more personal nature had propelled young Joaquín into the "vicious and bloody" life of an outlaw. When his brother Jesús was hanged and Joaquín was publicly whipped for allegedly stealing a mule they had legitimately bought, and after Rosita was gang-raped, Joaquín began to hunt and kill each of the Anglo perpetrators.

His deeds attracted the attention of many Mexican men who joined his band, but in particular Manuel García, also known as "Three-Fingered Jack," who became Murrieta's lieutenant and protector. None of the authors disputed Three-Fingered Jack's sanguinary nature or his hatred for the Chinese people in the region. The Gold Country in 1849 was populated almost entirely by men. Thus, women's domestic chores were taken over by Chinese and old or disabled Mi-Wuk and European men. In the socially disordered hierarchy of the mining camps, the Chinese were the most vulnerable. And a man with a gun was the law. But some authors argued that Murrieta could not have so calmly butchered the Chinese just because of their vulnerability or his racial prejudices.

Whether motivated by lofty ideals or ethnic rage, Murrieta adhered to the law of an-eye-for-an-eye. He died in 1853, at the age of twenty-three, killed and decapitated by Harry Love, a former Texas Ranger. Love received a reward of five thousand dollars from the California legislature for his deed when he showed them the whiskey-pickled head of Murrieta in a jar, together with the severed hand of Manuel "Three-Fingered Jack" García.

Many people who claimed to have known or seen Murrieta personally disputed Love's claim that the pickled head was indeed that of Joaquín. Speculation and rumored simultaneous sightings of Murrieta, alive, in places miles apart, spread over the Gold Country. Adding to the confusion and to the myth of his true identity was the presence of four other men in the region also named Joaquín—Carrillo, Botellier, Ocomoreña and Valenzuela—all of them considered outlaws at the time.

The name Joaquín Valenzuela was to me the most interesting of the quartet, since Paladin Valenzuela claimed to be a descendant of an "old Californio family." There was no credible record that Joaquín Valenzuela had indeed been a Californio. Not waiting for others to do it for him, Paladin was possibly reshaping himself as the hero of his own life. Did he hope that his life and exploits, like those of Murrieta, would one day become fodder for romantic minds and that he would become a legend in his own time? Was he already wondering if an older Antonio Banderas would play him in the Hollywood version of his life?

On that amusing query, I closed the handbound anthology and returned it to its place. I saw two copies of the *Life and Adventures of Joaquin Murrieta*, penned by Rollin Ridge aka Yellow Bird. When it was first published, no one questioned the facts and events in the story. And the Murrieta legend was born.

The first book was an 1858 mint-condition issue and surely a collector's item that Cantero had probably paid a pretty penny. I turned to the title page and was surprised to see an undated penciled-in dedication: "*A mi adorada bandida, quien me robó el corazón.*" I looked closely at the signature. It was illegible. I couldn't tell if it was Cantero's signature, since the check he had given me as retainer had been signed by Estefanía. However, I had often heard Mexican men talk about the women who had stolen their hearts as *bandidas*. Possibly, Cantero had bought the book for his wife precisely because of the traditional dedication in it.

I re-shelved the rare edition of Yellow Bird's book and began to thumb through the more recent pocket edition of the same book. Its front cover displayed a reproduction of the famous Nahl painting of Joaquín Murrieta in Cantero's study. Neither Carlos Manuel Cantero nor Jerónimo Valenzuela nor Diego Mendoza looked like that Murrieta.

Were I a filmmaker, I would probably cast Julio Moreno in the title role. But I would definitely give the role of Tornado, Murrieta's faithful horse, to Diablo. I chuckled and blamed sleep-deprivation for my mental wanderings.

I stopped reading and returned *The Life and Adventures of Joaquín Murrieta* and Valenzuela's aspirations to the place where they belonged—the shelf.

My spell of night chills was over, but I was still wide awake. In two hours I would be leaving the ranch. I didn't feel like going back to bed to just toss and turn until my cell phone alarm went off.

Back in my room, I turned off the lamp on the night table, drew the curtains and looked for the waxing moon; it had gone into hiding, but would probably reappear long before I went into my self-imposed exile.

My room faced east. The stables, the oak grove and the barn where the sheep slept were all far indistinct shadows now. Ensconced in an easy chair, I enjoyed the darkness of night, gazing upon the near-summer-solstice starry sky and listened to the soothing song of the crickets with my eyes closed.

"As long as the cricket sings, everything in the world is well," my grandmother Mami Julia used to tell me when I was little and she came to my bed to say good night.

The crickets still sang every night, but the world was worse than it had ever been. I thought of American mothers of all colors perhaps now mourning their sons killed somewhere in Iraq in the name of democracy; of Iraqi mothers burying at that precise moment their dead children and relatives; of Mexican mothers in Ciudad Juárez arising to another day of protest against the atrocities perpetrated on their four hundred raped, mutilated and murdered daughters. I wondered about Murrieta's mother, about how little a mother's warning to her son or her cry for justice means in this world. All of these mothers' funereal laments went unheard or ignored by those who had the power to stop the carnage.

Did Murrieta think of his mother as he lay dying, thinking of resting in her arms as a child still untouched by injustice, malice or murder? Justifiable circumstances or not, once a blade or a bullet drives through flesh and stops a heart from beating, be it the heart of one man or a thousand, how could innocence too not cease to exist?

The thought sent a chill up my spine. But I knew full well the source of my distress did not reside in my uterus or ovaries. It came directly from my conscience, from the deep contradictions in me, because I too carried a gun and sometimes two. I hadn't killed anyone yet, but every case brought me closer to that dreaded confrontation between my two selves.

"Stop it!" I said aloud. I was working myself into a mood darker than the night. Determined to fight it off, I opened my eyes. My blood literally froze. I was staring at a mountain lion stealing past my window. Fear whirled wildly in my chest as I imagined the lion watching me through the sliding door of Cantero's library a short while earlier.

I stood up slowly. In the dark, I circled around the easy chair and backtracked, as if the lion were also aware of my presence. With my fingers I felt for my night binoculars in my briefcase and looked through them. The large cat sniffed the ground and the air for the scent of the horses. Once sure his next meal awaited him past the corrals, he stole in that direction.

Looking to alert the Canteros to the lion's presence, I got dressed in a flash and strapped my holstered gun to my belt. I pulled the strap of my night binoculars over my head again. I heard the sound of the alarm code being punched and rushed to the front door.

"You saw it, too?" Cantero asked in a low voice.

He was wearing a brown T-shirt over a pair of brown sweatpants, ankle-length riding boots and a set of earmuffs around his neck. Two distinctly different rifles rested side by side against the wall. A heavy-duty flashlight lay on the floor next to them. He threw a saddlebag, probably containing the ammunition, over his shoulder.

"Have you ever used a tranquilizer gun?" He took off the scope of that gun and replaced it with another, then did the same with the rifle next to it.

"I've never had to use a tranquilizer gun. But I've fired a rifle. My partner—husband—insisted I learn to shoot more than pistols and revolvers."

When he handed me the rifle, I tried to come up with an excuse not to join him in the hunt. I couldn't think of any, so instead I asked, "Estefanía or Lula Marie?"

"I'd rather not have them join us."

He had said "us." I was drafted. Regardless, it was a no win situation for me either way because my conscience would not let me off the hook if any harm came to my client. I picked up the heavy-duty lamp and followed him to the back door.

"It's a pretty big cat, probably a male. I had no idea mountain lions hunt at night," I whispered.

"They do, especially if they're hungry enough. This cat may be starved."

"Any way he can get to the horses or the sheep?"

"Not really. But mountain lions are pretty resourceful and patient animals. They're usually shy and hardly ever come down to the foothills from the upper sierras unless they're following deer. But this cat has already killed small animals in the creek area, the forest rangers told me. I'm afraid he's already marked his territory. And he'll be back time and again."

"You're not going to kill him, are you?"

"Not unless he intends to have Diablo, you or me for breakfast," Cantero said facetiously. "I'll probably just tranquilize him and let the fish and game people deal with him."

He seemed in control, despite the neighing of the restless horses alerting us to the mountain lion's presence near the stables. He looked at me for an instant as if to make sure I would join him in the hunt.

I stepped out ahead of him, triggering the light outside the back door. We moved out of the spotlight and cautiously made our way to the stable.

The heavy iron bar locking the stable door was in place. But the scratches in the wood were a sure sign the cat had tried to get into it.

"Stay here. Keep the light off. I have another in there."

He turned the flashlight off, then set it and the riffle on the ground next to me. The large stable door creaked as he pushed it open and went in.

"I sure hope the cat didn't hear that," I whispered, cocking the rifle as quietly as possible.

I peered into the endless darkness. I blinked only when I absolutely had to. Using the night binoculars, I checked the branches of trees for strange lumps of shadow. An acorn dropping from an oak, the rustling of branch leaves by the night breeze, the faraway hoot of a barn owl, all conspired against my common sense. Time seemed to have stood still between my temples, despite the furious knocking of my heart against my breastbone. I had never before felt as vulnerable as at that moment. The best I

could, I harnessed my fear and forced myself to breath normally.
My life depended on it.

Cantero finally came out of the stables pulling two saddled
horses by the reins. His tranquilizer gun was already holstered on
the right side of a brown horse. He slid the rifle into the saddle
holster on the gray horse. He pushed the metal bar down to lock
the stable door again. Glad to be able to work out my fear, I
helped him tighten the saddle straps.

"Any sign of the cat?"

The sheep cried in the distance as if in answer to his question.
He quickly gave me a boost up on to the gray horse and handed
me the second flashlight, then he mounted and immediately
prompted his brown stallion. I prayed that what I knew about riding would kick in fast. I dug my heels into the flanks of the gray
horse. My inner thigh muscles stretched to the point of excruciat-
ing pain. But at the moment, pain meant action, and action still
felt better than fear.

We rode to the barn. There, Cantero got off his horse, handed me the reins and checked the barn doors. Using my night
binoculars, he walked around, scanning the area until he saw the
cat again. Pulling his horse, I kept pace with him. He mounted
again.

The horses cantered to the creek area, where we temporarily
lost the trail. Although it looked as if the cat was climbing up to
higher ground, Cantero was still set on tracking the predator. We
continued the search on foot on a parallel course, shedding light
on the ground while tugging on our horses. A cumbersome task
at best, but we eventually found the tracks again and followed
them across the creek, where the water was shallow and a jumble
of rocks made crossing easier, then on past the area where almost
twenty-four hours before Hilda Gallardo had been found dead.

The moon became visible again as it cleared the tops of the
trees. We could see farther ahead of us now. The thick underbrush
along the creek and up the slope still made it difficult for the horses to clamber to the meadow above, but we finally made it to the
top. A wide hiking trail went through the meadow. The night
breeze was stronger and gustier up there.

Cantero asked to use my night binoculars again. He scanned the whole area before handing them back to me. My eyes roamed aimlessly across the meadow, now bathed in moonlight.

For a second, my mind seemed void of thought while my ears became attuned to a clanging sound. Wind chimes. We had to be close to the house Finn and I had checked the day before, where I had found the two empty tapioca pudding containers. The chiming stopped.

"I think he's gone up to the higher hills. Let's get back to the ranch." He turned his brown horse around.

Finally! I had just pulled on the gray's rein when I again heard the sound of the wind chimes. But this time a sudden single scream echoed high in the wind. We heard another, then another, followed by the furious barking of dogs, the growling of the lion, the roaring of motorcycles and the high-pitched neighing of a horse.

"What the hell . . . !" Cantero exclaimed. "The creek area," he said and took off at full gallop across the meadow.

The screams stopped. But a dog still barked furiously. I lagged behind and soon lost sight of Cantero as he rode into the thicket.

Closer to the creek, the revving of motorcycles and the barking of dogs grew fainter. A shadow ran across the path a few feet ahead of me. I turned on the flashlight.

"Who's there?" I asked. I looked in all directions and waited, but I saw no one. I checked the branches of the trees. No lion either.

Cantero's horse was tied to a tree up ahead. He and the tranquilizer rifle were gone. I dismounted and tied my horse next to Cantero's. My first impulse was to run. But the possible presence of the lion and the cramps zigzagging from my calves to my butt convinced me otherwise. I walked as erect as possible, holding the rifle in front of me with both hands. My fear magnified every sound and shadow.

The odor of fresh blood was the first sign of the horror waiting for me by the side of the creek. A dog—perhaps a pitbull—lay dying, its body convulsing, its paws scratching the air as if it were still trying to fend off an attacker. The sight made my stomach turn. It took most of my dwindling will to contain the wave of nausea working itself up. I skipped over the dying dog and kept on going, afraid that the lion might come back to feast.

I came upon Cantero standing over a lump on the rocky bank of the creek. The beam of his flashlight illuminated a woman's bloody head. She lay face down. Not a wrinkle on her brown skin. A single, thick, long braid covered her jaw. I couldn't see any marks left by the lion's canines on her neck. But two lines of blood flowed from under her head. They mingled in their course to the ground, staining the collar and sleeve of her blue cotton jacket. Her jeans and white sneakers were muddy but showed no signs of blood.

"Did the cat kill her?" I asked in a raspy voice.

"No. As far as I can tell, she probably tripped and hit her head on the rocks. There's blood all over them."

Agreeing with a guttural "Uh-huh," I took my eyes off the body and felt in my bag for a sanitizing towelette. The vapors of the alcohol in it burned my nostrils but helped to get rid of the nausea. I patted my face and neck dry with a couple of tissues. I spotted a large stone by the stream where I could sit. On my way there, I stumbled on two hemp bags, which probably belonged to the dead woman. But then, I recalled seeing a shadow running across the hiking trail close to the area, so one of the bags might actually belong to that other person. When I checked the ground, however, I found only one set of shoeprints. I stepped around, careful not to disturb them.

My curiosity was piqued. My heart and stomach steadied. But not for long. I heard the snapping of fingers. I saw Cantero back-tracking. He was wearing his earmuffs. He stopped. He cocked his tranquilizer gun and swiftly lifted it up to his shoulder. The lion was back.

To protect my ears from the report of the rifles, I stuffed both my ears with the tissues. I aimed my rifle away from Cantero and cocked it quietly. The gun was light in weight. But its recoil could still throw me back. I would lose precious seconds before I could fire a second shot. So I went down on my left knee, my right leg bent in front of me to steady my aim. A muscle in my neck stretched and then ached as I surveyed the area through the very restrictive night scope. I momentarily lowered the weapon.

My mind was clear now, quickly processing sounds and sights. I breathed as normally as I could. When I saw the lion's silhouette tentatively approach the body on the ground, I raised the rifle and followed his movements through the scope. Cantero and I stood a short distance from each other, like two totem poles in the forest.

About a hundred feet from us, the feline stopped and raised his head. Encouraged by the normal sounds of the night and enticed by the fresh smell of blood, the lion was soon upon the dead woman's body and began to drag it away.

Cantero pulled the trigger. The dart hit the target in midriff. The lion raised his rear paw, trying to get rid of it. Cantero quickly reloaded. A second dart hit the cat below the left shoulder. The cat let go of his prey and let out a series of loud yelps. He looked around in confusion, then saw Cantero. But even with two tranquilizer shots in him, the lion was still up and moving toward Cantero.

"Go down," I pleaded.

I expected Cantero to fire a third dart, but he didn't. The big cat was now too close to him. I held my breath, took aim and fired, shooting the cat above his rear thigh. I felt the kickback of the gun on my shoulder. No time to soothe the pain spreading up to my neck and across my chest. The lion staggered but didn't stop altogether. I got ready to fire a second shot. But suddenly, the lion's legs gave out and he dropped on the ground and then he rolled over on his side.

Despite my makeshift ear plugs, the report of the shot had thundered in my ears. I pinched my nose, gulped in air, and cleared my throat a few times, then removed the tissues. Although fainter and intermittent, the sound of running water trickled down my ears again.

We approached the injured sleeping lion. I looked at the hole made by the bullet; blood still oozed from it. I had done that to him. But there wasn't time for regret and guilt.

"What can we do for him?" I asked.

"Clean his wound. We also need to tie him down. The tranquilizer isn't going to last forever. Wait here." He rushed up the path back to the horses.

I stumbled past the mountain lion to the place where the young woman's body was. There, I dropped to my knees, with both my hands wrapped tightly around the muzzle of the rifle. I wanted to say a prayer for her, for her mother, for my own daughter, for myself, for the lion. But my dry mouth and throat could hardly form the words. The rustling of the wind amidst the branches, the babbling of the streaming water, the lion's troubled breathing and my sobs were the only prayer said in her name. A name I didn't yet know.

After we finished tying the lion's rear and front legs, Cantero got a small flask from the saddlebag he had brought back with him and poured some whiskey in and around the cat's wounds. The lion didn't move.

"Not much else we can do for him." He offered me a drink from his flask. I drank from it even though I did not like whiskey.

He took a swig. "Were you aiming at his belly?"

"No. I shot him where I wanted to."

"Good shot then. You spared his life and saved mine."

I felt he wasn't voicing what truly concerned him. "I would have killed him before he got to you."

His only comment was a nod of his head. He took his cell phone out, punched a button and raised the receiver to his ear. "No signal. Try yours."

I dug my hand in my pants back pocket. "Sorry, I forgot my cell. I left it in my room, charging."

"I guess we'll have to do it the old-fashioned way. I'll ride back to the house and notify the authorities. Maybe the cell will work when I get to the Shadow Creek area. If so, I'll get back here sooner. Will you be all right?"

Since I really had no choice, I said I would. But I felt mortified. Being there kept me from pursuing those responsible for Virginia's abduction. On the other hand, I was also curious about the presence of the dead woman in such a remote area and more intrigued about her pursuers, who were on motorbikes and had brought their dogs to aid them in her capture.

We walked back to the place where we had left the horses. Cantero mounted and rode on. I was left behind as the guardian of the dead, the wounded lion and the living gray horse, who welcomed my return by pushing gently on me with his head. I rubbed the spot behind his ear, untied him and walked him to the edge of the creek to have his fill of the cool water. I dipped my hands in the water and patted my face and neck with my wet fingers. For my comfort more than his, I hugged the gray's head and rested mine on his neck for a little while.

"C'mon, let's check on the dog," I whispered in his ear.

I pushed the rifle into the saddle holster. The gray snorted and followed me up the hiking trail. I wasn't sure what I could do for the dog if it was still alive. But its ID tag might provide a clue about his owner, who most definitely was the young woman's pursuer.

I surveyed the ground along the trail. No matter how powerful the beam of the heavy-duty flashlight was, the search for evidence proved to be slow and hard on my already tired eyes. The dry furrows in the slopes had been carved out by streams of rain and melted snow. The motorcycle and dog tracks at the bottom of a runoff trail caught my attention. The young woman's pursuers had ridden down the narrow furrow to the wider path below, probably following the dogs. The bikes skidded. Then, the bikers circled and rode back up the way they had come down. The patterns left by the tires were similar, except for the jagged mark across one of them.

"What d'ya know? This biker sure gets around."

The gray's ears perked up.

"You know, Mami Julia—she was my grandmother—often told me there are always reasons why we find ourselves in a certain place at a certain time. If you're just patient enough and trust your intuition, you'll find out why."

The gray snorted. We resumed our walk up the hiking trail to check on the pit bull. I loosely wrapped the gray's rein around the slender branch of a bush, crouched beside the dog and pointed the beam of the flashlight to its neck. No collar or ID tag. But the signs of the cat's expert hunting skills were visible above its shoulders. I examined the bark of the tree trunk. The lion had probably climbed up to a branch when he heard the dog approach. He waited there until the precise moment, leaped and dug his claws into his prey to immobilize it. Then, his fangs swiftly broke through the smooth hair and skin and into the neck arteries. Probably

scared by the loud noise of the motorcycles, the cat didn't finish
the job. And the dog bled to death.

The fuzzy light of sunrise was visible above the foothills when
the gray and I walked back to the place where the dead young
woman lay. The rebellious moon was still up as if refusing to be
erased from the sky by the light of the new day. To see the dawn
before the rest of the world was a treat for those who dared to
look for their paths by moonlight. I couldn't remember who had
said that. But for me, the nightmare continued as I watched the
flies swarm over the bodies of the woman and the lion.

The vultures would soon be circling above us. Death would
have her feast at life's table one way or the other. But the young
woman deserved some respect in death as in life. I looked for
something to cover her body. Then I remembered the two hemp
bags she had been carrying with her when the lion attacked her.
With the gray right behind me, I hurried to the large stone by the
creek, where I had last seen them. I couldn't find them anywhere.
And I knew Cantero hadn't taken them.

I again remembered the shadow running across the trail. I
checked the ground carefully, confirming my suspicions when I
saw prints made by smaller shoes than the dead woman's joggers
and mine.

"Who do you think she might be? And what were they doing
here?" I whispered.

The gray stomped the ground and neighed softly. He pushed
against my arm. He scraped the ground with his left front hoof a
few times and shook his head repeatedly. His odd behavior made
me take notice. I turned the flashlight off. Just in case another lion
in the vicinity had spooked the gray, I pulled the rifle slowly out
of the holster and released the safety. Holding it in front of me, I
stood straight, careful not to make any sudden moves. I surveyed
the area from left to right. I heard the crunching of twigs to my
right, coming from somewhere in the brush by the creek. The
gray neighed softly. I doubted our visitor was of the feline kind.

"I know you're there," I said aloud.

I turned the light on. Then in Spanish I commanded the person to step out. I waited a few seconds, then repeated my warning
in English. A moment later, a woman crawled out from under the

bushes. Her long hair got caught in the thin branches, pulling her head back. Unable to get up, she moaned in pain and began to cry. But she raised her hands in the air.

I put the rifle down and went to her aid. She was shaking, but she tried to be still while I broke some of the twigs to free the strands of hair wrapped around them. She was very young, perhaps no older than eighteen.

"What are you doing here?" I asked her in a soft voice and repeated my question a second time in Spanish. "*¿Qué hace aquí?*"

The young woman stood up and stared at the body on the ground. "*Mi hermana Rosita,*" she answered. "My sister," she repeated in English.

"I'm truly sorry."

She began to cry. Her sobs soon turned to wheezing hiccups. I helped her to the edge of the creek. She splashed water on her face, cupped some in her hands and drank it.

I sat on the rock and waited for her. The gray came closer and rubbed against my upper arm with the top of his head. I returned the caress. The young woman came back and sat next to me.

"What's your name?" I asked in Spanish.

"Blanca."

"My name is Gloria. I'm not Migra and I don't work for the police. Okay?"

She sighed. "I can't leave Rosita, like she is, all alone."

"Would you like us to pray for her soul?"

When she said "yes," we got down on our knees. She got a hold of my hand and said a prayer in a language unfamiliar to me. She didn't make the sign of the cross when she finished her prayer. But she seemed calmer.

"Were you and Rosita lost? Where were you coming from?" I asked.

"No . . . yes, we are lost. We don't know where we are."

I noticed Blanca always spoke in the present tense. Her Spanish was sprinkled here and there with words in her native language.

"What language other than Spanish do you speak?"

"Mixteca."

"Are you from Oaxaca or Guerrero?"

"Oaxaca. But *nana*—my mother—lives in Fresno. Are we near Fresno?"

"Not too far. About four hours by car. What were you and Rosita doing here?"

"This is not where we want to be. Three years, my mother is here in El Norte. She leaves us with family in Oaxaca. Then, one day she writes to Rosita and me. She pays a *coyote* to take us across the border in Tijuana. We take a few things. Clean clothes, photos and a little money in pesos. We also take some dry meat and fruit and water. We take the bus to Tijuana. A man, El Pocho, he picks us up, in a van, no windows, only holes. It is so hot and I think . . . we die."

She began to cry again. I pulled a tissue out of my pocket and handed it to her. She blew her nose a few times. I didn't want her to revisit her pain, the hunger and thirst, the loneliness, her fears and unanswered prayers during her journey across the border. So I said, "You don't have to tell me everything if you don't want to."

"No. I want to tell. El Pocho, he says another *coyote* takes us to Fresno. We wait in an empty house. Dust everywhere. We are hot and hungry. Then the other *coyote* comes. He has a big hat. A blue handkerchief on his nose and mouth. His shirt has short sleeves, but is black. Black pants, too. He must be very hot, too, I think."

"Do you remember the color of his eyes or hair? Maybe how tall he was?"

"Brown eyes. Brown hair. He's this tall."

She raised her hand to about eight inches above her head. The man had to be about five-feet-nine inches tall.

"Good. Anything else special about him?"

"Yes. He has a Mexican flag and an American, too."

"He carried two flags in his hands? In the van?"

"No. Pictures. In his skin."

Blanca stretched her arm out and used her index finger as if it were a pin or needle pricking her skin.

"Tattoos?"

Blanca's eyes lit up. "He says we owe him money. Rosita says our mother pays them. He says no, we pay him. Rosita says no.

The *coyote* pulls a machete. He says, '*Dame el dinero.*' We give him our pesos. Not enough. He pushes us back in the van. He says we have to work for money we owe him. He says if not, he kills us and our mother."

"I know this is very hard. But, please tell me, where did the man take you? And what happened there?"

"The man takes us to a house first. I don't know where. Other women like us live there, too. Bad men with guns and dogs. We are scared. But the women are nice. Sara says she tries to escape."

"Who's Sara?"

"A woman there, with us. She runs and hides in a town. But the men catch her and bring her back. She says we're close to Sonora. Rosita and I think we are near the border again. At least they don't kill Sara. We think they don't kill us. Next day, at night, he takes us, six of us women, to another house. Not too far from here."

"Can you tell me about that house?"

"A fire in the house before. Wood covers the windows. They lock the door."

When I mentioned the Chinese wind chimes to her, her eyes opened wide.

"Yes. I like the sound. Every night I sleep better."

"Were any of the women . . . were you forced to have sex? *¿Las violaron?*"

Blanca shook her head a few times.

"Do you understand what that means? Are you sure?"

"Yes. No sex."

Given the circumstances, it seemed so unusual. But I wasn't about to complain for small blessings.

"Then how did the men make you pay what you owed them?"

"Every day, the *coyote* comes to take us to another building, with many sewing machines. We sew clothes to pay the *coyote* back. Every night, they take us back to the house to sleep. Two men always with us. They ride motorcycles. They have bad dogs."

"What kind of clothes did you all make there?"

"Some make pants, blouses, dresses. Others sew tags by hand."

"What did the tags say?"

Blanca closed her eyes and spelled out some of the more popular and well-known names in the clothing industry, including some unknown to me.

"Rosita and I sew by hand. They like our work. But Sara, she is the best. She knows much about clothes. All the women listen to her. She says what we do is against the law. Rosita and I know we have to escape. But how? The men, they take us back to the other burned house. They also take the clothes. We put clothes in plastic bags. I hear voices at night. The next day all the clothes are not there."

"What happened last night—rather this morning?"

"One of the men, he smokes a lot. The *coyote* tells him not to smoke because he can burn the clothes. But he smokes anyway. He comes and tells us we are moving to another house today. Sara asks why. He says some people, strangers come into the house. Not safe for us anymore."

I stood up and let out a "Dammit!" Finn and I had unwittingly precipitated the events that led to Rosita's death.

"What? You don't feel good?"

"My leg went to sleep. It's okay. Please go on."

"Then we all hear shouts. The dogs are outside. They bark a lot. And then we hear *him*." Blanca pointed at the mountain lion. "The man is smoking. He drops his cigarette. Then he runs out and back into the house. We see the cigarette still burning on the floor. Sara and all of us begin to fan it. A cotton blouse next to it is on fire. The dogs go crazy outside. The men scream. But the dogs bark more. Rosita and I know this is our chance. We tell the other women. They say too many of us. Only Rosita and I go. Sara says yes. They give us their blessing. They begin to throw clothes in the fire. Rosita and I, we take our bags and go quiet to the door. We hide behind the door. Sara shouts: 'Fire!' The men, they pull the dogs inside and run to the house. Rosita and I, we get out and begin to run. We hear the motorcycles, we run more hard. We hear the dogs close to us. But when we hear him, the lion, I hide. But Rosita doesn't. The lion, he jumps on the dog. The men attack the lion. We see the lion. Rosita runs. The lion runs after her. She falls. The other dog comes back and he and the lion fight. Then I hear a horse. The man on the horse makes the lion go away. The men, they come back. But the man on the horse, he goes after them. I go to Rosita and tell her we have to go. But Rosita does not move."

We heard the gallop of Cantero's horse. Blanca stood up, picked up her bags and got ready to run. I held her back.

"Leave your sister's bag. Can you find the place where the dead dog is? "

"Yes, I remember."

"Go there and wait for me. Get going. I'll get you to a safe place."

Blanca rushed for the edge of the creek. I saw her disappear behind a tree just as Cantero rode in and dismounted. I heard voices coming from the opposite side of the hill.

Wasting no time, I briefly told Cantero about Blanca, Rosita and their captors.

"She's in grave danger. I'm asking as a personal favor to trust me and let me hide her at the ranch for the time being."

"No problem. Go before the rangers get here. Take her to the shepherds. They'll help you. I trust them completely. And of course, tell Estefanía."

With Blanca precariously sitting behind me, I rode as fast as I could. Along the way, Blanca pulled on my sleeve and made me stop. "Here. The men bring us here. At night." She pointed at a shallow pool, hidden from sight by willow oaks.

"Why did they bring you and the other women here?"

"Wash our clothes and ourselves."

Cantero had said that at the time of Virginia's accident, Lula Marie had seen a flash of light and heard distant voices.

"One of those times, did you see a horse, all shiny?" I asked.

"A horse. Yes. Like a ghost. We are all scared. The men, they get us out of the water. We all run. They take us back. But I hear other horses."

"But no one was riding the shiny horse?"

"No. No horseman. No *jinete*."

"Was the horse you saw last night also shiny?"

"No, not shiny. But man rides the horse."

"And he helped you?"

"Yes. He attacks the bad men."

A half hour later, we caught sight of the sheep pens and the shepherds. I told them Cantero wanted the young woman kept hidden for awhile. No questions asked and no one to know. They immediately took Blanca inside.

I rode on to the main house. Estefanía and Lula Marie came out right away. The gray and I reluctantly parted company as Lula Marie took him back to the stables to feed him. I handed the rifle to Estefanía.

It had been difficult to talk with Blanca while we were riding at the fastest pace possible. I told Estefanía about the two sisters, the need to hide Blanca and about the significance of the motor-cycle tracks.

"These men should be brought to justice! What are we going to do about it?" she asked.

"I know there's a connection between these coyotes' pirate garment business and Hilda's murder and Virginia's disappearance. I feel it. But I want to talk to Blanca some more."

"Let's do that now, while her recollection is still fresh."

I went to my room and retrieved the photo of Virginia and Hilda. If Virginia had been taken to the abandoned house, Blanca might be able to identify her.

Estefanía had already packed a basket with food, milk and water. We rushed up the slope and past the stable to the sheep pens.

After Blanca ate and drank two glasses of water, I showed her the photo.

"She had a white cotton nightgown on, not the clothes in this photo," I explained.

Blanca didn't say anything at first. Then she pointed at Virginia's Virgin of Guadalupe medal.

"A woman, she has a medal of the virgin, big, beautiful like this. The men bring her. But her face—we cannot see her face. It's dark. Only candles. They say she's a sacred woman. She wants all the women happy. The men say to touch her, pray to her. Rosita and I, we do not pray. She is the devil, the woman, Rosita says. But

Sara and the other women pray to her. The men, they take the sacred woman away."

"When did this happen?" Estefanía asked in Spanish.

Since her mouth was full, Blanca raised two fingers.

"Two nights ago?" Estefanía asked.

Blanca answered with a head nod and a yawn.

"Do you know what the men did with the woman?"

Blanca shook her head.

"About the men with guns, do you know their names?" I asked.

"Only short names—Nato, Callado, Frisco."

"Did you see any gringos—red hair, blue eyes—with the men?"

"One gringo with red hair only. He comes a few times. At night. He talks to Nato, the *coyote* with the tattoos. They talk in the yard. All the women, we are always looking in the holes. We can't see his face. But the man, he is very, very tall. He has a radio. A walkie-talkie, Sara says. She also says we never get out of there. The man, he is a lawman."

Estefanía and I exchanged glances. She couldn't hide her rage anymore than I. Blanca was already showing signs of extreme fatigue. Estefanía started to ask something but changed her mind. She made Blanca lie down on a cot.

"I'll stay with her until she falls asleep. Please, Gloria, don't leave before I get back. We need to talk."

"I'll wait for a short while. But I really do need to get going."

The sun cleared the highest peaks of the sierra as I walked back to the house. It was now shining bright. I suddenly felt dizzy and had to hang on to the corral fence to steady my step. Sleeping was a commodity I could not afford at the moment. Virginia's trail was getting colder by the minute. Bringing Marshall to justice would take time. He would never confess to charges of piracy and slavery, let alone to kidnapping Virginia or murdering Hilda. We had nothing but Blanca's testimony against him, useless without other evidence to support it. In the meantime, whoever was holding Virginia could panic and kill her.

Lula Marie was already waiting for me at the kitchen door. "You're exhausted. You can't leave now. Lie down. I'll wake you in a couple of hours. Then we can plan your escape."

"I can't. I'm going to take a second look at the house where the women were held before Marshall has a chance to remove evidence."

"But you were already there, with Finn."

"True. But the men left in a hurry last night. No time to clean the place thoroughly. I might find something that helps me track Virginia down."

"At least go and freshen up. And have some coffee. Estefanía told me she wants to go with you."

I agreed. My body ached for a splash of cool water.

A while later, feeling cleaner and more alert, I joined Lula Marie in the kitchen. I lay down flat on the cool tiles and stretched my sore limbs and back. Lula Marie was lost in thought until I helped myself to some coffee and popped a couple of aspirins in my mouth.

"Paladin is involved in all this, isn't he?" she asked.

"Not sure. But maybe he knows about it and has looked the other way. Maybe he's the horseman Blanca saw last night, playing out his fantasy of being El Zorro."

I looked at her. "You really do care for him, don't you?" I asked.

"Guilty as charged. Don't ask me why."

"Love never answers to why. But what are you going to do about it?"

"Get myself out of this . . . sentimental trap. Please don't tell my sister." She gave me a sad smile.

"I'm not going to tell anyone. But I can't promise I won't go after him if he's involved in this whole mess."

The door opened. "Any time you're ready, Gloria," Estefanía said, holding on to the reins of two horses.

The gray and I were happy to see each other again. Estefanía climbed onto the saddle and sat erect on Diablo and waited for me to get on the gray. For a fleeting instant, in awe, I gazed at both as if horse and rider were one, a woman centaur. Cantero was right when he said that Diablo was hers. But she was also his.

We rode on. Past the oak grove and the creek beyond it, I pointed at the hiking trail Cantero and I had followed to the meadow where he and I had first heard the young woman's screams. Soon we came upon the paved back road to Sutter Creek and Jackson. Closer to the house, we saw fresh tire tracks, probably made by the motorcycles and vans used to transport the women and goods. I would have to follow that road later and pray it led to Virginia.

Estefanía and I tied the horses to a tree off the road and made our way to the house on foot. Finn and I had probably been there after the men had taken the women to the sweatshop. Everything seemed the same as before, except for a pile of ashes and charred garments, which confirmed Blanca's story. With a tissue I picked up and bagged a cigar butt that hadn't been there before.

"Finn might be able to run a DNA test and maybe prove Marshall's involvement. It's going to be tricky," I said.

"Not if Sheriff Thorpe goes along."

"What are the chances? The blue wall of silence—most cops won't rat on each other. They almost never air their laundry in public. Marshall's scandalous actions would reflect on the sheriff's name and the department's reputation and so on. How are we going to convince him to look into it?"

"Proof and more proof. Hank Thorpe is a good sheriff. Actually, he's the acting sheriff. He was brought back from retirement for awhile because the sheriff had to take a leave of absence. There was no second in command. Anyway, Finn will find a way to prove that Marshall is behind all this. Also, there is an eyewitness now. And perhaps the only way to keep her alive is by convincing the cops that she needs to be in protective custody."

"That makes sense. But you know she's going to be deported as soon as this is over."

"These criminal investigations and the trials take time. In the meantime, Cantero, Lula Marie and I can be her sponsors. She would be able to stay here and get a worker's permit."

With the Patriot Act in place and in matters of immigration enforced to a capital p as in paranoia, I wondered if that possibility was going to pan out.

"You seem to know quite a bit about immigration cases."

"I used to work as a volunteer with the Sanctuary Movement. It's obvious we need to reactivate it now. Regardless, this young woman and her sister were fortunate that their *coyotes* were not interested in exploiting them sexually or selling them into sexual slavery. Other women haven't been that lucky. Unbelievable, isn't it? Honor among *coyotes.* I suppose we should be—no—I'm grateful for their Godfather's type of twisted principles."

"Honorable *coyotes* or not, they might just try to do something to keep Blanca from testifying."

"Leave that to Carlos and me."

A few minutes later, we were back on the horses just as we heard a police siren approaching the house. From our hiding place we saw a county patrol pull up in front of the house. Deputy Marshall strolled leisurely to the back of the house, not even bothering to check the area.

"Maybe we should see what's going on at the creek, now that we know Marshall's here. I want to believe all of these events are related. It's frustrating to have so many pieces of the puzzle still missing," I said.

"Like what?"

"I'm sure Marshall is guilty of human trafficking and exploitation, not to mention piracy. Still, why did he kidnap Virginia? Why did he take her to see the captive women?"

"Control. He needed to keep the women under control. And in my opinion it is obtained by either muscle or wit. Marshall is most likely the muscle."

"And Valenzuela the wit? But is he also this Zorro-type man who keeps showing up everywhere? If so, he saved the women last night."

"Maybe. I'm sure you'll find out who El Zorro is. Why don't you join Carlos at the creek? I'm sure Finn is already there. I'll follow Marshall when he leaves."

"No. Forget it!"

"Look. The truth is that you can't be in two places at the same time—not unless *you* are Murrieta's ghost, of course. And let's face it. You're a stranger in these parts."

"But you're not getting paid to take risks. That's my job."

"And you're doing a fantastic job. But people are used to seeing me riding around here. Even Marshall wouldn't suspect me. He would notice you immediately and that would defeat your plan to go underground."

Before I had a chance to protest, she got off Diablo. Rider and horse disappeared in the brush.

I rode out to join Cantero. The rangers and the fish and game officers were already there trying to figure out the easiest way to carry the lion, awake and alive up to the van and Rosita's body to the medical examiner's wagon. Finn and Cantero were talking with a forest ranger and another man in a sheriff's uniform, probably Acting Sheriff Thorpe. I stayed out of sight until the rangers and Thorpe started up the slope on foot to reach their respective vehicles.

Finn greeted me with a smile. "Still hot on the trail?"

"Many trails, I'm afraid, but not sure yet which leads to Virginia."

I filled in all the details furnished by Blanca and gave Finn the evidence Estefanía and I had collected at the house.

"Marshall was already there, probably getting rid of self-incriminating evidence."

"I suspected he was dirty. Now we can do something about it," Finn said.

"And we have an eyewitness," Cantero added. "I'm going to have a talk with Thorpe as soon as I get back. We need to get protection for this young woman."

"Will the sheriff agree to it, considering the political fallout?"

"He's an old-fashioned honest cop. And he has nothing to lose. He'll do the right thing," Finn said.

"Anything new about Hilda Gallardo's murder?" I asked Finn.

"Pretty much what we concluded yesterday. The autopsy is scheduled for this morning. I'll call you when I get the report. What's your next move?"

"A talk with Benita and with Hilda's husband," I replied.

"Deputy Marshall already talked to Sal Gallardo, Hilda's husband. He filed his report. Apparently, nothing unusual happened that night, Gallardo claims."

"His wife is not at home most of the night, and Gallardo says there was nothing unusual! Either he wasn't home when he says he was or he's lying. But he's definitely somebody to watch."

"Are you still planning to vanish?" Cantero asked.

"I'll let you know later. I'm taking my stuff with me just in case."

The crime scene men were ready to go, and Finn joined them. Cantero offered his horse to carry Rosita's bagged body up to the medical examiner's wagon. I said a prayer for Rosita's soul and for Blanca's safety. Once again, the gray and I began our journey back to the ranch.

FIVE
BACKTRACKS ON BACKROADS

Emilia, Julio and Milagros had returned from Jackson. They all looked at me with an unbearable glitter of hope in their eyes. The usual no-news-is-good-news and other trite sayings got stuck in my throat. Emilia and Milagros went back to the staff quarters.

Rage and despair cast distinct shades of black in Julio's eyes. "Shouldn't you be out there looking for my sister?" For the first time his tone was confrontational.

"I will be as soon as you answer my questions. On the night Virginia disappeared, you went out sometime during the night. Where did you go? And why?"

"*El don* told me about a mountain lion and asked me to watch out for the cat. I heard Diablo. Went out to check on him. No sign of it. I slept there anyway."

"What time did you wake up?"

"At five, like always. Fed the horses. Looked for the cat's tracks. Found none. Then went to the house to clean up. My mom was up. She went to check on Virginia. My sister wasn't there. I went out again. Looked for her. Couldn't find her."

"Did you find any of Virginia's footprints?"

"I found some, but I lost her trail around the sheep pens. When I got back to the house, *El don* was there. He told me the rangers had found Hilda dead."

"What were you wearing that night you slept in the stables?"

"A black T-shirt, jeans, black boots and a blanket. Gets cold in the stalls at night . . . I see. You think I had something to do with my sister's disappearance? Wrong!"

"Should I believe you and Cantero or the surveillance tape? See, the tape that night showed a man all dressed in black, wearing a hat and chaps, sneaking out from somewhere behind the office building. It also showed your sister running in that direction a short while later. Cantero believes the man was you."

"But you don't."

"Not dressed like you tell me you were. If it wasn't you, then who? Any ideas?"

He held my stare and shook his head.

"This isn't the time to keep secrets from me. I'll find out eventually, but it'll be a waste of time. And let me remind you, time is running out for your sister."

"Even if what you say is true, and I'm hiding something from you, I can reassure you that it has nothing to do with Virginia or what happened to Hilda Gallardo. I swear. I'm sure you'll find out what the secret is. But not from me."

He strode to the door. His romantic affairs had probably nothing to do with Virginia's disappearance. But if he was the night rider, that surely was my business.

I went into the hall when I heard singing and the strumming of a guitar. I recognized the lyrics of *Alfonsina y el mar*, a song made famous by Mercedes Sosa, an Argentinean singer. I rapped on Lula Marie's door. The singing stopped.

"You're pretty good," I said, when she opened the door and invited me in.

"Not really. But thanks anyway. I play a little and sing, mostly when things get me down. Where's Estefanía? What's happening?"

"She's following the tracks we found at the house where the women were kept. She'll call me if or when . . . I'm on my way to have a talk with Benita, Emilia's oldest daughter. Then maybe with Sal Gallardo if I can find him."

"Please let me go with you. I've been trying to find a way to help you and this is it," Lula Marie pleaded.

Taken aback by her sudden request, I arched my brows.

"You think I'm just going to be dead weight. Benita and Hilda's husband know me. If I go with you, it might just get them to open up, not be defensive. You can coach me so I know what questions to ask or how to ask them," she argued.

She gestured a "C'mon" with her hands. "Give me your shirts and blouses, underwear, too. Levis take longer. We'll take care of those tonight."

She called out for Milagros, the gardener.

"What do you want my clothes for?" I asked.

"Milagros can do a short wash and dry. And we can be out of here in forty minutes. Meantime, you take a shower and eat something."

Tired as I was, I couldn't come up with a single objection to her plan. I gave Milagros my laundry.

The young woman was back thirty minutes later as I was putting on my makeup. She handed me a set of clean and ironed clothes.

"What am I supposed to do with these? My jeans are not ready yet?" I asked.

"Miss Lula says for you to wear this white blouse and your skirt and those cute sandals, too. No hiking boots," she replied.

Milagros was tickled, and I couldn't help but chuckle.

I asked Milagros to get my jeans.

I walked into the kitchen, wearing the cotton shirt, my jeans and hiking boots, and carrying my gear in both hands. Lula Marie was on the phone. She looked me over, shook her head and then sighed in resignation at my lackluster style. She pointed to the bowl of oatmeal, the glass of orange juice and the cup of coffee on the table. I had my meal while she talked.

"Problems?" I asked after she hung up.

"I was talking to my new manager at Oro Blanco. We have some very important decisions to make by the end of July. Nothing we can't handle if we prepare for it now."

The phone rang again, and she went to answer it. "Estefanía," she said, and pressed the speaker phone button.

"I tracked Marshall's cruiser, the van and the bikes to another old road near Jackson. The bikers went off the road there. But it's my guess that Marshall went on to Jackson. I have an idea where the van and the motorcycles were heading. An old church between Sutter Creek and Jackson. Meet me there."

Lula Marie wrote down the directions to the place.

"Let's go then," I said.

She gave me a military salute. "Right behind you, *mi comandante*."

Lula Marie drove fast, but she was definitely more in control than the first time I rode with her.

A half hour later, we glimpsed Estefanía and Diablo behind the brush where the dirt road ended. Lula Marie parked the pickup under a tree. My cell phone vibrated, startling me. It was a text message from my partner, Dora Saldaña, at Brown Angel Security & Investigations.

"Valenzuela and Marshall lv'd in S. Jose same time. Cops kept tabs on Val. Marsh joind Amad Co Sher's Dept yr be4 Val mvd to area. Cops susp'd Val drug Kpin, mostly MJ. Nvr prv'd."

I wondered if Marshall and Valenzuela were still in the marijuana-growing business together. The higher sierra foothills were an ideal place to grow the weed in summer and fall. But winters were too cold, so greenhouses would be needed. Valenzuela had perhaps been buying so much real estate for that reason. He was probably already growing marijuana right under everyone's noses. But was he involved in the pirate garment business, too?

I joined the sisters. Estefanía pulled the rifle out of Diablo's saddlebag but let the stallion roam free. She led us through the trees for about a hundred and fifty feet.

We stopped just before we entered a clearing in the woods. We circled the area until we had a clear view of a large building with very high windows. A smaller cabin stood next to it. A belfry with a small cross on top rose up from the main house—maybe an old but recently painted church. I couldn't see the van used to transport the women or the men watching them, but two motorcycles were half hidden behind the cabin. A large sign was visible between the building and cabin. I couldn't read what it said.

"They're probably keeping the women in the church," Estefanía whispered.

"What do we do now?" Lula Marie asked me.

"You two stay here. Keep an eye on the motorcycles. I'll check out the place and get back here. If I see the women, I'll give you the thumbs up. Then call the sheriff right away."

I scurried to the back of the old church. The rear door was locked. On each side of the building, the windows were too high. I sprinted to the corner and took a peek. A dog inside growled. I held my breath. The door opened. The ground crunched under someone's hard soled shoes. Loud sobs and women's voices inside.

"*Cállense, viejas, o les echamos los perros encima,*" a man said, warning the women to be quiet or else.

The door closed. I gave Estefanía the thumbs up. I quickly found my way back to the place where the sisters waited for me.

Estefanía had already made the call to the sheriff. She sat on the ground, resting the rifle and her back on the trunk of a tree. I did the same, opposite her. Lula Marie remained on her feet.

"Not about to get dirt on her Sunday's best," Estefanía joked.

Sunday. It was Sunday. I had left the Bay Area two and a half days earlier. I began to wonder why Justin hadn't called. The thought surprised me. Not that I hadn't worried about him when he was on a case away from me. But this wondering if he missed me was new. Was I beginning to think like a wife and not a partner or lover anymore? Uggh.

Lula Marie's voice brought me back to reality. "What's taking him so long?" She fanned her face and neck with her hands.

I closed my eyes. Bright stars blinked silently in my virtual maroon-twilight firmament. The astral lights shuddered and plummeted as the sky slid downward, uncovering the head and long braid of a woman, shimmering with a thousand tiny points of light. The woman's head began to turn as if to look over her shoulder, but stopped, letting me see only a bit of her profile. "Go to that place by the water. Find me," she whispered.

Startled, I opened my eyes at the same time that Lula Marie alerted us to the presence of the sheriffs. Estefanía and I were up in a flash.

Sheriff Thorpe and his deputies bellied down on the ground, not far from us. We heard the sheriff's voice through a bullhorn. "You in there, come out with your hands up." He repeated the command in half chewed Spanish.

Nothing happened. "*No importeh quien contigo. Dispehramos. Salen. Manos arebah!*" Sheriff Thorpe commanded.

"He could use a little coaching in Spanish," Lula Marie whispered.

Estefanía hushed her. In good or bad Spanish, the message was clear that the sheriff would not negotiate for hostages. I prayed his was just a ploy to get the men to surrender. I had to do something to make sure no harm came to the women. But what?

As if reading my mind, Estefanía grabbed my elbow and said, "Wait."

She slid the day binoculars over her head and gave them to me. She put the earmuffs on her ears and raised the rifle to eye level.

"Put your hand on my shoulder. Watch for Thorpe's signal. Squeeze my shoulder only once. Take your hand off."

She aimed the rifle at the high windows, hoping to convince the men at the church that they were surrounded.

"You're crazy," Lula Marie said. She took cover behind a tree and cupped her hands over her ears.

I crouched next to Estefanía, my hand on her shoulder, and watched the sheriff. Not knowing what signal he'd use with his men, I also watched his mouth. A minute later Thorpe raised his hand high and let it drop right away. I read the "Now" in his lips, squeezed Estefanía's shoulder, dropped the binoculars and covered my ears with my hands.

I didn't hear the glass pane shatter but it must have, alerting the sheriff and his deputies to our presence. But right then the door to the church opened. Two shotguns landed on the ground. Two men stepped out with their hands up. The sheriff and a deputy ordered them to face the wall, put their hands on it and spread their legs apart. The second deputy made his way into the house.

The sheriff looked in our direction. Estefanía pushed through the brush and threw the rifle out.

"Over here, Sheriff Thorpe. Estefanía Cantero. I called you."

He recognized her, lowered his weapon and waved at her. We rushed to join the sheriff. Estefanía explained who I was.

"A word with you later?" Thorpe asked me.

"Any time," I replied

Estefanía began to tell him about Marshall's illegal activities.

"I know. Your husband and I just had a long chat about the deputy."

Escorted by a deputy, four women filed out of the house and stood by a sign that said: "Welcome to the Dry Creek Christian Community Center."

"The women probably speak little English. Is it okay with you if Mrs. Aríztegui and I have a talk with them in Spanish?" I asked.

Thorpe gave us the go-ahead.

"Is there a Sara here?" I asked in Spanish. A woman in her early thirties raised her hand. "I'd like to talk to you."

Lula Marie volunteered to talk to the other women. "What do you want me to ask them about?"

"See if any of them can identify Marshall. Ask about the man with the tattoos and anything else you can think of that can help me locate Virginia."

I took Sara aside. She was saddened at Rosita's death but glad Blanca had survived. I showed her Hilda and Virginia's photo. I put my finger on Hilda. "Have you seen her before?"

Sara shook her head. But she took the photo from me and looked closely at it. "This woman, the younger, she was not here but at the other house."

"The house where you and the others slept or the sewing factory?"

"Where we slept. Nato said the woman is a saint. She's going to make things easy for us. I guess in heaven. Not here, not now."

"Does Nato have two tattoos, one in each arm?"

"Yes. Two flags. Very patriotic."

"Was Nato the one who took this woman saint to see you at the other house?"

"Maybe Nato. Maybe the lawman. I don't know. We were sleeping. Nato woke us up."

"Did you ever take a good look at this lawman?"

"A good look? Only one time, about a week ago. He had a uniform on."

"Was it a uniform like the one the sheriff is wearing?"

"Yes. But the lawman is very tall, a giant. He has red hair. He has . . . *granitos* . . ." Sara poked at her cheeks with her index finger.

"Acne. Do you know where they were taking the woman saint next?"

"I don't know. I don't believe Nato. She's probably not a saint. He was always lying. He said to me that I was almost paid.

Soon I would not owe him anymore. But that was six months ago, a long time."

"Did they ever let any of the women go?"

"Yes, two. Nato said they went back to El Salvador. But I don't know if they did. Maybe not."

"Do you know Nato's real name? Anything about him or the other men?"

"The men, they have *apodos*, you know. They never used their real names. Nato is the Tattoo man. The other two are Frisco and Callado."

"How about the lawman? What's his nickname?"

"Lawman," she said and smiled. "Everyone is scared of Lawman."

"Blanca told me that the men never . . . had sex with you, never . . ."

"Raped us? No, never. Nato punched Frisco hard one time because he was too friendly with me, joking all the time, teasing me, you know, just to laugh. I didn't mind. Why not? I have no shame. I would have done everything they wanted for a chance to escape from them."

"You tried once to escape. Were you punished for it?"

"I thought Nato was going to kill me. But he just punched me in the stomach and slapped me a few times and said, 'Don't try it again. Next time I throw you to the dogs.'"

"Are you sure these men never even attempted to have sex with you? It's so hard to believe."

"Not hard. They want something more than sex. They want money. You see we are cows to them. You don't kill the cows with the biggest *tetas*. And you don't want the cows pregnant. Then the milk is sucked up by the baby. You make no money. Besides, Nato, he is a very religious man, Frisco told me. Frisco said Nato gives a lot of his money to the poor and the church. But we are poor, I said. Frisco, he laughed."

Sara rubbed her knees with her hands. She looked flustered.

"What's the matter?" I asked.

"I can't go back. It's dangerous for a woman like me in Mexico. A good friend in Ciudad Juárez? We worked together in the *maquiladoras*. One day, she went to the grocery store and never came back. Many women like her. No one sees them again. No one knows what happens. And if they know, they don't tell because they might also get killed. I saved some money and left Ciudad Juárez. I went to Tijuana and crossed over, but ended up here."

She looked at the other women now talking with Lula Marie. "You see. We're the lucky ones. We're still alive. I can't go back!"

Her eyes begged but she couldn't bring herself to ask for my help.

"I don't know what we can do to help you all, but we'll do everything possible. You can count on that. The sheriff, I'm sure, will ask you to be a witness in court against these men, to tell what you saw. That means you can stay here longer. But just in case, it's important that you ask for a hearing with a judge before they take you to an immigration detention camp. If you don't, you'll have a police record. Next time they catch you, you'll go to prison."

"It's okay. One way or the other, I'm going to cross back again."

She looked at the photo in my hand. "Is the young miss, the saint, your daughter?"

"No, not my daughter. But it's important I find her. I'm thinking that Nato could have taken her to the place where you do the sewing, the factory. Would you be able to find the place?"

"I don't know where it is. They took us there in a van every day. No windows in the van. We cannot even see the driver. There are high, small windows at the factory. I can only tell you there are many trees and trees and more trees around the house. That's all I could see around the place and up the mountains."

I must have looked disappointed.

"I'm sorry," Sara added.

"It's not your fault. Tell me something. Blanca mentioned a man on a horse. Did you ever see him around the house where you slept? Maybe he knows where they took the woman saint."

"One night the dogs barked and barked and howled. I woke up. I heard the clip-clop-clip-clop. Fast. But that horse was angry, I could tell. People in my town say when you hear a horse doing that at night, that beast is the devil—*el mismo diablo*. I didn't want to see the devil. I got scared and covered my head with the blanket like a *tonta*. My grandfather didn't believe in the devil. He told me many times that men are the only devils."

Sara's face got red. She fanned it with her hands. "I guess I see the devil every day. He has tattoos on his arms and says he's a good man."

I put my arm around her shoulders. "You're very brave, Sara. We'll do our best to help you."

A deputy took her back to the Dry Creek Community Center. I joined the sheriff, Estefanía and Lula Marie.

"Did you by any chance find any tapioca pudding containers in there?" I asked Thorpe.

"None in plain sight. But Forensics will be here this afternoon. Does it have anything to do with Virginia Moreno's disappearance?"

Before I had a chance to answer, Estefanía said, "I was just telling the sheriff about Virginia."

"Did that young lady tell you where Miss Moreno is being kept?" Thorpe asked.

"I'm afraid she doesn't know. But those guys might know. Were you able to get anything from them?"

"They lawyered up. They're not going to talk until they work out a deal with the D.A., but most likely with the feds."

"The feds! I hadn't thought about that," Lula Marie remarked.

"Just the immigration issues alone . . . I have to notify the feds," the sheriff explained. Then he told me, "Mrs. Damasco, I'm going to go back into the community center. I'm assuming you'll be gone by the time I come out again. And you and I have never talked. And you have never talked to that young lady. Just the same, don't stray too far."

He smiled, tipped his hat and went on his way. We went back to the place where we'd left the stallion and the pickup.

Diablo reared on his hind legs a couple of times when he saw Estefanía. She mounted, and they took off down the slope to the road below.

"Those two are made for each other," Lula Marie said and laughed.

I didn't even attempt a grin. My mind seemed to be stuck on one word Sara had said: Diablo, Diablo, Diablo . . . I was breathless.

The pealing of bells, faraway, reminded me again it was Sunday. But the bells that were tolling were not Saint Patrick's. We were only a block from the church. Lula Marie drove three blocks past it and turned. She followed a narrow one-way street to a corner house with a picket fence and a tall pine in the front yard.

The smell of *carne asada* reached my nostrils. Like the mountain lion in the wee hours of the morning, I sniffed the air for its source. But the sudden memory of the carnage spoiled my taste for beef. By the time we reached Benita's front door, I was ready to become a vegan.

A young girl, about ten, with large black eyes, a ready smile and her hair in two long braids, opened the door. Virginia Moreno must have looked like her at about the same age. She grinned at Lula Marie.

"Annie, this is my friend Gloria. Is your mommy home, honey?"

Annie stretched her hand out to me. I shook it. She invited us into the living room, immediately asked us to sit down and offered us something to drink.

"Water, please," I said and congratulated Annie on both her beauty and her good manners. She skipped and hopped down the hall to the kitchen.

I took my sunglasses off and looked around. The living room was ample and uncluttered. Two burgundy upholstered sofas faced each other in front of a brick fireplace, a black coffee table between them.

A large, carved mahogany crucifix hung above the fireplace. Family photos were nicely displayed on the mantelpiece. Framed replicas of Da Vinci's "Last Supper" and Bosco's "La Dolorosa" were on opposite walls.

A playpen was next to one of the sofas. The pads around the playpen were covered with a marine blue fabric. Its small red boats with bright yellow sails were the only hints of life beyond religion.

A couple of minutes later, a man, carrying a two-year-old in his arms, greeted us. He put the toddler in the playpen and shook the rattler. The little boy grabbed it and immediately put it in his mouth.

"Tom Quiroz, *mucho gusto*. This is my son Freddy. My wife's not feeling well, *pero 'orita viene*. Please sit down," he said, switching from one language to the other with ease.

Tom was wearing a white, short-sleeved shirt. No tattoos anywhere I could see.

Annie came in and set a tray with a pitcher of water and two glasses on the coffee table and then politely excused herself. I put my sunglasses on the table, next to the tray. Lula Marie filled all three glasses with water.

"Any news about Virginia, Mrs. Aríztegui?"

"Not yet. That's why we're here. My friend Gloria here is helping us to look into what happened to Hilda and Virginia. But we need Benita's and your help."

"Yes, I heard you're a private detective. How can I help?"

"I understand that your family and the Gallardo family are good friends. When did you or your wife last see or hear from Mrs. Gallardo?" I asked.

"Friday afternoon. She seemed okay and, as usual, going on and on about Virginia's powers. It's all she talked about lately."

"Was she very worried about Virginia—I mean more than usual?" Lula Marie asked.

"Not particularly. She was always worried about my sister-in-law, always trying to convince the church that Virginia could cure all kinds of serious illnesses, help the blind see, the deaf hear, the lame walk, that sort of thing. Miracles. She always exaggerated, big, like she wanted everyone to know how great she, not my sister-in-law, was."

"Did anyone hate her or resent her? Maybe someone who didn't get the miracle he or she expected?" I asked.

"I really don't know . . . . She's . . . she was a good woman, a good nurse, for sure. It's just . . . I felt bad for the people who believed her, especially those who were going to die. It's cruel. I told Benita she should look for someone else to take care of Virginia."

"What about her husband? Did he approve of Hilda's religious activities?"

Tom bent forward and looked at Freddy in the playpen. A wave of red crept up from his neck to his cheeks.

"Sal never talked to me or anyone else about his wife."

"Did Hilda practice any kind of physical penance? After confession maybe? Or did she hurt herself in any way?"

"I see. You're asking me if Sal beat her up." He snuck a glance down the hall as if to make sure no one was listening.

I tried not to look surprised, but I was. He either did not know about the stigmata wounds in Hilda's hands and chest or was trying to throw me off.

"So Sal Gallardo did abuse his wife," I said.

"Don't know for sure. To be honest, I never figured Sal for a violent man. He's a good Catholic."

"But *good* Catholics can be abusers, too," Lula Marie said.

"Oh, for sure. *Claro que sí*," Tom immediately replied.

I heard the shuffling of soft-soled shoes and the closing of a door and then the sound of running water.

"My wife's up. Excuse me." Tom hurried down the hall.

Lula Marie picked Freddy up. Soon both of them were giggling and cooing. I tried to think of ways to speed up the interview. It was going to be difficult and time-consuming if Benita was still in the same emotional state as the day before.

Lula Marie put Freddy back in the playpen when Benita shuffled into the living room with an extremely solicitous Tom in her wake. The smooth cinnamon skin on her eyelids and cheeks was now tissue-paper thin and blotchy, her light-brown eyes bloodshot. Not even the abundant curly lashes or the curvy eyebrows or the full sensual mouth could animate her *dolorosa* countenance at the moment.

Why was she taking it all harder than everyone else? Milagros, the gardener, who was Virginia's best friend, had told me that Benita wasn't that close to Virginia and actually seemed to resent her younger sister. Perhaps the things said in anger or perhaps those not said in love kept gnawing at her conscience.

Benita's eye watered again when she saw Lula Marie. She readily walked into Lula Marie's comforting embrace. She blew her nose with the handkerchief Tom offered her.

Turning to me, she said, "You're the P.I. my mom told me about. I think I saw you at St. Patrick's."

"I am, and yes, I was there."

She wasn't as hysterical as she pretended to be if she could recall seeing me at the church and remembered my occupation.

"I'm sorry to be so direct, but I need to ask you some questions. They might help me piece together what happened to your sister Virginia and to Hilda Gallardo. Do you feel up to it?"

"Ask."

She sat on the sofa across from us. Seated next to her, Tom stretched his arm across her shoulders to support her neck and head. She stiffened. Her back arched away from his arm. Her head dropped slightly forward.

I didn't know how I was going to manage it, but I wanted Tom out of the room *pronto*.

"Basically, I'm trying to put together what Mrs. Gallardo did the day before and up to the time of her . . . passing. It might help me figure out what happened to Virginia."

"I saw Hilda at church that day. Deacon Fierro asked Tom and me and Hilda and Sal to go in and talk with him," Benita said.

"Fierro isn't really a deacon. I really don't know why everyone calls him that. You'd think he's actually the priest, the way he carries on," Tom said.

Benita gave him a fulminating glance.

"Why does Father Ignatius let this man tell everyone he's a deacon?" Lula Marie asked.

"Father Ignatius doesn't speak Spanish. And Fierro has been there forever, long before each of the priests came to St. Patrick's. People go to him, and he helps them, but you'd think he owns heaven."

"Why did fake . . . Deacon Fierro want to talk with all four of you?" Lula Marie asked.

Tom held back a chuckle.

"Father Ignatius asked him to talk to us about being godparents to two orphan baby girls. The babies' parents were Catholic, but the foster parents aren't. They wanted the girls baptized anyway," Benita replied.

"I thought Hilda wasn't a Catholic, that she was a Protestant," Lula Marie said.

"Hilda was raised Catholic. But she also worked with other Christian groups in the community. She says . . . said it was her 'apostolate,' her mission. She and Deacon Fierro had all kinds of workshops for people from different religions."

"At Saint Patrick's?"

"No. They had their meetings at another church's community hall, somewhere else."

"Going back to Friday, did Hilda seem all right to you?" I asked.

"She was jittery. She always talked up a storm, but not that day."

"Did she tell you what was bothering her?"

Tom shifted in his seat. Benita took a few short breaths through her mouth. Her eyes moved side to side under the eyelids.

"I don't know. She went into the rectory. I don't know what she was doing there. I left. I never . . . saw her . . . again . . . and now . . . Virginia's gone . . . and I . . ."

Benita gasped. She bolted to her feet. She struggled for a breath between quick apnea episodes. Her face was turning blue. She wasn't faking the attack, and I slapped her upper back to force her to breathe. A fit of coughing made her face turn red.

Annie rushed back into the room. She saw what was happening and swiftly picked up Freddy out of the playpen and rushed down the hall. Lula Marie went after them.

"Get some more water or some liquor if you have any," I told Tom.

He rushed to the kitchen while I made Benita follow my lead to breathe in and out a few times.

Still sobbing, she kept repeating, " . . . wished her dead. God's punishing me for it."

"You wished Hilda dead? Virginia? Who?" I asked.

"Hilda . . . I told her . . . to . . . go . . . to hell. So . . . ashamed." She squeezed my hand hard.

"Why? What did she do?"

" . . . Having an affair . . ."

"Who was she having an affair with?" I cursed under my breath when I heard the clinking of ice cubes.

Benita looked at Tom with wounded eyes. She fell to her knees and broke into sobs again. And I knew who the other man in Hilda's life was.

After we made sure the kids were all right, we left the Quiroz household. I asked Lula Marie to drive to the church, park and wait ten minutes.

"We have to go back, right? It's not like you to be careless with your things. I noticed you left your sunglasses on the coffee table," Lula Marie said.

"You don't miss a thing. Yeah. Benita has a lot to tell, but she won't talk in front of her husband. She thinks Hilda and Tom were having an affair."

"So that's what has her all bent out of shape. That weasel! My goodness! Do you think she killed Hilda? No, she couldn't. But maybe *he* could. Do you think he did?"

"I don't know. But something isn't right."

"He's pretty cunning, if you ask me. That whole business about Sal Gallardo being a wife beater, he worked it in so cleverly. But do you think it's true?"

"I'm not sure of anything right now. But when a wife gets killed, the husband is the prime suspect, especially if he abuses his wife as Tom implied. I can't afford not to take this rumor seriously."

"But what does all this have to do with Virginia's disappearance?"

"I can't tell you that either, not right now, anyway. But I know Benita has some of the answers. I'm going to ask her to meet me here at Saint Patrick's as soon as she can get away. Then I'll have a talk with Gallardo. Listen, if you need to go back to the ranch now, I can . . . "

"And miss out on all this intrigue and mayhem? Besides, I'm not going to leave you stranded with no wheels for a quick get-away. Let's call Benita."

Lula Marie punched in the phone number and handed me the receiver. Someone picked up but no one responded to my greeting. A child screamed so loud even Lula Marie heard it. Tom and Benita were yelling at each other. A smacking sound. The shattering of glass. Silence.

Lula Marie made a U-turn and took off with a screech.

In a flash, we were again at the Quirozes' front door, furiously knocking and ringing the bell. Holding her baby brother, Annie opened the door. She stumbled out. I grabbed her. Lula Marie snatched the little boy.

"Does your dad have a gun?"

Annie shook her head repeatedly. She ran and didn't stop until she reached the sidewalk. With Freddy astride her hip, Lula Marie ran after her.

The shards of the broken pitcher were strewn all over the floor, and I stepped around them. I heard groans coming from the back of the house. I resisted the temptation to get my gun out, hoping that Tom was indeed unarmed.

"Tom. Benita. Please come out. You're scaring your children. Let's talk."

Not even a sigh.

"Benita, are you all right? Answer me, please."

At the bedroom door, I peeked in. Tom Quiroz was on the floor on his back, wounded, and I tried to assess how bad he was hurt. All I could see was the stain of blood, fresh red, on his shirt, spreading perhaps from a shoulder wound. But he was still breathing.

Benita was kneeling before a crucifix, disheveled, a steak knife in her hand.

"Benita," I said, standing in the doorway.

She turned and stared at me with vacant eyes, but she dropped the knife. She rose, stumbled toward me and fell into my arms. I grabbed her by the waist and steered her out of the house. She dropped to the ground at the sight of her children. Annie rushed to her mother's side. Lula Marie, with Freddy still in her arms, followed right behind her. They helped Benita sit up.

"Tom's hurt. I don't know how badly. I'm going back in," I whispered in Lula Marie's ear.

I walked back into the bedroom as Tom, having managed to sit up, was unbuttoning his shirt. I checked his wound.

"The knife ripped the skin open, but it's mostly a flesh wound. You're going to need stitches, though. You should have a doctor check it."

"No, no doctors. Doctors mean police. *¿Mis hijos?*"

"Your children are okay. Lula Marie is looking after them and your wife. But you need to take care of that shoulder."

I helped him to the bathroom, then headed for the front door.

"He's going to be okay. It's not a deep wound. He's in the bathroom cleaning it up. He doesn't want to go to a doctor. As he said, the doctor would have to report the injury to the police. How're they doing?"

"Benita hasn't said anything. Probably still in shock. I think just for tonight these two should be apart, especially for the sake of the children. Things might look better in the morning."

"Do you think Estefanía and Cantero will let her and the kids stay with Emilia tonight?" I asked.

"I'm sure they will." Lula Marie let out a soft laugh.

"What's so funny?"

"Not this, of course. I was just thinking that the ranch is quickly becoming the Heartbreak Hotel."

I heard the door of the bathroom open. I went back in.

"I need your help." Tom handed me a first-aid kit.

After I dressed his wound, he looked out the door and made an effort to get up.

"Not a good time right now. Maybe you should let Benita and the children spend the night at Emilia's."

He buried his eyes in his palms and wept.

"Can you tell me what happened?" I asked.

"My wife . . . she wouldn't stop, on and on about Hilda and me. My wife is *muy celosa. Y yo ya estaba cansado*—I was fed up and angry, and I yelled at her. She was wild, threatening me, and then she got a knife from the kitchen . . . She didn't mean to stab me. You have to believe me. She had never done anything like this before. *Nunca*. Yell at me, yes, but never in front of our children."

"Were you and Hilda . . . involved?" I asked.

"No. We weren't. Not now."

"Not now. But you were at some time or another?"

"Yes. But it was before I married Benita. It happened only once, the day after Sal asked Hilda to marry him. Hilda drank a lot then. She was drunk that day. She told me she'd always been in love with me. But I was already in love with Benita. I was putting money away so we could get married. Then that night Hilda showed up at my apartment. I know it's difficult to believe, but she just kept . . . she forced herself on me."

At the sight of my arched eyebrows, Tom blushed.

"Okay, no excuses. But after Hilda married Sal, she stopped drinking. She became really, really religious and then she got her nursing degree. Benita and I got married and moved to Jackson. A few months later the Gallardos also moved to Jackson. Hilda and Benita met at Saint Patrick's. Hilda was very friendly to Benita. Y*o andaba que me cagaba de miedo todo el tiempo*. I was scared that Hilda would tell Benita what happened. *Y yo de pendejo pues le dije*. I thought that maybe if I told my wife how it happened, that it happened before she and I got married that. . . . the biggest mistake ever. You gotta believe me. I swear I never had anything to do with Hilda again."

"I don't doubt what you tell me is true. But why would Benita, feeling the way she did about Hilda, recommend her to the Canteros? Did she feel guilty or did she want to make up for her ill feelings toward Hilda?"

"Beats me. I really can't figure it out either."

"Did Sal Gallardo know about your . . . one-night stand?"

"If he did, he never said anything to me."

"But you're sure he beats his wife up."

"Not really sure. But he must've. Hilda said as much the day before yesterday. Maybe he just hit her once."

"Why didn't you tell me that you saw Hilda the day she got killed?"

"I . . . it wasn't anything important. And I didn't want to say anything in front of my wife."

"You'd better tell me now."

"I was on my way home from work. It must've been about seven. I went by Saint Patrick's. I heard honking behind me. It was Hilda. I parked. She parked behind me. She looked scared and started crying, saying something about Sal and how cruel he was. I assumed he beat her up. She put her arms around my neck. I swear I didn't hug her or kiss her. But what d'ya know? Benita was walking out of the church right then. She saw us. She got it all wrong. I told Hilda to talk to someone else about her troubles, maybe the fake Deacon Fierro. Better yet, the cops and file a complaint against Sal. I got back in my car and drove home. I felt really bad for Hilda. But my wife . . . she didn't even let me explain. Then the next morning Hilda was dead."

"Were you and Benita home the night Hilda died?"

Tom gasped and gave me a how-dare-you look. He tried to get up but pain humbled him down.

"Benita slept in Annie's room. But she was home all night, I'm sure. I was, too. You can ask Annie. And yesterday, my wife and daughter got up early and went to Annie's school to help. The school was having a bake sale to raise funds for the kids' field trips. I stayed home with Freddy. Ask the neighbors—they saw me here. And ask the other parents at school 'cause that's where my wife was. I didn't know about Hilda and Virginia until Julio called . . . about nine yesterday. You gotta believe me. We didn't have anything to do with Hilda's death."

"I do want to believe you. But given what just happened, I had to ask. The sheriff will be asking you and everyone else the same questions. I'm amazed no one from his office has come to talk to you."

"A sheriff's deputy already came around asking questions. But he just asked us if we had seen Hilda Friday. We told him we saw her at church, and that's the truth. He left right away."

"By any chance, was that Sheriff's Deputy John Marshall?"

"Yeah. I think that was his name."

"Friday, did Hilda say anything about Virginia? Did you think Virginia was in danger?"

"She just said that she had to see Virginia, that my sister-in-law could fix anything, that she had the power. She talked and I listened. But see? Hilda always talked like that—crazy. And not just about Virginia's powers. Everything she did. Look. She and the fake Deacon Fierro started a religious group, Misión Manos de la Virgen. The Misión members had to pay dues and put in a number of hours a week to help with many community projects. Hilda and Renato Fierro worked very hard to raise funds to rent space for their meetings, that's true. My wife and I went to one of their prayer meetings. We never went back. It was all mumbo jumbo—Native American ceremonies, revival sessions, praying in tongues, you name it. And this was even before Hilda started going around saying that Virginia had the power to heal."

"Were those meetings at St. Patrick's? Didn't the priest object to it?"

"Not at the church. The priest would have objected. No. But Fierro was good at what he did. He finally got some bigwig in town to give them lots of money to buy a building to have their meetings. So the Misión people repaired an old abandoned Baptist church outside town."

"Are you by any chance talking about the Dry Creek Christian Community Center?"

"That's it. It's not too far from here if you follow the old road to Sutter Creek, you'll see it. Can't miss it."

"Thanks. I'll ask Lula Marie to bring the children in while I talk with your wife."

So, there it was. Fierro was the X factor in the equation. "The bigwig" had to be Valenzuela, as Estefanía and Cantero had indicated. What if Deacon Renato Fierro was also the man that Sara and Blanca had called Nato, which could be short for Renato? If so, he was directly connected to Hilda through their community work and to Marshall through their pirate garment business. I knew who I had to talk to next.

I called Lula Marie to the door. "I think it's safe to let the children back in while I talk to Benita. But I'll need your help."

Benita had regained her composure somewhat. Her eyes rose past the top of the pine in the front yard to the sky. She then looked at Lula Marie and me.

"I'm so selfish. Virginia's gone. Hilda's dead. And I can only think of myself. But I can't help it. I guess my marriage is over," she told Lula Marie.

"It doesn't have to be. Obviously, you and Tom have a lot to work out. But he really loves you and the children."

"But he betrayed me."

"Before you two got married, he tells me," I said and then asked. "Do you really believe that he was carrying on behind your back all this time?"

Benita didn't answer my question.

"What's important now is that you two learn to trust each other again. And that won't be easy, but it can be done," Lula Marie added.

"You really think so? I hope *que la virgencita me haga el milagro*. Why would the Virgin do it for me? It's so hard for me to be good. I'm evil!"

Benita was fishing for sympathy. But before Lula Marie got hooked, I asked, "Are you evil enough to kill someone?"

Benita sprang to her feet. Her face was flushed. Lula Marie was shocked but kept quiet.

"You think I killed Hilda? Is that it? I couldn't. I'm not *that* evil."

"I never said you were evil. You did. All I know is that just now you lost control and stabbed your husband in the shoulder, in front of your children. Give me a good reason why I should believe you didn't kill Hilda."

"Why would I kill her now? I've known about their affair for a long time. If I wanted to kill her, I would have done that a long time ago."

"But you'd never seen her hug your husband before."

"That's true. But you're wrong. I didn't want to kill her. I wanted *him* to pay for it. He was married to me, not her. He was responsible for what happened to us." She began to cry and grabbed my arm. "I'm really sorry I hurt him . . . and my children. But I swear . . . I didn't kill Hilda. I didn't."

"All right, I believe you, until I find out otherwise. But right now I need to find Virginia. So tell me, did Hilda say anything about Virginia?"

"Nothing. She stopped talking to me about Virginia 'cause I asked her to. Tom's right. She just wanted to use my sister. Why are you asking? Did Hilda kidnap my sister?"

"No. But I'm sure she knew someone was going to. Can you think of anyone Hilda might have confided in?"

"Not her husband. She had no love for that man. Maybe she told Deacon Fierro. They were always going on and on about Virginia. They had lots of people really believing that Virginia had powers to heal and grant miracles. These people in the Misión Manos de la Virgen group kept pushing the Catholic Church to have my sister canonized. The deacon and Hilda had these weird ideas about a whole bunch of stuff, not just about my sister. But the diocese wasn't buying any of it. I don't blame them."

"Do you know where I can find Deacon Renato Fierro right now?" I asked.

"Yes. It's Sunday. The Deacon . . . Renato is at Saint Patrick's. I've seen him there until about six Sunday evenings."

I stood up and picked up my handbag.

"Maybe you and the children should spend the night at your mom's. We can take you," Lula Marie offered.

"No. It won't be necessary."

"Are you sure?"

"I'm sure. This is between Tom and me."

Benita walked back into the house and hurried to her husband and children. Tom put his uninjured arm around her and kissed her forehead.

Lula Marie and I picked up our belongings on our way out. The Quiroz family waved good-bye from the porch. It was three o'clock.

"Do you really think she killed Hilda?" Lula Marie asked on our way back to the ranch.

"I tend to believe she didn't. But it's just a hunch."

"So why be so hard on her?"

"I had to make sure. Benita's good at playing the victim and getting sympathy from anyone around her, and, for the most part, people respond to her. But I can't afford to play up to her need for attention. And let's face it, next time it won't be me asking the questions."

"Good news," Cantero said as soon as Lula Marie and I walked in. "The D.A. will be offering those two thugs immunity. Marshall is in trouble. The only problem is that the deputy went AWOL. The sheriff issued an APB and a warrant for his arrest. I'm sure they'll have him in custody before long."

"What about Paladin? Is he implicated in all this, too?" Lula Marie asked.

"We don't know yet. Those men refuse to say anything about him or anyone else involved until they get immunity and protection for their families."

"What's going to happen to Blanca in the meantime?" I asked.

"The sheriff agrees that she's safer at the ranch for the time being. She's considered a witness, and she and the other women will be moved to a safe house soon."

I looked at my watch. It was nearly four. I had barely two hours to hunt down Deacon Fierro if he wasn't still at St. Patrick's.

"I'm sorry, but I need to get back to Jackson. Lula Marie will explain. And I won't be back here until this is all over," I said.

"At least come in and have a snack. You must be starved. I know I am," Lula Marie suggested.

"Thank you but I can't."

Cantero walked me to my car.

"Can you recommend a place where I can stay in or around Sonora if I need to?" I asked.

"Why don't you stay at our Oro Viejo winery? It's just outside Sonora and a perfectly secluded place. As a matter of fact, Estefanía and Lula Marie will be driving there this evening. They'll be taking Diablo. Julio will arrive tomorrow with a couple of other horses. They have to meet with a horse buyer in San Juan Bautista on Tuesday. Call on them if you need help."

Cantero gave me directions to Oro Viejo. He also called the winery manager and the housekeeper to let them know I'd be coming in, perhaps very late.

"Good luck," Estefanía said.

"Sorry, but it's only a ham and cheese sandwich and water—all I had time to make," Lula Marie said as she hugged me and put a paper bag in my hand. She drew the sign of the cross on my fore-head, like Mami Julia used to do when I left for school every day.

I drove off, feeling like a traveler setting out on a journey of no return, even though Sonora was only forty-some miles from the Cantero Cross Ranch.

I called Justin. I briefed him on the important events and facts. I didn't mention what I had done to the mountain lion. We had been married only a few weeks, but there I was, already keeping secrets from my husband.

I sped down Highway 49, back to Saint Patrick's in Jackson. After parking in the public lot behind the church, I walked to the rectory and rang the bell. A swarthy man, in his early fifties per-haps, rather thin and wearing a surplice over a black cassock, answered the door. I immediately recognized him as the man who had led the rosary the day before.

The late afternoon was still quite warm and the rather thin man was literally hot under the collar of his cassock. But he appeared otherwise composed. His light brown gaze was benevo-lent, his demeanor that of a humble man. For an instant, he too looked at me as if he'd seen me before but made no mention of it.

"How may I help you?" he asked. He pulled back his surplice and cassock sleeves to look at his watch on his right wrist.

"I'd like to have a word with Deacon Fierro," I said, holding back a gasp and quickly taking my eyes off the stars and stripes on the skin of his inner arm, which was partly hidden by the watchband.

"We're very busy right now. We're preparing the liturgy for the week. Come back in a couple of hours. What's your name?"

"My name is Gloria Damasco. And I can't wait. You probably know I've been hired to look into Virginia Moreno's disappear-ance. I understand that before she died Mrs. Gallardo talked to you about Virginia's safety. I was hoping you could help me clar-ify a few things."

He waved his palm in front of me and said, "I'm afraid I can't help you."

"Because?" I looked directly into his eyes.

Alternating bolts of defiance and arrogance zigzagged across his eyes. But he quickly recovered and changed back into the meek man he believed a holy man should look and act like.

"I'm sorry, but I can't reveal anything Mrs. Gallardo might have told me in . . . you understand . . . ."

Cunning, treacherous fake Deacon, I thought, but to him I said, "I'm sorry, Father. I had no idea Mrs. Gallardo had said things to you in confession—a sacrament, of course. I thought you were Deacon Fierro. Forgive me, Father."

"I really must go," Fierro said, after clearing his throat. In less than a second, he was behind locked doors.

I'd called his bluff. And he'd just blinked. But cornered, he was more dangerous than ever. It was better to let Sheriff Thorpe and his men deal with him. Mother Church would have to withstand yet another scandal, I thought as I started the Volvo.

I drove to a parking spot with a full view of the sanctuary and the rectory. If Marshall had any allies in the sheriff's office, I didn't want them to find out what was about to happen. I didn't have Thorpe's cell phone number, so I phoned Cantero, told him what had just transpired and asked him to phone the sheriff.

"Wait. Estefanía is calling him now. Don't hang up."

I waited. A group of tourists walked down Court Street, looking at the county court building across from the rectory and taking pictures of each other in front of it.

"Okay. Sheriff Thorpe is on his way. But stay on the line. He wants you to keep an eye on Fierro in case he tries to get away."

"That's exactly what I'm doing."

A cyclist pedaled up the street. He wore a navy blue jersey and pants and a yellow helmet. He got off his bicycle and lifted it onto the sidewalk. After securing his bike to a tree, he walked to my car and tapped on the passenger window. I lowered it just enough to hear what he had to say.

"Still detecting?" he asked, as he took off his sunglasses and helmet.

"You do get around, too. What brings 'El Zorro' to this part of town?"

Diego Mendoza laughed.

"Gloria, are you still there?" Cantero asked over the phone.

"Still here. Nothing happening."

I sandwiched my handbag between my leg and the door, then unlocked the passenger door. Diego got in. I signaled for him to be quiet.

"Thorpe sent a couple of his men, and the city cops have also been notified. Get there as quickly as you can," Cantero said.

"I'm already there."

To Diego I said, "I can't explain it to you right now, but something's going on at the church. I have to meet the cops there. You can either come with me or get on your 'horse' and ride out."

"I'll see you there. If not, I'll find you. We need to talk."

A Jackson patrol car parked across from the church, but the two cops sat in it, just keeping an eye on the group of tourists. Five of the tourists, two men and three women, crossed the street and went up the steps to the sanctuary, probably hoping to tour it. They had no luck in gaining access and began pounding on the door.

Diego pedaled past me and into the small parking lot in the back of the church.

Someone opened the front door of the sanctuary, but I couldn't see who, since the visitors gathered in front of the door-keeper, probably trying to persuade him to let them in.

"It's closed for the day," one of the men shouted to his wife, who was standing next to me. The door closed. The men and women began to walk slowly down the stairs. A third man walked behind the two male tourists. The sneaky fake Deacon Fierro was wearing a short-sleeved shirt and khaki pants, a baseball cap and sunglasses, and had a large paper bag in his hand.

I saw Diego, helmet in hand, coming up the walkway between the sanctuary and the rectory. I ran across the street to meet him.

"Do you know Deacon Fierro and what he looks like?" I asked.

"I sure do. But I don't see him here."

"Look at the tourists coming down the stairs."

"Oh, yeah. I think that's him with them."

"We can't let him get away."

The wailing of two sirens died down somewhere behind the church. Two sheriff's deputies came running around the corner, unaware that Fierro was playing tourist. I tried to get their attention, but they didn't even look in my direction. They were busy trying to disperse the growing group of bystanders. From across the street, one of the cops commanded the group on the stairs to get down immediately. They did as told. Fierro stuck to them.

"Dammit! Where's that sheriff? Fierro's gonna get away."

Diego raised an eyebrow and said, "The law ain't here. It's obviously your call. What can I do?"

"Just like that, no questions asked?"

"Yep."

"We need to stop Fierro, right now, by whatever means. Let's just do it!"

I went up a couple of steps and shouted, "Deacon Fierro! Wait!"

Years of responding to someone's call made the fake deacon automatically raise his head and look for the caller. At first glimpse of me, he froze. He quickly recovered and began to run down the stairs. But he didn't see the yellow helmet flying through the air at him. It hit Fierro on his left shoulder and upper arm. Helmet and deacon tumbled down the bottom steps. The paper bag flew out of his hand and landed a couple of feet away.

Fierro fell on his injured arm with a thump. By then, I was close enough to hear the snap of the bone as it broke. He shrieked. But he quickly attempted to roll onto his back. I was right beside him when the split bone ripped the skin just below the tattooed Mexican flag on his arm. It stuck out like the broken mast of a pirate ship. Blood spewed out, smearing the Mexican flag before running a course to the ground.

The tourists were pushing against the cops who were holding them back. The sheriff's patrol was turning the corner. Trying to get Thorpe's attention, I took my eyes off the wannabe deacon. When I looked at the ground again, he was trying to grab the paper bag. The pain must have been unbearable, but his instinct for survival was stronger.

I stepped on his hand, mostly to immobilize it. I had only a few seconds before the sheriff and his men reached us.

"What did you do with Virginia Moreno?"

He squirmed and squealed.

"Where are you keeping her?" I dug my heel into his hand. "Where?"

"Gallardo's woman, ask Gallardo's woman."

I stepped back when I felt someone's hand on my shoulder.

"Mrs. Damasco. I didn't expect to see you again so soon," Thorpe said.

"Nice to see you, too. Check the paper bag."

"We'll take it from here. Go over there and sit down. Wait for me."

I took only a couple of steps back. He crouched to check on the deacon's injuries.

"Call dispatch. We need a bus," he told one of his deputies. "Check in the paper bag," he commanded the other, a woman deputy who quickly put on her latex gloves.

She took a small pistol out of the bag and smelled it. "A small caliber. Not recently fired, boss. But get a load of this."

The deputy held out the bag for her boss to look into it.

"Jackpot! How much?" Thorpe asked, retrieving the contents.

"Fifteen K, maybe more," she said, eyeballing the three thick wads of one hundred dollar bills.

"What have we here?" Thorpe remarked when the deputy pulled out a plastic bag with an ice pick in it.

"It looks like blood, maybe a murder weapon?"

Something else rattled in the bag, and the deputy emptied the contents into her hand. One of Carlota's Tears dangled from her thumb and index finger. Hilda was wearing them the night she died. But Finn had found only one of the earrings outside the Moreno's home at the ranch.

"Read him his rights. Murder, kidnapping, conspiracy to commit fraud—hell, throw the book at him," the sheriff ordered.

Fierro could hardly utter a yes at the end of the deputy's Miranda litany. But he began to cry when he saw a real deacon and the parish priest talking to one of the local cops. "Forgive me, Father, for I have sinned," he begged. But both clerics ignored his plea.

The sheriff stepped aside to talk to them, and then the priest told everyone gathered there to join him in prayer in the sanctuary if they so desired.

Thorpe let the Jackson cops know it was all right to let people through. The priest and the real deacon led their flock up the stairs and into the sanctuary.

I looked for Diego Mendoza, but he was nowhere in sight and neither was the yellow helmet. I also needed to get going. The news of the arrest would soon reach Gallardo. I wrote a quick note to the sheriff, telling him I'd be in touch later. I asked the deputy to get it to Thorpe. She rushed to the sheriff's side, but she didn't hand him my note.

I talked to Cantero while I walked back to my car. I could hear Lula Marie and Estefanía's cheers in the background.

Leaning on the trunk of a tree, Diego waited for me.

"Where's your bike?" I asked when he got into the car.

"Back at the parking lot behind St. Patrick's."

I buckled up and started the car.

"Where are you going?" He grabbed the handle to open his door.

"We're going to Sal Gallardo's house. Tell me how to get there."

He buckled up. "You are a tough cookie," he said. "Turn right at the corner and follow the street to the end."

"How did you know where I'd be today?" I asked him.

"Would you believe me if I said it was a coincidence?"

"No. None of this is news to you. You were at the rosary yesterday, old man, because you already knew Fierro and Marshall were in cahoots. You already knew about their damned illegal pirate business. I think you also knew the trail would lead me to this fake deacon soon enough. So it was a matter of time."

"It's true. When I saw you and Mrs. Aríztegui going into Benita's house, I knew you were only a step away from Saint Patrick's rectory and Fierro."

"Why did you keep quiet about all this? These poor women were kept captive, living in filth, financially and emotionally exploited. And one of them is now dead, trying to get away from Fierro and his goons. And in all this, we're supposed to be glad that the women weren't raped or sold as sex slaves, because there's honor among Catholic *coyotes*! And because this poor excuse of a man gave his money to charities! And then you chose to keep it all to yourself for your own private reasons. You had no right, you hear me? No right!"

Diego was livid. He swallowed hard and said, "True. All true. But I had no idea Hilda was going to end up dead and Virginia missing. You have to believe me. I didn't learn about the sweat-shops and that slavery business until Hilda told me two days ago. But she was talking about her husband, not about the others. I had to check it out before I started accusing people left and right."

I blew air out my mouth. "Okay. I probably would have done the same. Tell me the rest and quickly."

"Sheesh! Okay. Hilda told me that she was in the confession-al at Saint Patrick's, waiting for the priest when she heard Deacon Fierro's angry voice. He was arguing with another man. She was afraid to look, so she just listened for awhile. Fierro was demand-ing more money. The other man wanted more women. Hilda had no idea what they were talking about. But then she heard her hus-band's name mentioned. 'You or Gallardo, I don't care who, but get down to Bakersfield and quick,' the other man said. Sal had told her that his trips to Bakersfield had to do with training so he could keep his job as a security guard.

"Hilda heard Fierro protest, but then the other man asked him if he wanted the women dead. Fierro didn't say anything, so the man told him to start making arrangements. It was obvious the man called the shots. When the men stopped talking, Hilda snuck a quick look. When she saw the back of the sheriff's uni-form, she panicked. They left; she went home."

"I guess Marshall was the man in uniform."

"My guess, too, though she didn't say."

"What did Hilda do next?"

"Can't you guess? What kinda woman are you?"

"The best. Would you please get on with it?"

"Do I have to do all the work here? Sheesh. Anyway, Hilda did what most women do. She went through every closet and every drawer in the house. But she couldn't find anything that implicat-ed Sal in any shady business. No mention of Fierro and Marshall anywhere. But she was obsessed and determined to get to the bottom of it. So she also checked the garden shed where she knew Gallardo kept an old trunk and a file cabinet, both locked.

"When Gallardo was asleep that night, she took his keys. In a file cabinet drawer, she found a small box of love notes a woman with the initials AC, had written to Sal. In the box, there were also very syrupy poems Sal had written for his mistress. The last poem was dated May 15, 2005, and celebrated some sort of anniversary."

Diego looked around. "Do you have anything to drink here?"

I reached behind his seat and pulled out a bottle of water. He drank almost half of it. "Where was I?" he asked.

"About to tell me what else was in the cabinet."

"Plenty. The second drawer contained a few file folders. In one of them, Hilda found a deed in Sal Gallardo's name for a property in Tuolumne County, on the outskirts of Sonora. She brought it to me and asked me to find out what that was all about. Hilda was a religious fanatic, but she wasn't by any means stupid. She knew that under California law she was entitled to half of the property. She wanted to make sure Gallardo was the sole owner. For obvious reasons, Gallardo didn't come to me to acquire the property."

"Would you get to the point, please?"

"Okay! It was a deed to a house and five acres of land. The mortgage was backed by none other than Paladin Valenzuela."

"So Hilda confronted her husband, and she ended up dead."

Diego was quiet after he told me to take a left at the next corner.

"What exactly does Valenzuela have on you?" I asked.

He let out a long sigh as if he'd been waiting an eternity for someone to finally ask him that question.

"When Valenzuela first came to Jackson, he asked me to take care of . . . a couple of cash transactions for him. He offered me enough money to get my real estate business going. I found a way to help him. But I had to sign a . . . document to get it done. He goes down, he takes me with him. That's all I'm going to say, for your sake and mine."

"We're here," he said a few minutes later. "But Gallardo isn't home. His dark blue SUV isn't in the driveway. He never keeps it in the garage."

"The front room and porch lights are on. Maybe he isn't home, but someone is."

"Yeah. Maybe his mom and daughter are there. We'll see."

Sal Gallardo's mother, Doña Chuchita, opened the door. If she grieved for her daughter-in-law, she kept her sorrow well-hidden underneath her tan dress with a purple and red flower design and her thick loud makeup.

"We stopped by to see if you and Candy need anything, Doña Chuchita," Diego said in Spanish.

I figured Candy must be Sal and Hilda's daughter. Diego introduced me as a friend and former client. But he didn't give the woman my name. And she didn't recognize me.

"I'm really sorry for your loss." I shook her hand.

I glimpsed down the hall and saw a stack of cardboard boxes filled to the top with framed pictures and women's clothes.

"How's Sal doing?" Diego asked.

She shrugged her shoulders. "My son doesn't show much. You men don't know how to talk about your feelings."

She gave me a woman-to-woman kind of look and said, "My granddaughter, you know, she's too young to understand. I have to protect her."

"I know. It's better to keep Candy as far away from this horror as possible."

"That's exactly what I told *m'ijo*. *M'ija* is going to take care of Candy until the burial."

"Ah, you have a daughter, too, here in Jackson? It's nice to have your daughter so close."

"She lives in Sonora, but it's not that far. My granddaughter Candy will be better off living with my daughter. But the police won't tell us when we can have the body. We don't know when we're going to have the funeral."

She turned around, picked up a photo of Hilda and Candy lying on the coffee table, walked to an open box and dropped it in.

"We must be going, Doña Chuchita. But here's my card. Call me if you need anything, anything at all," Diego offered.

She took the card, patted his hand and walked us to the door.

Outside, I immediately asked, "Where does Gallardo's sister live?"

"Probably in the house in Sonora."

"How do you know?"

"I checked the property out for Hilda, remember? I saw Sal's sister letting herself in with a key."

"Write the directions to that house, please, and anything you remember about the SUV."

Out of chivalry or chauvinism, he felt compelled to ask, "Will you be all right?"

I reassured him with a "You betcha."

I drove Diego back to Saint Patrick's. I wondered if he was going to pedal all the way to Sonora. Not him. I was sure he had some four-legged or four-wheeled HP at his disposal somewhere else in Jackson. But at the moment that was the least of my concerns.

SIX
BEYOND ASTRONOMICAL DARKNESS

Darkness came suddenly as I drove to Sonora. I stopped at a service station to use the restroom. My arms and legs were as stiff as tree branches, and I stretched them. The grumble in my stomach reminded me I hadn't eaten since midmorning. I took the ham sandwich out of the paper bag. I followed each bite with a copious swig of water. I ate only half the sandwich and put the other half back in the bag for later, and I started out again toward Sonora.

Paladin Valenzuela and Sal Gallardo were probably already aware of the arrests and of Deputy Marshall's getaway. Gallardo couldn't risk leaving the area without creating suspicion. Speculation, rumor and innuendo were all I had about Paladin, mostly coming from the Canteros. From what they told me, Paladin had acquired a great deal of property but his dealings seemed to be legitimate. And I only had Diego's word that Marshall had approached Paladin to help him kidnap Virginia and that he had agreed to do it. If Paladin was trying to get legitimate, there had to be a powerful reason for him to get involved in any of Marshall's schemes. And so far, there wasn't a shred of tangible proof that he was directly involved in cattle and horse rustling, in Marshall's slavetrade or in the cowardly deacon's bizarre murder scheme. But Fierro had definitely implicated Gallardo and his mystery mistress in Virginia's abduction.

For Gallardo, kidnapping the Santísima Niña might have been the best way to keep Hilda from going to the authorities or divorcing him and getting most of his money. He might have asked Marshall for help. But Gallardo had to be an indispensable asset in the deputy's illegal business to risk it all by abducting Virginia.

In her search for help, Hilda reached out to Tom Quiroz, but he turned her down. And she was left with only the deceitful fake deacon, not knowing she was seeking help from death himself. Fierro made her murder look like a case of stigmata and left her body in a public place, both signs of remorse. But what was his reason for murdering his partner in Christ? Perhaps Hilda had confronted or questioned the deacon about his and Marshall's conversation outside the confessional at the church? Possible. The pit in the murder plot was the scene of the murder. The fake deacon and his men operated out of Jackson. And Hilda's body had been transported from somewhere around Sonora to the Shadow Creek park. So my money was still on Sal Gallardo.

I called Finn. "Sorry to bother you so late."

"Not late for us in forensics. I'm still at the lab. The sheriff wants results fast."

"Anything I should know?"

"We're just now processing the evidence in the paper bag. The lab is running tests to make sure the blood on the ice pick is Mrs. Gallardo's. But the only thing we're sure of right now is that the fingerprints on the murder weapon are not Fierro's."

My pulse went from sixty to the speed of light in a second. "Whose then? Sal Gallardo's?" I asked.

"I'll have to get back to you on that. It shouldn't take long. He's worked as a security guard so his fingerprints should be on file. The feds are arriving soon. Maybe then we can speed up the processing of all this evidence. Listen, I have to go, but just so you know, a call came in a while ago. Marshall was spotted somewhere near Jamestown, just a few miles from Sonora. The Tuolumne County sheriff's office has been alerted."

"Maybe Paladin Valenzuela is hiding him. His ranch, La Herradura, is somewhere between Jamestown and Sonora, if I remember correctly."

"Could be."

"Do you happen to know if Sheriff Thorpe is looking for me?"

"I'm not sure, but I don't think so. Thorpe's a smart man. He wants you free as a bird, if you get my drift. But be careful out there. I'll call you as soon as I get the results of the prelim tests."

Of course the sheriff was cutting me some slack. I could tread swamps where the law couldn't wet even a toe without a search warrant. I just prayed that I would not find myself at the noose end of a rope.

Only the Ghost of Sonora could be in two places at the same time. I wasn't a ghost yet. And I had to get to Gallardo's place. So I called the only other person that had access to Paladin Valenzuela's La Herradura ranch. I hoped his heart answered my call.

"You and Paladin—*andan en la misma onda*. He called just a few minutes ago," Diego said.

"What did he want?"

"He says a game of poker, but probably just company. I told him I'd try to get there before midnight. But I don't think I'm going to be able to. So what are you calling me for now?"

"I just thought you'd like to know that Marshall has been seen around Jamestown. Since Valenzuela's ranch is somewhere between Jamestown and Sonora, he's probably hiding there. What do you think?"

"It's possible . . . No."

"What?"

"I know what you're up to. And the answer is N-O. I'm not going there. No sirree."

"It wouldn't take much. You could either join Paladin for a game of poker or just watch the ranch and keep an eye out for Marshall. Just watch. If you see Marshall, call me or call the Tuolumne County sheriff anonymously. I need to keep an eye on Gallardo. He's involved in all this. And I'm sure he knows where Virginia's being kept. But Marshall might also know and might try to do away with her. Obviously I can't be here and there. I'd really appreciate it if you could help. Please."

"You're good. You should be in sales."

"Not interested. How about it?"

"Okay. Tell you the truth, I'll just stand guard. I don't feel like playing cards or being social tonight. But Paladin isn't home yet anyway. He'll be home in about an hour. I'll let you know if I change my mind."

"Good enough."

I punched in Cantero's phone number. My cell's light flickered but the call went through. The connection broke off after about a couple of minutes. But I managed to tell Cantero about Finn's findings so far and Marshall's whereabouts. I pulled out the cigarette lighter in the Volvo, attached the cable to charge my cell phone and stepped on the gas.

I drove into Sonora as light was only a glowing line on the western horizon. Highway 49 became Washington Street, the town's main thoroughfare. It was unusually active for a late Sunday evening. Although its many jewelry, clothing and antique stores were already closed, the countless noisy bars lining the main street on both sides were still busy. Both Sonora and Tuolumne County patrol cars cruised back and forth, keeping an eye on the young, rowdy bar patrons.

Ahead, I saw the Y intersection Diego had told me about. I veered left onto Mono Way East, later took a left on Hess Avenue, and then a right onto Phoenix Lake Road.

I was driving slower on a winding road and had a few cars behind me. At the first opportunity, I let them pass me. Five vehicles wheezed by, but none of them a dark blue SUV. Two and a half miles past Bear Club Road, I found the dirt road that led down to Gallardo's property. I slowed down and took a look at the large house, partly hidden behind a row of trees. Either no one was home or the windows were covered with dark, heavy curtains. But the exterior lights were on, one right above the front door.

Trying to find a more suitable place for a stakeout, I drove farther up the road. Four vehicles were parked on a wider ledge that served as a rest area. I could have a much better view of Gallardo's house from there.

In the light of the near full moon, I made out the silhouettes of people sitting on crates or folding chairs and looking at something through their binoculars. A telescope on a tripod and some another round contraption sat on the roof of an old VW bus. A power line was hooked to a buzzing generator on the ground. Amateur astronomers, I thought. They hardly turned their heads when they saw my headlights, seemingly more interested in scanning the eastern sky, just above the dark tops of the Sierra Nevada.

I thanked my lucky stars for coming upon the flock of stargazers. No one would suspect me if I were in their midst. I parked a few feet down the road and left my belongings in the car, including my handbag. I took my night and day binoculars with me, set my cell phone to vibrate and put it into my shirt breast pocket.

"Welcome," a rather scrawny young man said in a soft voice and pointed to the crate next to him. "They're here. Just a few minutes ago, we saw them, three small ships. We think they landed."

Even better. I had just joined a band of terrestrials looking to make contact with extra-terrestrials.

"We were here June second and the twelfth and also the fourteenth. It was awesome." He looked at me and asked, "What's your name? I don't think I've seen you before."

"Gloria. What's yours?"

"My name is Solo. That one is Darius, our guide," he said pointing at the hefty man on top of the VW, now looking through his telescope.

"Solo as in Han Solo?"

The young man laughed. I wondered if the woman sitting in front of us was Princess Leia, looking a bit older and fuller than in Star Wars. A rather sophisticated camera sat on a folding chair next to her.

The woman hissed a hush. Solo and I went back to our sky search in silence. I then lowered my binoculars until I had Gallardo's house in sight.

"I gotta piss," Solo said aloud a few minutes later, a loud comment probably meant to piss off the woman in front of us. But she ignored him. And he walked to the other side of the road to find a more private place.

I kept an eye on the house below while Darius, their leader, voiced some degrees of longitude and latitude east or northeast from time to time. As if on cue, everyone gazed up in that direction to find only astronomical disappointment.

I heard Solo's fast footsteps behind me. I turned around. The headlights of a vehicle spotted his run across the road. The driver saw him but seemed not to slow down. Solo made it across safely. But the driver slammed on his brakes, coming to a screeching halt in a cloud of dust.

Solo stood next to me, panting. When the dust settled, I saw the dark blue SUV. The passenger window lowered. I cursed under my breath. I'd left my gun in the car.

"This is private property," the driver shouted through the passenger window. "Getoutta'ere! You're trespassin'." He stepped out of the vehicle, carrying a baseball bat.

Everyone else in the group stood up to face him. But Gallardo had seen me at the church so I hid behind Solo, who reached back and touched my arm to reassure me he would protect me.

In the moonlight, I couldn't tell if the man was really Sal Gallardo. He was wearing a baseball cap that shaded the upper half of his face. And I couldn't tell by his voice since, at the church the day before, I had heard him speak only in monosyllables.

A powerful beam of light from the top of the VW bus crept down then up until both driver and SUV could be seen clearly. The man looked up as he covered his eyes with his hand. I caught a glimpse of the pouting mouth, high cheeks and a thin mustache and goatee.

Solo pushed on me to step back. "We're not trespassing, sir. This is the people's land," he said in a very polite tone.

I heard a thump behind me.

"Go get him, Darius," the woman next to me said.

I felt someone's hands grab my elbows. Before I knew it, I was being literally lifted and put aside. Darius moved past me and into the circle of light. He was holding a metal pipe, and he struck his hand with it several times.

"You were saying, sir?"

Gallardo's eyes shifted from side to side.

"Now, we're not doing anything wrong. We're here only to welcome our celestial guests. So I suggest you move on and let us go on with our vigil, sir." Darius stepped forward.

Gallardo stepped back but brandished the bat in the air with both hands. He then got back into his SUV. "I'll be back. And if you haven't left, I'll call the sheriff. Bunch of creeps! *Hijos de la chingada.*"

The SUV took off with a screech and disappeared behind the next bend down the road.

"Should we move out to the main road just in case?" Solo asked Darius.

"Yeah, we'll do it but later."

Darius climbed up the stepladder. His VW bus shook and squeaked. I expected it to topple over, but it withstood the test. And we all went back to our sky watch in silence.

Down below, Gallardo arrived at his house. He parked. The hatch door popped up. The front door opened and two young children spilled out with the light. Gallardo embraced them. A woman stood at the door, and took one of the bags from him and then walked back in. All I could see of her was her rather slender frame in jeans, a tight top and her abundant curly hair.

"There they are. Three of them," the woman in front of Solo and me said.

She stood up and babbled a coordinate and the names of two constellations, Ophiuchus and Hercules—the serpent bearer and the mighty warrior. She immediately began to snap a sequence of photos.

With the help of my day binoculars, I located the groups of stars that resembled the teapot shape of the bearer, holding a snake in each hand, and the N shape of the mighty warrior's body. The moonlight blinded me. When I finally was able to focus, I saw only one light. It looked like a giant, fuzzy, glowing bumblebee. But its light didn't flicker so it wasn't a jet. It moved too fast to be a weather balloon. Its flight seemed erratic at first. Soon I saw that it was moving from right to left and then up and down at forty-five-degree angles each time and then around the area it had just covered.

"It's a pattern, a cross in a circle. Is someone getting it down?" Darius asked the group.

"I am. I am," a delighted Solo chanted.

Darius pointed the floodlight up. He began to flip the lamp's cover to send a message to the "celestial guests."

I didn't know Morse code or any other code used to transmit ship-to-ship blinker messages during World War Two. But I was sure Darius's message had a "welcome" somewhere in it.

For five minutes I became oblivious to anything but the celestial phenomenon. Then, as suddenly as it had appeared, the pulsating, glowing bumblebee sketched its last cross in a circle pattern, flew past the serpent charmer's head and the warrior's knee and disappeared in the darkness between them. Everyone sat there in contemplation, sighs breaking the silence from time to time.

Darius was the only one still looking through his telescope, but it wasn't at the sky.

"We'd better get outta here. That guy's coming back," he said.

He took his telescope off its tripod, and he handed the pieces to another man on the ground.

I saw Gallardo driving up the winding road. Everyone gathered their belongings, equipment and crates and began to load them into their respective vehicles. I rushed to my car, slid in and waited. Gallardo showed up a few minutes later. He didn't get out of his vehicle but waited until everyone drove out. In my side mirror, I saw the SUV turn around and head back down the road. I started out and drove down the hill, away from the Gallardo's place.

Near the intersection with Bear Club Road, I slowed down and parked off the road to let the car behind me pass. Instead of going downhill, I drove uphill some distance until I found another rest area. It was large enough to hide the Volvo. I ran across to the other side and found a perfect spot to continue my watch. I went back to my car and got my surveillance gear and my gun.

I shuddered at the thought that a snake might be hiding under the brush or behind the rocks there. But I harnessed my fear and sat on a large rock. I now had an unobstructed view of Gallardo's front door and of the smaller structure previously hidden by the main house, most likely a detached garage or storage area.

The outside lights went off a few minutes later. The family was in for the night. I debated whether to go back to my car and get some sleep, too. I flipped my cell phone open and checked the time. It was five past ten. It seemed reasonable to wait for another hour.

I watched the area below and the sky above. I smiled at the memory of the extraterrestrial bumblebee sighting. I had to agree with Solo. It had been an awesome experience. And if my skepticism weren't running interference, I would already be a convert and believe that the light in the sky was indeed an alien spacecraft. I was still curious about the cryptic message the celestial guests had seemingly been trying to convey—the cross in a circle.

It was an ancient symbol, common to many civilizations. Until Nazi Germany adopted it as the swastika, it had been the written representation of the Norse god Odin. For some Mexican symbologists it was the symbol for the Mayan god Kukulkan, known to the Aztecs as Quetzalcoatl, the Plumed Serpent. At present, the symbol has been appropriated by the White Supremacy movement.

So there I was on a rock between heaven and hell, with a White Supremacist alien spacecraft hovering beyond the Sierra Nevada range. I was watching out for an alleged ritualistic murderer who had also kidnapped a young woman said to be a saint able to perform miracles. The absurdity of it all was worth a laugh.

A half hour into my watch, my cell phone vibrated. I expected to hear Diego's or Justin's voice. I was surprised when Finn greeted me.

"Burning the midnight oil, I see. What's going on?" I asked.

"I don't know how the press found out . . . probably the feds told them. They just arrived an hour ago. But the TV network people are now camped outside the department. It's hotter than a boiler room in here. So we're all working around the clock."

"Which of all the shocking news attracted the networks?"

"Oh, the ritualistic aspect of Mrs. Gallardo's murder is the cherry on the cake. They love Marshall's story and the sheriff's department's 'alleged' involvement in human trafficking across the Mexican border. And third, that the same deputy involved in the slave traffic was also the lead investigator in the murder. They haven't found out about Virginia Moreno's saintly powers and her kidnapping yet."

"Something to be thankful for."

"Amen. But that's not why I'm calling you. We haven't been able to determine whose fingerprints are on the ice pick. But we have ruled out Fierro's prints. The medical examiner found traces of skin under Mrs. Gallardo's fingernails. Prelim tests show we're dealing with a perpetrator, blood type "O" and—you're not going to believe this—double X chromosomes."

"A woman!"

"Yep. Now that the FBI is running the show, we have access to their databases. So I sent the fingerprints on the ice pick to their Integrated Automated Fingerprint Identification System—IAFIS. If this woman's prints are in the national fingerprint database, we might have a match within hours. They'll be doing the DNA testing, too. I'll keep you posted. What's happening at your end?"

"I have Gallardo under surveillance. The fake deacon implicated him. But he also talked about Gallardo's woman being involved in the kidnapping. From what you tell me, she might have killed Hilda. Just the same, Gallardo is most definitely involved in transporting the women across the border to this area, and I still think he's the kidnapper."

"Do you think Virginia's still alive?"

"It's just a hunch. But I don't know exactly where she's being kept. I also have someone watching Valenzuela's ranch near Sonora. I'll keep you posted."

I quickly reviewed the list of women in direct contact with Hilda. Not knowing their blood types, I had to trust my feelings about them. Blanca and her sister Rosita were not even on the list. My intuition told me that neither Emilia nor the gardener Milagros nor Lula Marie was capable of duplicity and murder. Estefanía might keep secrets from her husband, but the possibility of her killing Hilda seemed far-fetched.

Benita Moreno Quiroz was the most likely suspect. She was capable of violence, and she had crossed over from verbal to physical abuse. A woman would definitely try to eliminate the competition. But she had taken her anger out on her husband, blaming him not her rival for putting their marriage in jeopardy. I nonetheless put Benita second on the short list.

Gallardo's mother was an older short and thin woman. Although her dislike of her daughter-in-law was obvious, she did not try to hide her feelings or make excuses for them. To overpower Hilda, who was taller and heftier than she was, and then to kill her seemed beyond Chuchita Gallardo's physical ability. She took third place on the short list.

Then there was Gallardo's sister. From watching her through the night binoculars, I had a sketchy image of her body shape and build, her shoulder-length curly hair, and her height, but not of her facial features. Nor did I have any personal information about her, not even her name. However, I knew someone who might know her. But before I called Diego, I got in touch with Cantero.

"It's a TV circus out here. They're creating all sorts of traffic jams on Highway 49. Estefanía and Lula Marie already left for our winery in Sonora. They should be getting there in about twenty minutes. They took Diablo. Julio will follow with the other horses tomorrow morning. I need him here tonight."

"What about Emilia and Milagros?"

"They're here, too."

"And Blanca?"

"She's staying with the shepherd and his wife in Jackson. Luckily, they left before the press got here."

"Have you talked to Finn?"

"Yes. He called a while ago. He's sure Fierro didn't kill Hilda. Are you at the winery already?" Cantero asked.

"No. I'm keeping an eye on Gallardo. He has another house in Sonora."

"So you think he killed his wife. Did he also kidnap Virginia?"

"Not exactly. But Fierro implicated Gallardo's mistress in Virginia's abduction. So I'd like to stick around for awhile longer. See what develops. I'm hoping Marshall will pay a visit to Valenzuela at La Herradura. If he does, we got him," I said.

"Call Estefanía if you need help."

I heard him curse. A photographer or reporter was attempting to gain access to the ranch. Cantero apologized, rushed a good night in, and hung up.

Right then, I wished I hadn't resisted getting addicted to technology and had one of those multimedia gadgets to see what was being reported. I called Diego instead.

"I was beginning to think you'd forgotten about me," he said as a greeting.

"That could never happen. What's happening at your end?"

"I've been here for awhile. Paladin came home about fifteen minutes ago. No sign of Marshall. Can I go now?" He sounded like a little boy at detention, asking his teacher to let him go home.

"Nah. But tell me, what's Gallardo's sister's name and what does she look like?"

"Her name is Isabel Gallardo, never been married, about thirty years old. She's kind of . . . homely. But she does have beautiful straight hair down to her a . . . very, very long. She has a nice shape, about five feet two. What else do you want to know?"

"Wow! You're good. Does she have any children?"

"I just told you she's single . . . I see. No, no children. Why?"

"Now, Gallardo has one child, right?"

"Yes, Candy, six years old or thereabouts. Why?"

"The woman at the house with Gallardo is at least five feet four, flatter on all counts and has shoulder-length curly hair. She also has a child, younger than Candy. I'm thinking she's the other woman, the mistress the phoney deacon mentioned."

"Could be. I've never seen the woman, and until a few days ago, I didn't even know she existed. All these questions about this woman, why? And this is the last time I ask. Answer my question or I go home."

"An ultimatum. Tch. Tch. Okay. Remember the ice pick found in Deacon Fierro's paper bag? It was the murder weapon. But the fingerprints on it aren't Fierro's or Gallardo's. And apparently Hilda managed to scratch her attacker. She was killed by a woman."

"No shit! So you think either Gallardo's sister or his lover might have killed Hilda."

"Possibly. So far, I've eliminated every other woman who had contact with or knew Hilda, except for one. You just described Gallardo's sister for me. The woman in the house with him doesn't look like 'sis' at all. Now, I have to find out who this other woman is."

"Just when you think you have it all figured out . . . Go figure." He let out a nervous laugh.

"At least one of us hasn't lost his sense of humor. Please, give it another half hour at La Herradura. But call me before you go home. And thanks."

"And you keep me in the loop. Okay?"

"I will."

My stomach made enough noise to scare away any night creepy-crawlers or white supremacist aliens around me. I had left the half sandwich, bottle of water and thermos of coffee in the Volvo. However, my bladder demanded relief first. If any aliens were around, they probably were already familiar with a woman's anatomy and the parts I was about to expose. I went behind the bushes, nonetheless, all the while foolishly checking the ground for snakes. When I was finally ready to go across the road and get to the food, I looked up, gasped, stumbled and almost fell back on the rock where I'd sat before. I quickly straightened out, blinked and looked again. I snapped the holster strap off and slid my gun out.

A man stood next to the Volvo, seemingly unfazed by my moves. He was clad all in black and was wearing chaps. His face was shadowed by his hat. His arms hung straight down. He raised his head slightly. His cheek, chin and neck were covered with black luster. The moonlight ebbed and rose on the slick surface of his shirt with every breath.

If I could get him to talk, I might be able to identify his voice.

"It's about time we met, Murrieta," I said.

Silence.

"What's the Ghost of Sonora doing here? What do you want with me?"

The distant revving of an engine replied.

I aimed my gun at the breathing spirit. "You move and I shoot!"

I glanced at Gallardo's house down below. A white car was climbing up the hill. But when I looked across the road again, the living spirit had fled.

I got into my car, lowered the window still looking for the masked man, then started out. A horse neighed and I heard the pounding of hoofs on the ground. I checked my rearview mirror. Tornado and the Ghost of Sonora appeared behind me, ran past the Volvo and disappeared behind the next bend in the road.

I wanted nothing more than to chase after this Murrieta impersonator and wipe the black glossy smears off his face. But my obligation to the Santísima Niña came first. The white car, a Toyota, moved quickly past my hiding place. It was dark and all I could make out was the man's baseball cap. I counted to thirty before I began my run after Gallardo. He stepped on the brakes every time he came to a curve in the road. I did the same to avoid getting too close to him. Every so often, I checked my mirrors, but the Ghost of Sonora had vanished.

Closer to the Y intersection with Phoenix Lake Road, I sped up to make sure Gallardo veered to the right. I followed the car downhill to Hess and a block ahead to Mono Way. When I got to the corner, the light was turning red as the driver took a left. I waited an interminable five seconds. Gallardo could have already turned onto any of the streets fanning out from Mono Way. Since the traffic was insignificant in either direction, I made an illegal left turn and raced down the street.

Highway 108 came into view as the Toyota entered the ramp onto it. Gallardo was heading west. Valenzuela's ranch was between Sonora and Jamestown down that same highway. Gallardo worked for Marshall, and if Marshall was at Valenzuela's La Herradura, a meeting of the head honchos was about to happen.

I immediately called Diego to alert him and to ask him for the lay of the land and the house at La Herradura. He was getting ready to go home and reluctantly agreed to wait for me at the Cal-Trans parking lot off the frontage road near the ranch. I was to look for a yellow, tall, portable toilet and some Cal-Trans road repair vehicles there.

I followed the Toyota at a reasonable distance for a few miles, drove past the exit sign for the Cantero's Oro Viejo Winery and eventually came to the sign for La Herradura. The Toyota took the exit ramp and turned left at the bottom. Gallardo was already waiting at the ranch gate when I got to the bottom of the exit. I had a glimpse of the two-story Mediterranean-style house, illumi-nated by ground spotlights. The gate opened as I turned right. Gallardo drove in. I drove on to the Cal-Trans parking area.

Diego, dressed as an old mining prospector, thick mustache and hat, didn't waste any time. The instant I was out of the car, he led me to his pickup. He pointed the beam of his flashlight onto two sheets of white paper on the hood where he had sketched the main house and the area around it.

"There's only one more or less safe way to gain access to the house. Here, through the cooler room and pantry. It has an outside door; it's always locked. But the connecting door to the kitchen isn't. Use this to get into the cooler room."

He twirled a skeleton key between his thumb and index finger.

"I won't ask how you got it. I'm assuming you didn't find the incriminating documents Valenzuela has on you, or you wouldn't have a need for camouflage."

He didn't answer.

"Where do Gallardo and Valenzuela usually pow-wow?" I asked.

"In Paladin's business office."

With his index finger, Diego traced the route I was to follow once in the kitchen: on to the hall, right, down and then left. Two doors, the one on the left was the game room. Diego would be asked to wait there for Paladin. The other door led into Valenzuela's home office. Past the office, the hall widened. There was a small sitting area at the end of that hall.

"You'll see a mirror on the wall just before you get to his office. Crawl under it."

"A camera behind the mirror?"

"No. A reverse two-way mirror. Paladin doesn't like surprises."

"What about the security guards? I saw one at the gate."

"Uh-huh. He usually has one of the dogs with him. Two other dogs are kept in a kennel next to the stables, about two hundred feet from the main house. The second watchman patrols the outer areas in a Jeep. He'll be back at the gate in about an hour, maybe forty-five minutes. Both guards pack, so be careful. Then, there's Gordo, the house manager. He's up until Valenzuela retires for the night. There's a home alarm, too. The pad is next to the front door. Now, get in the back, behind the passenger seat. Stay low until we're in. When it's safe, get out and go right. You'll see the cooler room. Wait. I'd better change clothes."

He took his regular clothes off the garment hook in there.

"Okay, get in. And don't peek."

"Don't flatter yourself," I said and got in. I lay down on the floor, sandwiched between the back and front seats. The butt of my gun dug painfully into my own butt just below my waist, exciting all kinds of pain and pleasure nerve endings. Pain won over pleasure, and I shifted positions.

Diego threw the prospector's clothes in. They landed on my face. I rolled them up and squeezed the bundle under my neck.

We arrived at the gate in a cloud of rust-colored dust.

"*Buenas*, Gonzalo. Mr. Valenzuela is expecting me."

"He didn't tell me. Let me call him, Mr. Mendoza."

Valenzuela okayed the visit over the intercom. The gate opened.

"Tell Gordo to let you in the game room, Mr. Mendoza."

"Sure thing."

A couple of minutes later, the pickup came to a full stop.

"Gordo loves to talk. I'll keep him busy in the front room for about ten minutes so you can get in the house before he walks me to the game room," Diego piped in. "On the count of three."

We both got out and shut our respective doors. I crouched beside the pickup. Five long steps and Diego was ringing the doorbell. I snuck a glance over the truck bed. The Toyota was parked on the other side of the front door. A dog growled and barked but was immediately hushed by the gatekeeper. I took my gun out. The front door opened. Greetings followed.

The ground lamps shed much of their light on the area around the walls. So I decided to run quickly along the open path toward the rear as soon as the front door closed. The humming of an engine and the snorts of horses were barely audible in the distance. The thumping of my heart was loud in my ears.

I let myself into the cooler. The strong smell of hams and other cold meats permeated everything. The room had no windows but a dim nightlight provided enough light. I walked around the full sacks and boxes of food stacked on the ground. Light showed underneath the door to the kitchen. I could only hear the humming of kitchen appliances.

The door creaked lightly as I pushed it open. I raced past the quartz-topped counters, full of every conceivable small appliance, across to the other door. I heard laughter and talk. I snuck a glimpse but couldn't see the men in either the living room or the adjacent dining area. I agreed with Lula Marie that Paladin had a penchant for heavy, dark velvet upholstery and window coverings. But his taste in hardwood flooring and area rugs was impeccable.

I took a few tentative steps out the kitchen door. Diego and Gordo were still in the foyer. Gordo had his back to me. Diego gave me the go-ahead.

A staircase rose where the halls met. The beige carpeted halls were ample, dimly lit by tiffany wall sconces. The sitting area at the end of the second hall was more like an alcove. Heavy green velvet panels hung on each side of the recessed arc. They were loosely tied with thick golden cords. A console table stood between the drape panels. The Tiffany lamp on it was off.

A trickle of light from the hall wall sconces illuminated a bundle, like a large sack full of laundry, on one of the loveseats there. I wondered what Gallardo had brought with him.

The wooden floors under the carpet creaked as I took a step. I walked closer to the wall to avoid the more heavily treaded center strip.

Diego and Gordo were now in the kitchen, judging by the clinking of crystal on metal.

I squatted and duckwalked under the large two-way mirror. Valenzuela's office door was ajar. I snuck a glance and quickly moved to the other side of the door. I heard whispers. A woman sobbed and pleaded for something I couldn't quite make out. Valenzuela issued a warning hush, followed by a promise to look after the supplicant.

But where was Gallardo, I wondered. He might be in the game room. No chance to find out. Gordo and Diego's voices and laughter sounded nearer. The office door closed. My heart took flight. No place to take cover except for a corner of the alcove, half hidden by the narrow but long green velvet side panels. In my haste, I bumped against the loveseat. I heard a long sigh coming from the bundle on it. I touched it. It felt warm. Something moved underneath my fingers. I scurried behind one of the drapes.

Mashed against the recessed wall, I waited until I heard a door open and close and Gordo's good night. He rapped twice on the office door and then headed down the hall. A couple of minutes later, the door to the office flung open. A woman stepped back out the door. "If he finds us," she said.

Her voice sounded somewhat familiar.

"Shush. You're my own flesh and blood. I'm not going to abandon you. Sal can threaten all he wants. But you and my grandson are spending the night here where I can look after you. You can leave tomorrow. Moisés will drive you to Watsonville."

I hadn't seen that one coming. Gallardo's mistress was Valenzuela's daughter, and the bundled up child sleeping on the seat was his grandchild. I had finally come upon Paladin's powerful motive for covering up Gallardo and Marshall's slavetrade and pirate business.

The child sighed. Paladin's daughter glanced over her shoulder at her son. My heart flipped in my chest. Lula Marie's housekeeper Aster was the last person in the world I expected to see there, let alone to be suspected of killing Hilda Gallardo or kidnapping Virginia.

"Promise me you'll let her go free. She doesn't know anything. She hasn't seen anyone's face. We all have been very careful. I wouldn't want . . . I'll be cursed, damned if anything happens to her . . . . Please," Aster said, sobbing.

"Moisés has it all arranged for tomorrow night. La Niña will be all right. And everything will be taken care of. You'll see." Valenzuela's tone was reassuring and caring.

Virginia was alive! At least until the following night. Moisés—whoever he was—had seemingly been keeping her captive all this time. I pressed against the wall when I saw Valenzuela begin to walk to the loveseat.

"Take him upstairs. Get some rest. I'll check in on you before I turn in," he said.

"I want to go now," Aster pleaded.

"Not a good idea. Besides, I need Moisés where he is right now. Trust me. He'll be here tomorrow afternoon. Besides, if you gave him the cocktail I gave you, Sal won't wake up until very late tomorrow. You did do it as I said, right?"

"Uh-huh."

"So you're safe here. Get some sleep."

Valenzuela picked up his grandson and carried him down the hall and up the stairs; Aster shuffled behind them. I didn't dare move until I heard him go into the game room to meet Diego.

Pain shot up my butt and swiftly ran a fiery twin track up my back. Limping, I made my way to and up the staircase. Although I now knew what motivated Paladin and had heard his promise to Aster that Virginia was safe in Watsonville, I needed to make sure that he wasn't lying to his own daughter and didn't have Virginia stashed somewhere in the house.

Light spilled out from underneath two of the four closed doors upstairs. I put my ear to the first door and heard Aster humming "Twinkle, Twinkle, Little Star." The second room had the looks of a master suite—king-sized mahogany bed, matching dresser and nightstands. I stood in awe at the threshold for a minute. Valenzuela's bedroom was unlike any other room in the house. The atmosphere in the master suite was at once airy, elegant and welcoming, perhaps the effect of the cathedral ceiling, the light peaches-and-cream wall paint and the copper sconces spotting the art on the walls. Displayed against the opposite cayenne-colored accent walls were two Rupert García's prints, a striking mixed media Ana Lilia Salinas painting, and several of Mary Andrade's "Day of the Dead" color photographs. The sage and copper-colored linen drapes matched the bed covers and the upholstery of easy chairs in the sitting area.

This was Paladin Valenzuela's mind-heart sanctum. And for a fleeting instant, I understood something about Lula Marie and what she loved in him. But that love story would have to wait, I thought as I rushed through the walk-in closet and the master bathroom, with its white marble walls and black vanity and cabinets and two of Pancho Jiménez's red and black ceramics on tall stone pedestals, like guardians flanking a large Jacuzzi tub.

My window of opportunity could close any minute, so I rushed out and checked the other two bedrooms and guest bathroom, more in sync with the downstairs décor. And I was satisfied that Virginia wasn't there. My stop the next day: Watsonville.

I stood at the bottom of the stairs and listened. Gordo was in the kitchen, I was sure. There was only one other way out. I walked briskly to the front door, but just before opening it, I checked the alarm pad next to it. It wasn't armed yet. I pulled the door just enough to look out and listen for any sounds of danger. The night was eerily quiet.

I slid through the opening, pulled the door shut noiselessly, and sprinted to the side of the pickup. Soon I was lying on the floor of the rear cab, trying to find a somewhat comfortable position for a long wait.

An occasional bark from the dog at the gate kept me alert until I heard Diego's voice as he said good night to Valenzuela and the sound of his footfalls as he walked to the pickup. He turned on the engine as he whispered, "Are you there?"

"I'm here," I replied.

A moment later, the grating of metal reassured me that we were out of harm's way. I sat up.

Diego looked at me in the rearview mirror. "We have to stop meeting like this," he snickered.

"What did Valenzuela have to say?" I asked.

"I told him I'd heard Marshall was M.I.A. He said he got a call from Marshall, telling him to run. The deputy is on his way to the Mexican border."

"With California?"

"Yeah. Tijuana or Mexicali or any point between them. Anyway, Paladin didn't seem worried at all. I've gotten to know him. And I don't think he was involved in that whole business. How about you? Did you find out what Gallardo was doing there?"

"Gallardo wasn't there."

"What? But I thought you told me . . . so who?"

"Did you know Valenzuela has a daughter and a grandson?" I asked.

"He's hinted about having a daughter someplace. I've never asked about her. I figured that if he really wanted me to know, he would have told me about her."

"So you don't know who she is."

"Haven't the faintest. So are you going to tell me who she is? Better yet, what does she have to do with all this?"

"Aster, Lula Marie's housekeeper—she's Valenzuela's daughter and the other woman in Sal Gallardo's life."

"Holy shit! Is she—do you think she's the woman who . . ."

"Who killed Hilda Gallardo and had Virginia kidnapped? It looks that way. Murder in this case, wrong and sad as it is, makes as much sense as murder ever does. Aster was eliminating the competition. But her reason for kidnapping Virginia is still a big question mark."

"What're you gonna do? Notify the Amador County sheriff?"

"Only about Marshall's whereabouts. Who's Moisés?"

"The bartender at the Golden Nugget Taverna. Why?"

"Before I answer that, let me ask you one more question. Do you know if Paladin owns a house in Watsonville?"

"Your question just answered my question about Moisés."

"Ah, so Moisés owns the house in Watsonville."

"In the Pinto Lake area; he hopes to retire there. He's shown me photos. He's always telling me what a bargain he got. He bought the house about ten years ago for next to nothing."

I briefly related the conversation between Paladin and Aster.

"It sounds to me like Paladin doesn't intend to harm Virginia, that he's actually been keeping her alive," Diego said as he pulled next to my car.

I couldn't help a laugh.

"What?"

"You do admire the man. It shouldn't surprise me. He's practiced angel and devil in equal parts—no one more fascinating to a younger man."

He pouted and ignored my comment.

"I went to Watsonville with a group of Oakland volunteers a week after the 1989 Loma Prieta earthquake. It's about an hour and forty-five-minute ride from Oakland. How far is it from here? And how do I get there?" I asked.

Diego shook his head. "You're all business, ain't ya?" For the first time, his comment was meant to hurt.

"I am, but only when someone's life depends on me."

"You're right. I don't know where that came from. I'm sorry . . . let's see. You have to take Highway 108 east to 120 then to I-5 south; and I believe 152 west to Watsonville. About four hours, give or take. Where are you staying tonight?"

"At the Oro Viejo winery, if someone is still up to let me in."

I took out my cell phone and looked for Lula Marie's number but didn't press the talk button.

"You can crash at my place if you need to. Call me. Otherwise I'll talk to you tomorrow and give you the exact address in Pinto Lake-Watsonville."

Surely he was tired, but exhaustion wasn't what I heard in his voice next. "About Virginia—good or bad—I'd prefer to hear it from you. Will you let me know?"

"I promise. Listen. You don't have to answer, but what will happen to you if Valenzuela is implicated in all this? The feds are going to go over everything with a fine-toothed comb. And I'm assuming you haven't gotten your hands on those documents you talked about."

"I have no idea what's going to happen. I'll own up. Do the crime, do the time. Whatever. But Paladin just told me that he's all legitimate now, what he always wanted to be. He said his paper shredder has been running nonstop since Saturday. 'Don't worry,' he said. 'We'll get out of this in one piece.' Notice he said, 'WE.'"

"Why don't you just ask him for the papers now?"

"I've been thinking about doing just that."

"Better do it before tomorrow. But before I go, I want to ask you something very personal, if you don't mind."

"Ask away. You now know most of my secrets. What's one more?"

"Are you gallivanting all over the Gold Country masquerading as the Ghost of Joaquín Murrieta?"

He straightened up in his seat. "*Me estás madereando*, right?"

"No, I'm not kidding."

"Hello! I won't get on a horse if you offer me a million dollars. I just wear the get-up. I don't ride the damned beasts. Hmm . . . now I know why you've been calling me El Zorro. I wish."

We both laughed. I grabbed my handbag and said, "Thanks for everything. I owe you."

He got out and went around, opened the door for me and then walked me to my car. He unexpectedly drew me to him and hugged me tight.

"You owe me nothing. Take care of yourself."

Lula Marie answered her cell phone immediately and greeted me with an "I'm so glad you're all right." I apologized for calling so late and told her I was on my way.

"I'm up. It's been a crazy day. So I had a long nap as soon as we got here. Come whenever you're ready."

"Gracias. See you soon."

I then dialed Finn's cell phone number.

"Goodness. When are you going to get some rest?" I asked.

"Believe it or not, I'm getting ready to go home. What's happening?"

"I just found out that Marshall is heading for the Mexican border—could be Tijuana or Mexicali."

"I'll let Thorpe know right away. He's bunking at the office tonight. Thanks. Call me tomorrow?"

"I'll do that."

In twenty minutes I was driving through the gate of the Oro Viejo Winery. The surveillance cameras on the arc above kept track of me as I pressed the intercom and identified myself.

"Drive up about forty feet. At the Y, take the right up the hill to the house," Lula Marie said.

The road wound up past vineyards on both sides and farther up a corral and small stable. I expected to hear snorts, but not even a soft neigh broke the night's silence.

The house sat on a low hill. It was a two-story, gray or greenish-gray Victorian, with a small upstairs balcony right above the wide porch. A large garden, enclosed by a white picket fence, was flanked by twin tall palms.

I got a change of clothes and put them into my cosmetic bag, which went into my hardware bag. Lula Marie stepped out to greet me. She led the way up the stairs to a guest room next to the stairs.

I hoped that Lula Marie would also be tired and not expect a detailed report. Barring her total emotional meltdown at the news, we were still looking at another hour minimum before we went to bed. So I toyed with the idea of not giving her the bad news just yet. But I didn't get a chance to bow out gracefully.

"You must be starved. We can talk while you eat," she said, already going down the stairs.

I was exhausted and the bed looked soft, warm and inviting. But the Ghost of Sonora had spoiled my meager supper, and it had been hours since my last meal. I was hungry.

An omelet, toast and tea were on the table when I walked into the kitchen. And for the next few minutes, I ate while she sipped her tea.

"You look worried. Has something happened?" she asked.

"Plenty, but it's going to be hard for you . . ."

"Whatever it is, I can take it. Is it about Cantero or Estefanía Feliz?"

"No. And not about the Morenos, either. In fact, I have a good lead about Virginia's whereabouts. I think she's still alive."

"Thank God. So that's the good news. Tell me the rest."

"It involves Paladin Valenzuela."

"Who else but . . . ? Is Virginia at La Herradura? Is he keeping her there?"

Not able to come up with a way to sweeten the next set of news, I said, "The woman who allegedly killed Hilda Gallardo and had Paladin Valenzuela kidnap Virginia is your housekeeper Aster. She's in fact Valenzuela's daughter and Sal Gallardo's mistress."

To my astonishment, Lula Marie laughed. Perhaps it was the shock, but she had obviously not believed a word I'd said.

"This isn't the script for a *telenovela*. I'm not making it up."

She sucked in her breath. "How sure are you?"

"Very sure. I'm sorry."

She sobbed softly while I told her what I had uncovered at La Herradura. It took her awhile to regain her composure.

"I've been such a dupe. I trusted Aster so completely."

"You were not the only one. I never suspected her, not until the truth was staring at me, literally in the face. I suspect she's been playing chameleon all her life."

"Did you call the cops on them—father and daughter?"

"I can't do that. I'd risk never finding Virginia. I might even have to run interference with Gallardo. I don't think he's aware she left him. Aster might have drugged him to get away."

"You think so?"

"Wouldn't the sound of an engine in the quiet of night wake you up? And Paladin asked whether Aster had given Gallardo the 'cocktail' he had gotten for her. At any rate, I'm hoping Aster will lead me to Virginia. Talking about father and daughter, what's Aster's last name?"

"Cellier. I'm guessing she used her mother's name, though she probably hoped she'd soon be the second Mrs. Gallardo. I can't believe she did what she did. Maybe Gallardo made her do it."

I shook my head. "It's hard to tell who was using who. She obviously manipulated her father into kidnapping Virginia for whatever reason. But if she murdered Hilda, she's gone on to an entirely new and more frightening level."

"But you just said if . . . so you're not sure."

"It's not that easy for most people to drive an ice pick into someone while staring them in the face, even in self-defense. But when jealousy and rage mix, they're powerful. Probably a crime of passion, as the saying goes. Did she ever talk about herself, her family maybe?"

"That's the thing. She did. She told me her mother came from Haiti to Florida in 1980 and relocated to California in '81. Aster was born in San Francisco in '83. Funny, she never really talked about her father. I assumed he had either abandoned her and her mother or he was dead. I had no reason to make it my business. Little did I know . . ." Lula Marie sighed.

"How long has she worked for you?"

"About three years. She had just moved to this area. She had references and a social security number. They checked out. I had no idea she was involved with Hilda's husband. Once, I did ask if her son's father was helping out. She told me he did. And that was all. I respected her privacy."

"What was she like all those years?"

"She's been a good worker. For the most part, she was friend-ly, although, at times, she seemed moody and very tired, almost fatigued. At other times she seemed excited and optimistic. Her son seemed to be in poor health, and every so often she couldn't come to work for a few days. I was sympathetic. She's a single mother trying to make ends meet with a sickly child. I trusted her implicitly. I just can't begin to comprehend . . . Oh, my God. I just thought of something awful. Maybe she's the one that left the notes threatening me. Don't you think it makes sense? I mean, I was dating her father, and she didn't like it."

"You've got something there."

"Do you think maybe she also stole Carlota's Tears?"

"How would she know the combination to Cantero's safe?"

"She had access to everything in my house. She must have figured out where I keep the safe combination."

"Where do you keep it?"

"I have a photo album on my dresser. You know—probably you don't know—but I have the memory of a free range chicken when it comes to credit card numbers, etc. So I wrote those numbers down in the album. Not easy to tell what all those numbers are. But one of them is the combination to the safe. She must have figured it out . . . must have."

"I guess we won't get any answers until after all of this is over."

"So what do you think's going to happen? Do you have any idea where Virginia is?"

"If I'm right, probably in Watsonville, Pinto Lake to be more precise."

"Pinto Lake . . . Pinto Lake. Why does that sound familiar?"

"Does Aster have relatives there that you know of?"

Lula Marie snapped her fingers. "I know why. That's where the shrine to the Virgin of Guadalupe is . . . oh, Blessed Mother of Jesus! And guess who told me about it and took me there? This is unbelievable!"

"When were you and Aster there?"

"About two years ago. You think she's planning to take Virginia there and kill her?"

"I'm not sure. Can you tell me about the shrine, where it is, what it looks like? It's important."

"Hmm. Not many pilgrims were there the day we went, though it was Guadalupana Day, December twelfth. But the *ofrendas* were festive—lots of fresh flowers in plastic or crystal vases and tall votive candles, written prayers and testimonial notes and a few *milagritos*. To tell you the truth, the image of the Virgin was very small, but I guess etched by divine fire on the bark of an oak tree."

I was amused by the "etched by divine fire" remark. "Disappointing?"

"Yeah, it was."

"I'd love to hear about the rest but not now. I need to know the exact location. Do you remember?"

"I don't quite remember the name of the road to Pinto Lake—something like Deep . . . No. Give me a sec, it'll come to me. Teh tah-teh Road. Teh tah-teh Road . . . Green Valley Road! I'm almost sure. Let me see. We got to the lake. There were two recreation areas. Mexicans favor the first park we came to. But we didn't go into the first parking lot. You'd think the Virgin of Guadalupe of all virgins would choose to appear in the Mexican park. She didn't. Instead, she appeared at the Anglo park, which is the second recreation area. Care to guess why?"

"Not right now. Let's talk about it again after I find La Santísima Niña. So the shrine is in the second recreation area. How did you get there?"

"We went through a residential area to get to the park, drove into the parking lot. From there, we walked the trail down to the edge of the lake and turned right to get to the shrine. It's in the middle of an oak grove there, right on the bank."

Lula Marie laughed softly.

"Not about to throw down another religious gauntlet, are you?" I asked.

"No. I remember talking to a woman, a skeptic, there. She told me she used to work with Anita, the woman who claims the Virgin appeared to her, back in 1992. She said Anita was critical to the point of cruelty, opinionated and the worst kind of snob. She used to look down on her coworkers at the cannery. She behaved as if she were *la mera, mera*—the boss. So I asked Anita's friend why she thought the Virgin had chosen such a sinner to be her witness. She shrugged her shoulders and said she doubted the Virgin had chosen Anita. It was more like Anita had chosen the Virgin."

"It sounds like the coworker believed the whole thing was some kind of ruse. Do you?"

"Who's to say what the truth is. But I often wonder what moves women like this Anita to pursue all this and risk going to hell for all eternity."

"I'm not sure. Some people seem to need more attention than others. Maybe fear."

"Fear! Of what?"

"Fear that when she dies, nothing but bones will remain, that eventually she'll be forgotten."

"Hmm. True, I guess. Most of us have only the promise of an afterlife to fight total and merciless oblivion. Faith seems to be the only way we can face death with some dignity."

We sighed, and looked at each other and burst out laughing.

"It's morbid to be talking like this at two o'clock in the morning," Lula Marie said.

"You're absolutely right. I'm going to bed. Good night."

I took a warm shower, set my cell's alarm for seven and plugged it into the charger. I'd hardly closed my eyes when I found myself walking down a dirt path to the water's edge. I heard a horse's trot. But this time it was real. I opened my eyes and jumped out of bed. But I couldn't see the stable from my window. And I was too tired to think about anything but rest. I was lulled to sleep by the sound of water lapping around the slender reeds on a lake bank and by a woman's voice saying, "Find this place and you'll find me."

Now I knew where that place was.

SEVEN
THE TORTUROUS PATHS TO HEAVEN

The heavy car careened and plunged into the water, sucking me in. A terrified face stared at me from behind the window. She looked around in confusion. Moonlight filtered in. I was looking into my own eyes. Someone behind me grabbed my arm and pushed on my shoulder. A scream gathered force in my throat. I kept it in, but a stream of tiny bubbles escaped through my mouth. My chest felt like a balloon filled with hot air to the bursting point. I didn't want to let go of my breath, but I did. Suddenly, I was on land, crawling, then running. Women chanted. A child cried. A horse neighed, reared on its hind legs. Hoofs struck the air. A shot, then another shot, a bloody face and a scream . . . .

My throat was on fire. The scream still burrowed in my ears. Diminishing by whole and half notes, it became the cawing of a distant crow. I opened my eyes at the knock on the door. When I didn't answer, Lula Marie stormed into the room.

"Are you all right? I heard you scream."

"Sorry. It was just a . . . dream," I said, unwilling to talk to Lula Marie about my visions. "What time is it?"

"Close to seven. Breakfast is ready anytime you are."

"Thanks. I'll be there soon."

My haggard face stared back at me from the bathroom mirror. I put some makeup on and eye drops to alleviate the burning sensation in my eyes. But there wasn't much I could do about the suffocating fear that I might fail to save the woman and the child in the car and, even more frightening, that I might kill someone before the day was over.

I had a sudden need to call my mother and my daughter. The three of us had breakfast together every Monday. But they still got together when I wasn't in town. My mother and daughter were my links to my past and my future. But most of all, they were the source of my strength and courage. We talked about nothing and everything.

Tania's voice was so much like a little girl's every time she said, "I love you, mom." I could never hear that softly said, long "Bye" of hers and not think of her as my little girl, no matter how old and accomplished a woman she was now. I had never given much thought to it, but as soon as I told my mom I loved her, I wondered if I too sounded like a little girl—her little girl.

I marched down the stairs to join Lula Marie for breakfast. She wasn't her usual talkative self. Then, all of a sudden, she said, "I don't mean to say that you're not normal, but is it normal to have death dreams?"

"I'm sure most people have them. But having a death dream doesn't mean that the dreamer is actually going to die."

"Don't you know? Dreamers never die!" she said in jest.

"It's good to see you laugh again."

"Ahh, what's one to do? But seriously, do you have them— death dreams—often?"

"Sometimes, but I don't worry much about them."

"So what is a death dream?"

"It's the theme with variations. You or someone you love is being threatened. Someone pursues you and wants to do you harm. Or you actually see yourself dead."

"But it's not the same as knowing when and where you're going to die, is it?"

"Like having a premonition? No. Why do you ask?"

"Sometimes, just before I wake up, I find myself in Santiago, chatting with my parents and my son. I hear chiming. It's three o'clock on a glorious Sunday afternoon. Then suddenly, some-how, I know I die, right then and there. I wake up with a headache."

"I wouldn't worry too much about it," I said.

"You're right. It's silly. You know the saying, '*Nadie muere en la víspera.*' And it's true; no one dies before their number comes up."

"It reminds me of a Somerset Maugham story," I said, trying to change the subject.

Lula Marie's eyes lit up. "Ah, Somerset Maugham. The doctor turned spy, then writer. British vintage. Which story?"

"It's called 'Appointment in Samarra,' but I call it 'The Death Story.' It's the one about the servant of a rich man who sees Death staring at him at the marketplace in Baghdad. In a panic, he borrows his master's horse and gallops to Samarra to escape his fate. His master goes to the marketplace and asks Death why she stared at his servant. Death explains that she did not stare at the servant, that she was merely surprised to see the servant in Baghdad because she knew they had an appointment that night in Samarra."

"*Genial,* just precious! I remember it now. Sad, isn't it? Death's been quite busy in Baghdad and Samarra lately."

The door to the breakfast nook opened. Estefanía stood just outside it, taking off her stable work coveralls and rubber shoes. She hung all of the items from hooks that were outside. She reached for a washcloth on the counter and began to wipe the sweat and dirt off her face and neck. The greasy smears on the towel were as black as her hair. She sat down to eat.

My cell phone vibrated, and I stepped out into the hall to take the call.

"I have that Pinto Lake address for you," Diego Mendoza said.

I wrote it down.

"What's your next move?" he asked.

"I'm going to stake out La Herradura. Moisés, the bartender, and Aster are not supposed to leave for Pinto Lake until this afternoon, but why take a chance."

"You have the address. Why not just go to Watsonville and wait for them there?"

"No, I have to follow them all the way there. They might have Virginia stashed someplace along the way. Anyway, I'm leaving for La Herradura in a few minutes."

"Tell you what I can do. After my appointment this morning, I have some paperwork to do and phone calls to make. All I need is my laptop and cell phone for that. I can work at the Golden Nugget. I've done that many times before. That way, I can keep an eye on Moisés there."

"What if he isn't working today?"

"Then I'll sit outside his place. I know where he lives. Either way, when he leaves for Sonora, I'll give you a heads-up, that way you can relax or take care of other things. And before you ask, yes, I'm sure."

"Okay, then. I'll wait for your call. And by the way, thanks for the tip about Marshall's whereabouts. I passed it on to the Amador County sheriff. I kept you out of it."

"Gracias. Later."

Estefanía was on the phone when I walked back into the kitchen. "Great news!" she said to me and handed me the receiver.

"Marshall was arrested outside Indio, California, a couple of hours ago," Cantero said. "Blanca is now officially a prosecution witness. So are the other women. The sheriff has them in protective custody. We of course are going to do everything possible to help them stay in this country legally. Or at least get them work permits."

"That's even better."

"My wife just told me about Lula Marie's housekeeper, Aster Cellier. I can't believe she was able to get away with all these lies and secrets for so long. And a murderer! We're lucky she didn't kill Lula Marie in her sleep. Have you told the cops about her?"

"No. Aster knows where Virginia is. If I turn her in, I might never find Virginia or, worse yet, I might find her too late."

"You're right. But I bet that hyena, her father, also had Aster steal Carlota's Tears from our safe. I'm going to ask Emilia if that woman was here just before the robbery."

"It's possible. But it isn't clear how the earrings ended up in Hilda's possession."

"True. But I'm sure you'll find out why."

"Count on it. By the way, I think it'd be better if you don't tell Julio or Emilia about Virginia's possible whereabouts just yet."

When I tuned into the conversation between the sisters again, Lula Marie was saying, "So what's wrong with having faith? People need something to believe in."

"I believe in advocacy here on earth rather than faith and prayer. You want to add the prayer to your advocacy, that's fine

with me. It's your prerogative. Right now, I need a shower."
Estefanía rushed out.

A red tsunami worked its way up Lula Marie's cheeks. When she saw my puzzled look, she said, "Nothing important, really. It just irks me that she always walks out in the middle of a good argument. I need a smoke right now. Coming?"

"No. You go ahead. I want to get going soon, and I need to get my gear ready."

I walked back into the kitchen fifteen minutes later. I heard the buzz of an engine and the crunching of tires on gravel and looked out the window. Tail up, Diablo cantered from side to side of the corral. He reared, then trotted to the fence to greet Julio. The stallion sniffed his handler's face and snorted softly in his ear. Julio went to take care of the other horses. Diablo whinnied until Julio was back at his side.

"He's quite a sight, isn't he?" Estefanía said behind me.

The compliment might have been meant for either the horse or the horse whisperer. But she was right on both counts. She joined me at the window. She was sporting an all-black western outfit and boots and was holding two dark leather chaps and a black hat in her hands. She saw me looking at those items. She smiled.

I returned the smile. She went out the door as Lula Marie walked back into the kitchen.

"Is Estefanía taking Diablo with her?" I asked.

"She sure is. The lucky devil's going to have fun making a mare in San Juan Bautista very pregnant."

Just before they went into the stables, Estefanía rubbed Julio's arm.

"Hmm. There they go again," Lula Marie said.

"Sometimes things aren't what they seem. Have faith," I said. She enjoyed the comment.

I was definitely getting restless. If all that talk about illicit love and death didn't kill me, inactivity would. I got my gear. Lula Marie walked me to my car, hugged me tight and waited until I took off.

Diablo was grazing in the small corral. I stopped the car and got out. He looked up, saw me and came to the fence. I caressed his face.

"See ya," I said.

He neighed. His head bobbed. I drove on.

The last morning of spring 2005 was swiftly moving to an end. I pulled into a service station. This Monday wasn't just the longest day of the year, it was also the warmest. The breeze did little to disperse the smell of gas fumes as I filled the tank of my car.

At a country grocery store down the road, I picked up copies of valley and Bay Area newspapers and a variety of food and drinks to have during the trip.

Since Diego Mendoza was keeping an eye on Moisés at the Golden Nugget Taverna, I decided to see what was going on at Sal Gallardo's place. I'd have to run interference in case he got too close to La Herradura. Virginia's life depended on Aster's freedom.

Waiting for the left turn onto Mono Way, I spotted Gallardo driving his SUV out of a bank's parking lot. His daughter was strapped to the car seat in the back. I made a U-turn and followed him at a safe distance through the downtown area and several other parking lots. Driving very slowly, he finally headed back to Mono Way and two miles down he turned right onto Tuolomne Road and then onto a dirt driveway. He retrieved a large bag and a doll and helped his daughter out. They went in the house.

I drove on, parked a half block from the house and checked my Tuolomne County map.

Ten minutes later Gallardo was back in his vehicle alone, driving past me down Toulomne Road. According to the map, the serpentine road led to two smaller towns and went through another Mi-Wuk Rancheria in the county. It was a busy road and drivers got upset and honked their horns at Gallardo, who drove way under the speed limit.

About fifteen miles down, Gallardo made a left turn at a signal. A few miles down, he turned onto a drive up to a parking lot. The arrow on a sign pointed the way to the Black Oak Indian

Casino. The gaming building was much smaller than the Jackson Rancheria's casino, where Diego and I had had our first meeting.

I parked and walked in, but stayed in the foyer between the outer and inner doors. Gallardo stood in the middle of the parking lot, dressed in a white *guayabera* shirt and pants that blazed in the sunlight. He scanned the area around him. After a handshake and a brief exchange with a security guard by the entrance, he shuffled to the door.

I entered the casino ahead of him and hid. He came and peeked into the café next to the front doors. He rocked slightly as if he'd just awakened from deep slumber and was still feeling groggy and disoriented. By then, he had to be aware that Aster had slipped him a "cocktail" of sedatives, although he might not know that Paladin Valenzuela had provided it for his daughter.

Gallardo checked around an island of penny slots across the aisle, then walked the whole casino floor, stopping every so often to check some areas in particular. He eventually made it back to the penny slot island he had first checked. I gathered those were his beloved Aster's favorite machines. He dropped on to a tall stool there.

I sat next to him. Perhaps I could get some answers from him. At least I would keep him away from La Herradura. I got two one-dollar bills and fed my machine.

He took no notice of me. Gone were the swaggering ways and the don't-mess-with-me attitude he had displayed at St. Patrick's. He had no weapons to fight his own heart, nothing to shield him from Aster's rejection of him.

"Aren't you Mr. Gallardo?" I asked in Spanish.

He glanced at me. He didn't answer, but he made no move to leave.

"Please accept my condolences for your loss."

He replied with a barely audible "Gracias." But this time he stared at me and blinked a few times.

"We met at St. Patrick's Church, at the rosary said for your wife's eternal rest," I said.

He leaned forward as if he were getting ready to stand up. But despondency or drugs weighed on him like a ton of fool's gold. He reeled and landed back onto his stool.

"I know who you are," he deadpanned. He had switched to English.

"Then you know why I'm here."

"You're wasting your time, lady. I did not kill my wife." He rubbed the stubble on his cheeks and his goatee.

"That's between you and your god and the sheriffs. I'm not here as your judge and jury, or your jailer for that matter. I'm here only to find out what happened to Virginia Moreno and why. That's all I'm interested in."

He came alive. "Oh, yeah, La Santísima Niña—that's what my wife calls her. My wife's dead but La Santísima Niña is still fucking up my life."

"You know that's not true. Virginia Moreno has done nothing to you. She's just a young innocent woman. Your wife wanted, perhaps needed desperately to believe in something or someone. But you can't blame this young woman for your wife's indifference toward you or whatever else is going on in your life now. What *is* going on?"

I had just jumped into the shark's tank. He glared at me but said nothing. I glared back.

"If you ask me, you're just a man who . . . has loved two women who . . . betrayed him," I added.

He turned to face me. Relief segued anger in his eyes. Someone had finally acknowledged the unfairness he'd been the victim of at the hands of love. But I was sure his gratitude would be short-lived. So I pressed on. "By the way, Deputy John Marshall was caught trying to cross into Mexico. And Renato Fierro is already in custody. It won't be long before those two sell each other and everybody else out, especially you."

Gallardo smirked. His nostrils flared. But he remained seated.

"Listen. I believe you didn't kill your wife and that you're not directly responsible for Virginia's kidnapping. But you helped dispose of your wife's body, and you know who took Virginia. Those two counts make you an accessory to murder and kidnapping on top of the federal charges."

His voice was abysmally low as he said, "All I did was bring those women over the border and move Marshall and Fierro's merchandise. I wanted a better life for Aster and my son. For my daughter, too. But I never touched those women. I didn't take Virginia Moreno. And I didn't kill my wife."

"Who killed your wife, then? And where's Virginia?"

He shrugged one shoulder and then the other.

"The night she died, your wife was wearing emerald earrings that belonged to her employers. I know that Aster Cellier stole them and gave them to you. Did you think it was going to take so little to buy your freedom out?"

Bull's eye! He rubbed his thin mustache down with index finger and thumb, hard.

"Then Aster had the bright idea of kidnapping Virginia, didn't she? Was it to keep your wife Hilda under control by threatening the Santísima Niña's life?"

He shook his head, but his breathing quickened.

"Look, there's nothing I can do to you. But think about your two children, your family. If you turn yourself in now, you might cut a deal and even avoid going to prison."

"Like hell! Aster and I will never, you hear me, NEVER go to jail! We'll never let that happen. We rather . . . I'll . . . ."

He straightened up, fixed his collar and pulled his white *guayabera* shirt down. I tried not to stare at the shape of the gun stock underneath it. He made a move as if to reach for his weapon.

I stood up and reached into my handbag. I aimed my pistol at him. Staring in his eyes all the time, I said, "It's your call!"

"You really think I'm afraid of dying?" He rolled his shoulders back.

"No, but you don't want to die alone. You want *her*—Aster— to die with you. I kill you or you kill me. You'll be dead or in jail. But she'll still be alive."

Gallardo's shoulders sagged. He gave me a last look, a desperate look, then turned around and walked out of the casino.

I collapsed on the stool and wondered why in hell I had just flirted with death. I would have to deal with my idiocy later. I flipped my cell phone open and called Diego.

"This guy is bent on killing Aster and himself. I have the feeling that he and Aster made a pact to die together. She might be backing out of the deal. But it's a matter of time before he heads to La Herradura," I said.

"Are you calling the cops?"

"I can't call the cops just yet. If they catch up with Aster, I might never find Virginia alive. I need Valenzuela's number. He won't know who gave it to me. I swear."

Diego hesitated but finally gave me the number. I found a pay phone and dialed it. Valenzuela answered the phone on the first ring.

"Sal Gallardo has a gun. It won't be long before he's headed your way." I hung up.

In a matter of minutes, I had gone from defending the innocent to protecting the guilty. It was the right thing to do, but the certitude left a bitter, acrid taste in my mouth.

It was exactly one o'clock when I squeezed between a Cal-Trans pickup and a Ford Taurus. A half mile up the road, the Cal-Trans workers were repairing potholes in the road. The spot I chose offered a clear view of the gate at La Herradura. Spectacular views of the sierra and a portable toilet facility were added pluses.

My eyes drank in the beauty of the mountains. Memories rushed up those roads as I thought of my family's annual camping trips in Yosemite Valley. My heart skipped a beat every time El Capitan came into view. The three-thousand-foot granite monolith was bathed in a kind of light I had not seen anywhere else.

"The light is like a thin blue cloud up here," I told my dad at the time, not knowing how else to describe its opalescent quality. It was heaven's light, and I would get to enjoy it for all eternity if I was good, he said. I never confessed to my dad that for the nine-year-old girl in me, Yosemite Valley was already heaven on earth.

My phone vibrated. Justin was at the other end. We talked briefly, and I promised to call him from Watsonville. Then I called Finn to get an update.

"The sheriff told the FBI guys that if anything happened to Virginia and she was still alive when the feds leaked it to the TV networks, he would have no trouble going public. And he would charge them all with obstruction. And believe it or not, the feds stood down." Finn laughed.

"I bet you don't see that often. But it doesn't surprise me. They're more interested in what's going on at the border, I'm sure. What about Deacon Fierro?"

"He and the others are not talking. Fierro wants immunity on all counts. Then he'll give up Deputy Marshall and everyone else and tell us what he knows about Mrs. Gallardo's death. But we already checked his home and vehicles. And we also got a warrant and checked the Gallardo residence. As far as I can tell, Mrs. Gallardo wasn't killed at Fierro's or her own home. And we have no reason to believe that Virginia was held there either. But when Sheriff Hank Thorpe added burglary to the charges, Fierro did say that Sal Gallardo gave his wife Carlota's Tears, or so Hilda told him. She probably had no idea they were stolen and was actually planning to sell them and fund a family shelter in Sonora."

"I have a pretty good idea how Carlota's Tears ended up in Gallardo's and then Hilda's possession. I still have to prove it, though. But listen, Gallardo owns a house here in Sonora. I think Hilda was killed there."

I told Finn how to get to Gallardo's house.

"But could you wait a couple of hours before you notify the Toulomne sheriff's office. I need to buy some time for Virginia."

"No problem. So what about Virginia?"

"It's very important that you keep this to yourself for now. Virginia is being held somewhere around Watsonville, in the Pinto Lake area. That's where I'm going next."

"Watsonville. I know one of the local cops there, Lieutenant Salvador Molina. Would it be all right if I called him? I can tell him only that you're collaborating with us, but that you'll explain everything when you get there. You might need his help."

"It's bound to get messy down there and I could use Molina's help to smooth things out for me with cops and sheriffs. Okay. Call Molina. But I can't stress enough the need for discretion."

"Agreed."

I shut my cell phone off and rested my eyes. Immediately, I began to shiver, but not as a result of a sudden hormone withdrawal. I was gulping air in and going back down into the water. It was dark. A little boy cried out for his mother. I heard the woman's voice again, saying, "Find this place and you'll find me."

I couldn't listen to that voice any longer. It was driving me crazy. I opened my eyes and saw Gallardo driving down the frontage road to La Herradura. Just then my phone did another rattle dance on my lap.

"¿*Qué pasa?*" I asked Diego.

"Paladin's bartender Moisés is leaving the Golden Nugget now. He's driving a new dark red Lincoln Continental, four-door sedan. He should be there in about a half hour. Good luck."

Through my binoculars, I saw Gallardo drive up to the gate and get out. The guard got on his cell phone. Gallardo stood his ground. Whatever the gatekeeper said next didn't sit well with the spurned lover. Gallardo tried to grab at the guard through the bars. But he suddenly jumped back. I got my answer when I saw the heads and paws of two dogs charging the gate. A second later, a Jeep Cherokee came to a screeching halt just inches from the gate. A man armed with a shotgun jumped out of the Jeep.

Gallardo backtracked. The gate opened and the second guard stepped out. He made Gallardo unbutton his white shirt and hold it open, frisked him and then escorted him through the gate. Gallardo had had the good sense to leave his gun in his SUV.

I trusted that Diego was right and that Paladin Valenzuela was not a killer. My brain was constantly rewiring circuitry to do the right thing—who to spare, who to save, when to do it. This time I decided to let the drama play out all on its own.

After fifteen anxiety-laden minutes, I finally saw Gallardo walking through the gate and getting behind the wheel again. He drove past the Cal-Trans parking area. But five minutes later he was back. He parked under a tree, next to the portable toilet. Valenzuela had obviously failed to convince him that Aster and their son were not there. He would be waiting when they finally ventured outside the ranch.

Gallardo's presence complicated things for me. Warning Valenzuela again was not an option. He'd know for sure I had the ranch under surveillance.

But when I saw the Jeep Cherokee charging out of the gate and driving directly to the Cal-Trans parking area, I realized Valenzuela was already a step ahead of Gallardo. I slid down in my seat. I heard the men's loud voices, the slamming of car doors and the sound of the two vehicles picking up speed. I peeked. Gallardo was zigzagging up the road toward the freeway, closely followed by Valenzuela's security goon.

Paladin Valenzuela would never know how grateful I was to him at that moment.

The Lincoln Continental drove through the gate at twenty minutes past two and rode out fifteen minutes later. Aster was in the passenger side, her son in a car seat in the back. She looked over her shoulder and waved at her father. The Lincoln whizzed by. I gave it a few seconds and started out.

I drove below the speed limit, but my heart was racing. I concentrated on my memory of El Capitan, my father and I basking in the blue opal light of a summer afternoon long ago. It helped my heart slow down to its normal pace. I raced to catch up with the Lincoln.

After three and a half hours of driving, my butt and legs were getting numb. I shifted in my seat. Despite the sunglasses, the phosphorous luminous light, peculiar to California summer sunsets, blinded me. I didn't see the sign for the junction with Highway 152 West and took the exit at the last minute.

It would take our convoy another hour to get to Watsonville. Moisés, Aster and her little boy had already stopped three times to either gas up or use the toilet and grab something to eat.

Delighted, I had watched Aster's son run after the pigeons, his mop of black curls ruffled by the breeze, his chubby dimpled arms and hands in the air, waving good-bye to the birds when they flew away from him. I hated to know what was in store for that little boy. I wanted to find an excuse to hate Aster. But I couldn't. She was a solicitous, caring mother. It was hard to believe she was someone capable of torture and murder. Was she at all thinking of her son when she drove the ice pick into Hilda's chest?

If Aster went to prison, Valenzuela might just abduct his grandson and flee with him. He probably knew by now that his chances of ever gaining full entry into Lula Marie's heart and into her world were almost nonexistent.

Lula Marie loved him, no question about it. But Estefanía and Cantero believed Paladin Valenzuela was a thief and a scoundrel, they would never accept him in their family. It would take Lula Marie all the courage she could muster to break away from her family and follow the dictates of her heart. And I didn't see her doing that. So she would have to quash her love for him until it became only a sigh of nostalgia, perhaps even a stab of regret on that Sunday's three o'clock appointment with Death in Santiago.

I turned my attention to the road. The golden glow of the sunset had been swallowed by the marine layer rolling up and over the coastal mountains. The road narrowed, twisted and wound through the eerily beautiful mountain forest. The smell of dewy eucalyptus, pine and cypress foliage found its way in. The tops of the tall trees were hardly visible in the mist, and I could see only up to the next bend on the road ahead. I had lost sight of the Lincoln.

As I drove over the mountain pass, I began to feel anxious. I instinctively looked in the rearview mirror. As far as I could see, there were no cars behind me. But I still had to fight the strong impulse to drive faster. Then, unexpectedly, I was out of the fog and the forest and on flat terrain. The red disc of the sun, sinking quickly below the horizon, was still visible from there.

A while later I saw the headlights of a large vehicle in the rearview mirror. It had to be traveling way over my seventy-five miles per hour. The dark blue SUV was soon behind me and then it zoomed past me. I stepped on the gas.

In Watsonville, Sal Gallardo still drove fast down Main Street. He didn't even see the dark red Lincoln Continental parked outside a Mexican Taquería. I parked across the street from the restaurant where I could scan the small dining room. Aster and Moisés were not there. In the Lincoln, the boy toddler was alone and asleep in his car seat.

Most of the stores and shops on both sides of the street were closed. But the lights in a small alteration shop were on. I snuck a look in it. Moisés was talking to another man, perhaps the shop owner. I went back to the car and waited.

Moisés came out of the shop carrying a garment in a clear plastic bag. Aster walked behind him holding a shopping bag. They had both changed clothes and were now wearing black shirts and pants. They got in the Lincoln and were soon on their way up Main Street to Green Valley Road.

A couple of miles down, Moisés took a right. A half block down the street, he drove up the driveway to a ranch-style house.

An old Chevrolet station wagon was parked under the street light. A man, also wearing black clothes, stepped out of the Chevrolet and waved at Moisés. I looked at my watch. It was almost eight.

I slowed down past the house. A white-haired woman limped out the front door and onto the driveway. He handed her the garment bag. She hurried back into the house, followed by the two men. Aster and her son remained in the car.

At the cul-de-sac two blocks down, I made a U-turn and parked a half block from the house. Gallardo's SUV was nowhere around. I had the feeling he knew by now where to look for Aster. They had been together at least four years. Surely she had talked to him about the Virgin's lake shrine, maybe had even taken him there.

Moisés and the older man came out of the house a while later. A woman dressed in a long, shimmering, pastel-blue dress and a darker, sparkling, flowing cape and hood stepped out of the house, aided by the elderly woman of the house.

I couldn't see the face inside the hood. I could only trust my intuition, telling me the caped and hooded woman was Virginia Moreno.

I was almost sure their plan was to leave her at the shrine by the lake so an early jogger or pilgrim would discover her the next morning. They counted on her being relatively safe there. And they would honor their promise to keep her alive.

The two men were extremely solicitous and helped the caped woman into the station wagon as if she were blind. It occurred to me that she might be blindfolded or, worse yet, drugged. The elderly woman made her way to the Lincoln. Aster got out and pulled her son out of the car. But he began to cry hard as he wiggled and squirmed and he finally pulled away from the other woman's hold. Aster picked him up and put him back in the car.

Taking Virginia from them at gun point right there would have made sense if I had been sure Moisés and his accomplice were not carrying weapons. I couldn't risk getting Virginia or the little boy hurt in the crossfire. So I had to play by their rules.

I joined the pilgrimage to the holy shrine after both vehicles had turned the corner onto Green Valley Road. I kept my distance for awhile. The Lincoln and the station wagon made a left turn onto a street past the lake park. But I had to wait for a couple of cars making the turn at the intersection. Two motorcycle cops were directing traffic, heavier than expected on a Monday evening. I wondered what was going on at the park.

The Lincoln and the Chevrolet station wagon were behind two cars trying to get into the parking lot. A large group of people milled around in the picnic area. Some were dressed in dark robes and hoods, others in gauzy light cotton gowns and capes. Young girls led a miniature horse out of a large van, decorated with flowers.

I caught sight of a hand-painted poster on an easel announcing the "2005 Solar-Lunar Midsummer Celebration," sponsored by "Plenitude: A Monterey Peninsula Witches Coven."

According to the program, the rituals were beginning at nine. Music and chanting would cease at ten. No bonfires were allowed. Witches could remain in the park, but only in silent meditation and divination, from exactly eleven forty-six, the time of the solstice, until daybreak, when the moon would be at its fullest. All activities had been authorized by the Pajaro County sheriff's office.

I assumed that the few men clad in black shirts and slacks, now lighting candles and keeping the fires burning in the barbecue pits were the male witches or sorcerers. I had to hand it to Moisés, Aster or whoever had masterminded such a plan. The solstice-lunar festivity offered an even better cover than the proverbial mantle of night.

There were a few SUV's in the parking lot, but none of them was Gallardo's. The Lincoln and the Chevrolet were finally able to get past the traffic jam. They veered onto an unpaved road at the end of the street. There were other vehicles parked in a grassy area large enough to accommodate the spillover from the main parking lot.

I circled the grassy area looking for a spot and for the two other vehicles. I saw the station wagon parked behind clumps of tall grass. The driver wasn't in it. The Lincoln was nowhere in sight. I finally had to maneuver into a very narrow parking space about fifty feet from the station wagon.

As I ran to that spot, I heard the sustained note of a flute and then the witches chanting to the beat of tambourines. Midsummer rituals had begun.

With my binoculars I scanned the area around me and the muddy path along the shore. The driver of the station wagon was standing next to the Lincoln, partly hidden behind a row of pink and white oleander about two hundred feet from me. I began to run toward them but slipped on the mud and fell down.

As I got up, my eyes slid over the lake surface. A rowboat crossed the luminous reflection of the moon on the water. A man was slowly rowing and steering it toward the opposite shore. The boat was not too far from where I was. A woman sat very still on the boat, like a statue. Her cape shimmered in the moonlight. Moisés was taking Virginia to the shrine.

I could easily lose sight of the boat if I had to run all the way to the opposite shore. Swimming was the logical option. I just hoped the lake would not turn out to be the watery grave in my vision. Shivering already, I took off my jacket, slid off my joggers, the binoculars and my holstered gun. I used my jacket to make a roll with my clothing and gun, my ID wallet and the car keys in it. I hid the bundle under the single white oleander bush there. I secured my flashlight between my loosened belt and my pants waist.

I was getting ready to jump into the water when I heard the rustling of clothes, the ground crunching and the heavy breathing of someone running in my direction. I took cover behind the oleander bush. The driver of the Chevrolet ran past me and disappeared behind the tall grasses. But he was being followed by someone else. Gallardo stopped right in front of me, gun in hand.

He didn't seem to be aware of my presence there. I scurried to the other side of the bush.

I heard the revving of a vehicle as it picked up speed. It had to be the Lincoln. If Moisés was on the boat with Virginia, then Aster was behind the Lincoln's wheel. I knew what was coming and had to fight the impulse to step out and try to stop Aster.

Instead of running away from the car, Gallardo sprinted to it. Moisés had stopped rowing, and the rowboat lulled midway between shores. Virginia was now standing on it.

I heard the screeching of tires, a thump and a scream immediately after. I looked. A lump of shadow lay on the path. But Aster had lost control of the car. It skidded and plunged into the water. Its front bobbed for a second. Then it began to slide slowly toward the bottom as if sucked in, an inch at a time, by a giant anaconda.

Moisés was now furiously rowing back. Virginia had taken off her hooded cape and had thrown it into the water. I waded in and began swimming as fast as I could toward the car. There was an innocent child in it. I prayed Virginia would be all right. When I got to the spot, I pulled out my flashlight, turned it on and dove. Swayed by the rip current created by the sinking car, I lost my sense of direction. But I kept going down until, unexpectedly, I bumped into the driver's side of the car, which was now resting at the bottom.

I was sure the water level inside the car would start rising any second. I pointed the light beam at the car window and saw Aster's terrified face. She pounded on the window. Still strapped to the seat, she struggled desperately to free herself.

My first impulse was to try to open the door. A thought about equal inner and outer pressure and the fastest way to drown stayed my hand.

Finally unbuckled, Aster managed to climb over her seat. I directed the beam to the back seat. The car seat was empty. The little boy hadn't been strapped in it.

Aster struggled desperately to pull her son up. He was wet. His head hung to his side. She hit his back hard. He came to, and she held him close. My lungs felt as if they were on fire. Larger bubbles floated out.

The water level inside the car rose faster now. The light of the full moon trickled down through the water.

I felt something brush against my shoulder. Someone grabbed my arm. I turned so suddenly that another gust of bubbles blew out of my mouth. The light beam fell on a woman's face. It was Virginia. She got a hold of my flashlight, aimed it at the door and then pointed up with her thumb. Moisés, next to her, pulled me away from the rear door of the car. He gestured for Aster to hold her son close to her chest and roll down the rear car window. Aster seemed confused. I wasn't sure she could manage all that she had to do. But I could no longer wait and swam up. With one last thrust, I broke out of the water, coughing and gasping for breath.

The radiant countenance of the full solstice moon gazed upon me as I gulped mouthfuls of air in and went back down. Halfway down I saw the beam of the flashlight getting brighter. Moisés was swimming up. Virginia was behind him, her arm around the body of the child. I didn't see Aster. Moisés shot out of the water and dove again. He went past us again on his way back to the bottom.

Slipping, falling and crawling, Virginia and I managed to get Aster's son and ourselves onto the muddy bank. While I counted and pushed on his chest, Virginia blew air into the boy's mouth. We worked on him steadily. Finally, we heard the gurgling of water and a gasp and then his troubled breathing. We sat him up. He began to sob and cried out for his mommy. I took off his wet shirt and rubbed his limbs and torso to warm him up and I pulled him close and held him tight.

Virginia was wringing her braid, twisting it so hard I thought she would pull her scalp off. She took off her wet dress, leaving the sleeveless full undergarment on. She threw the dress into the lake. Holding the little boy, I staggered up to my feet. All sorts of confusing thoughts and questions were going through my mind, but there was no time to make sense of anything.

I looked around for Gallardo. He was lying on the ground, dead or knocked out by the impact of the car.

Virginia took the little boy in her arms. Suddenly, as if to abate my confusion, she said, "He's the reason you and I are here now. You had to look for me to get to him."

I was hearing Virginia speak for the first time. Hers was the voice of the woman who had guided me the past few days through the darkness of the solstice hour, but not to the end of my journey or hers.

"My name's Virginia. What's yours, little man?" she asked the boy and softly brushed his wet curls away from his eyes.

"Jerry."

"You have to come away with us right now. Okay, Jerry?"

"Uh-huh."

In the distance, tambourines played on. The miniature horse snorted and whinnied, and another horse answered. Then I heard the sound of splashing water. The rowboat was no longer drifting. It was moving away from the shore, as if pushed by someone. The ripples pushed Virginia's dress farther out. It spread like an oil stain on the water.

I ran to the oleander bush and pulled my jacket bundle out, retrieved my holster and gun from it, and slipped my joggers back on. My clothes were still wet, but I didn't feel cold anymore.

I looked across to the picnic area when the tambourines went quiet. The faster and louder pealing of triangles announced the beginning of the silent vigil that would end at solstice. I glimpsed the ripples in the water, much closer to us than those made by the boat. I couldn't tell who was wading along the shore or if toward or away from us. But Gallardo's body was no longer where he'd fallen. I did a lighthouse search and saw the crouching white silhouette in the tall grass scurry to a spot nearer the water's edge. Gallardo was alive.

"Let's get out of here. It isn't safe," I said as I helped Virginia and Jerry up.

"It's better if I carry him piggyback," she said.

I helped Jerry up and onto her shoulders as I watched the wader crawl to the shore. Moisés had also survived. Gallardo was upon him immediately. They soon fell to the ground, wrestling. I lost sight of them in the cluster of tall grass. But I could hear the echo of slaps, punches and expletives of the two men fighting. Then, the cussing stopped. There were soft groans, fading like the last line of a song. Jerry whimpered.

"Let's go. Now!"

"Hang on, little man. We're going for a ride."

We stayed out of sight as long as we could, but the ground was so uneven and slippery, finally we had to step out onto the grassy area. We began our risky run through the clearing to the road ahead. But just before we reached it, Sal Gallardo saw us. He was still about thirty feet behind us; he'd soon gain on us.

Some of the witches were beginning to leave when we got to my car. The two motor cops were gone. A black pickup pulling a horse trailer was driving up the street.

"Get him into the car. Lie low. There's a cotton blanket on the back seat. Cover him and yourself with it."

Virginia did as told.

I put my gun between my thighs, got my key and started the car. Jerry whimpered as Virginia calmly asked him to lie still. I heard the single pealing of a musical triangle.

Steam rose from our hot wet bodies, fogging up the windows. I turned on the defogger. I pressed 911 on my cell phone and then handed it to Virginia.

"Tell the operator you're Gloria Damasco. Tell her we're at Pinto Lake, the Witches' Sabbath area. Ask the operator to patch you through to Lieutenant Salvador Molina at the Watsonville Police Department."

With partly limited vision and a prayer, I backed out of the parking spot without turning on the lights. When I could finally see out the windshield, I had to wait for a couple of cars ahead of us to get moving. Then I saw Gallardo standing at the exit of the main parking lot.

"What's happening with Molina?" I asked Virginia.

"They're trying to find him."

A van on the way out of the parking lot stopped to wait for people crossing the street. It shielded us from Gallardo but also made it impossible for us to drive out. The other driver honked and revved his engine, but Gallardo would not budge. A couple of male witches were walking to their vehicles. Gallardo pointed his weapon at them.

"He has a gun," the warlocks shouted. Other drivers left their cars in the middle of the street and scurried to safety. There was no way out for us, so I quickly maneuvered the Volvo back into the same parking slot. Not a siren could be heard in the distance.

"You see the restrooms?" I asked Virginia.

"Yes."

"When I tell you, get Jerry out, run and hide there. Try to stay low. Keep Jerry out of sight. Take the blanket. Keep Jerry quiet. I'll come to you."

Virginia handed me the phone. I got out of my car, my gun in my hand behind my back.

Gallardo was insanely determined to remain there. But he took cover behind a tree, blocking his view of us.

"Go now," I told Virginia. She crawled out of the car. Wrapped in the blanket, Jerry climbed on her back. She pulled both ends of the blanket under her arms and tied them. She made her way to the path as fast as she could.

Gallardo decided to make his move. He fired a shot in the air and took off running in the direction of Green Valley Road.

I ran down to the women's restroom after Virginia and Jerry. There, I called out to them. No one answered. I checked all the stalls to no avail. I looked into the men's restroom just in case, surprising a caped sorcerer walking in. I pushed out past him.

Outside, I turned right, then left and back, like a weather vane moved by a gusty, whimsical wind. Then I became aware only of the lapping sound of water inside my ears. "Find this place and you'll find me." This time I was certain it was Virginia's voice and the place was the shrine.

I rushed down the path to the oak grove by the water's edge. The stronger scent of gardenias and the glow of flickering candle lights at the shrine guided me down the sloping trail. In the dark, I tripped on the root of a tree, fell and rolled down the dip onto the clearing below, grazing my elbow on some wooden object there. I held the gasp in but not the tears. I rubbed my elbow and sat up. I had landed in the middle of the shrine.

Votive candles and lights in glass containers rested in rows on a tall long altar-like wood counter. To my teary eyes, each lit candle looked like a glowing cross. I closed my eyes and wiped the tears off. The burning crosses became mere candle flames again.

But their dancing lights made me feel as if I were in a hall of mirrors, where nothing was what it seemed.

I rose and stepped back until I found a place darker than the rest. Mashed against the trunk of a pine tree, I let my eyes readjust and tried to distinguish true shapes from spectral optical effect. I heard the rustling of dry leaves. I turned my head and made out a shrouded figure standing there.

"We're here," Virginia whispered.

"Thank God. Why didn't you wait for me in the restroom?"

"That man . . . he was walking into the men's restroom when we got there. And I didn't think we were safe, so we came here. But I knew you would find us."

"Is he asleep?"

"Not really. Just quiet."

Cloaked in the light cotton blanket, she held Jerry in her arms. The flickering candle lights reflected on her face, and she seemed suddenly transfigured. A heat wave traveled up my arms to my neck and cheeks. Virginia rested her head on my shoulder. I was surprised to feel twin streams running down my cheeks.

Virginia and I scrambled up to the dirt path, leading back to the picnic area. We walked along the darker side of the trail. Jerry was heavy in her arms, but she wouldn't let me carry him. I caught a glimpse of Gallardo's white outfit down the path. I was sure he was determined now to get his hands on his son, since he could no longer die together with Aster. I pulled Virginia and Jerry down.

Gallardo made a run to the bushes across the path. I looked through the binoculars and spotted someone else, hiding behind a park bench, not too far from him.

Jerry stirred in Virginia's arms and mumbled a soft "Mommy." Virginia pulled the blanket off her shoulders, wrapped him in it and laid him gently on the ground.

"Dark Dancer," she said.

Not the time to be calling for Diablo. I whispered a hush. Her neck felt hot when I touched it. Suddenly, my scalp felt as if electric eels zigzagged just underneath the skin from the nape and jaw to the crown of my head. A shiver ran up my spine and my hair stood on end.

"She's here. It's time," Virginia said, louder. She stood up and took a tentative step. I grabbed her arm, but she resisted me.

Gallardo came out of his hiding place, looked at the bench, at Virginia, at me and then he cocked his head and his gun. We all heard the neighing of a horse nearby. I trembled. The end of my vision was near. But whose death would be mourned at solstice?

I pointed my .9 mm at the hand holding the gun, too close to his torso. If I had to shoot him, I would damage more than his hand.

"Take Jerry. Hide behind that oak tree," I told Virginia. She did as told.

A police siren wailed in the distance. A horse and his rider appeared across the path from Gallardo. "Dark Dancer," I heard Virginia say again.

Gallardo stopped in his tracks. The rider jumped off and ran in our direction. Gallardo sprinted to safety behind a bush.

My heart sank when I heard Jerry's louder voice calling his mommy and his daddy. I heard Virginia's muffled hush but it was too late. Jerry's cry sent Gallardo on a fearless sprint in the open. He would get to his son, no matter the cost.

"Stop right there or you're dead!" I shouted.

Far from cowing down, he aimed his gun at me. I lunged to my left and hit the ground as Diablo appeared between Gallardo and me and reared on his hind legs. Gallardo backtracked to stay clear of the horse. Diablo reared again. I got back on my feet. Gallardo pointed his gun at Diablo. I held my breath, took aim at Gallardo's arm and fired. He went down on his knees, put a hand on his chest, fell onto his side and then his back. Diablo galloped away. Someone screamed.

"He isn't dead, he isn't dead. He can't be," I kept repeating as I rose to my feet and began my tentative walk to the spot. Then, as if in slow motion, I saw the shadow that was hidden in the bushes by the bench come out. Aster's countenance waxed in the moonlight as she rushed to her lover's side. She picked up the gun. I lifted mine, ready to fire again.

"Don't do it, Aster," I warned.

She didn't even turn to see me. She pointed the gun at Gallardo's head and fired. Then she raised the gun to her head and fired again.

The night air reeked of gunpowder and fresh blood. I didn't want to smell it. I didn't want to see their lives spurting from their wounds. But no one else was there. With a shaky hand, I felt her neck and then his for the life that was no more.

Something warm and humid rubbed against my arm. I sprang to my feet. Pain shot up and down my back. I saw the raven's black head and mane and the two white stripes just below the left ear. I rested my head on Diablo's neck and wept.

"Virginia and Jerry need you. I took them to the shrine. The cops will be here shortly. I'd better go." In a daze, I recognized Estefanía's voice. I looked up and saw her face hidden behind a layer of black gloss. She got hold of Diablo's reins, mounted and rode out.

The walk to the virgin's shrine took every ounce of energy and concentration I had left in me. Carrying Jerry over her shoulder, Virginia came out of her hiding place behind the oak that bore the Guadalupana image. Jerry began to cry, and she made me hold him. As if by magic, a sudden calm spread inside me.

"Shh. It's all right, baby." I pulled the blanket over his head so he wouldn't see his parents' bodies as we walked past them on our way back to the picnic area.

Far off, it seemed, the peals of a triangle welcomed the witches' hour. The solstice had come to pass.

POSTMORTEM/POSTVITA

A battalion of city cops and sheriff's men, among them Molina, were getting out of their patrol cars when Virginia, Jerry and I reached the picnic area. Most of the witches and warlocks and their vehicles were gone. My car was among the few left. An ambulance was parked by the entrance to the parking lot. Some of the news crews were arriving, too. A different kind of Sabbath was starting.

While the other cops busied themselves cordoning off the area and pushing back the television crews, a group of curious bystanders wandered in. Molina approached us and said, "Who are you?"

I gave him my name. Virginia took Jerry so I could reach in my pocket for my ID card.

"You're the P.I. the Amador County sheriff told me about." Without waiting for my reply, he asked. "Are they—you, all of you, okay?"

"She and I are not injured, but I'd like a medic to check the boy. He almost drowned. "

He called a paramedic over. "Check him over and let me know."

"Is it okay if she goes with him?" I asked.

Molina agreed with a nod. "I need your gun, too."

He stretched out his hand. I surrendered my .9 mm to him. He smelled it and pulled the magazine out.

"One shot recently fired."

"Before I answer your questions, I wonder if you'll let the young woman and the boy wait in my car when the paramedics finish their exam."

"Where's your car?"

I pointed at the Volvo across the way.

Our Q and A session was interrupted by the paramedics, who told Molina Jerry was all right.

"I'm going to ask all of you to wait for me in your car."

He threw a glance at Virginia, who, tired, had just put Jerry down.

"I'll help you with him." He picked Jerry up.

"Hey, Lieutenant," a cop called out, and Molina stopped and turned. "Two, man and woman. Should I call for another wagon?"

"You'd better call for a second and a third. There's someone else injured, maybe dead. His name is Moisés. I don't know his last name. You'll see him, past that parking area, about a hundred feet down the bank." I pointed to the place.

"Did you . . ."

"No, I didn't. The dead man did it."

Jerry began to cry, and Virginia reached for him.

"We'll wait for you in the car," I said.

"No, it's going to be a long night." Molina said.

He called out to another officer there. "Escort them to the department." To me he said, "I'll talk to you there after we wrap things up here."

At the police station, my hands and clothes were swabbed for gunpowder residue. Our police escort went with me to the parking lot and watched while I retrieved some underwear, a pair of pants and a shirt from my overnight bag. Back in the station, I went into the restroom, changed, put my wet jacket, shirt and pants in separate evidence bags and handed them to the cop outside the door.

Then I sat with Jerry while Virginia used the restroom. The officer in charge of us brought us dry blankets, a small carton of milk and cookies for Jerry.

I called home. "It's over," I said when Justin picked up.

"Are you all right?"

"As well as can be since I just shot a man, maybe killed . . . I can't talk right now. I just wanted to let you know Virginia's found and I am okay. I'll call you again when I get back to the Cantero's ranch. I love you."

"I love you, too, *amorcito*. Get some rest if you can."

I stared at the phone in my trembling hand for an instant. I wanted to smash it, smash something against a wall.

"Was that your husband on the phone?" Virginia asked, holding my hand.

"Yes. We've been married only a few weeks, but we've been partners and friends for, oh—about, hmm—forever."

Virginia was tickled. Jerry had fallen asleep in her arms, and she laid him on the bench.

"Maybe this is a good time to call his grandfather," I said.

I stepped aside to make the call. It took Valenzuela a long time to answer.

"Paladin Valenzuela?"

"Speaking."

"Your grandson Jerry is at the Watsonville Police Department. He needs you. It might be a good idea to come get him before Child Protective Services shows up."

In a deep, broken-up voice, he said, "I'll be there."

I heard the click at his end. He did not ask nor did I inform him of Gallardo and Aster's deaths.

Jerry begin to stir and then opened his eyes. He looked at me and smiled.

"I'll hold . . . I need to hold him," I said as I picked him up.

Two hours later, a social worker from Child Protective Services came to talk with us. The worker looked disgruntled and with good reasons. No one wanted to be awakened in the middle of the night. In no uncertain terms, she told us we had to surrender Jerry to her immediately.

Virginia took it upon herself to talk with the worker. They sat together and Virginia related what happened in a soft voice. At some point I saw Virginia reach for the woman's hand and hold it in hers. Before my very eyes, the woman's face softened and her attitude changed. She was smiling when she gave Virginia her card and asked her to give it to Jerry's grandfather as soon as he showed up.

I was in awe of Virginia, not because I believed she indeed had saintly powers. She was what people in the spiritual mantic arts called "an empath," someone who had an uncanny ability to know what grieved or troubled those she was in contact with. By appropriating their pain, feelings, fears and conflicts, Virginia knew just what to say to allay their fears, encourage their faith in themselves and to comfort and bring them peace. But this kind of empathy was also a dark gift, a state of mind and spirit that made the gifted constantly vulnerable to the dire needs of others, with little hope of shutting off the stream and finding peace herself.

I knew that Diego's love for her would never be reciprocated. Virginia loved everyone but could not be in love with anyone in particular. My heart went out to him. I moved away from Virginia and called him.

"I'm sorry to wake you but I thought you'd like to know right away."

"Is she all right?"

"Yes."

I could hear his sighs of relief between bouts of laughter and sobs. "Did she ask for . . . never mind . . . thank you," he said.

"You're very welcome."

I shut my phone off. Virginia opened her eyes as I sat back on a seat across from her and Jerry. She came to sit next to me.

"Is Diego all right?" she asked.

"He is. His heart will be, too, in time."

She was quiet.

"Are you aware that people think you can grant miracles?" I asked.

She mulled her answer over and then said, "People make their own miracles possible. I just help them to believe they can. Sometimes it works and other times it doesn't."

"What about Hilda? Why did you let her use you?"

"Hilda needed to believe in miracles more than anyone I know. I just helped her to help others."

I held her hand. "You know Hilda's dead."

"I thought so. I haven't sensed her since the night I last saw her," she said and made the sign of the cross. "I wanted so much to help her that night she came to me. I could feel her unhappiness, her pain and anguish, like a ball of black fire pushing hard against the walls. I went out the back door to talk to her. She told me I had to get away because some bad men were looking for me, that they were going to hurt me. She was scared, looking over her shoulder all the time. She told me to go to that place where I'd had my accident. She said a man, a good man, would be waiting for me there to take me to her later. He would keep me safe. Whatever happened I should stay with him."

"Did you meet the 'good man'? What did he look like?"

"I don't know what he looked like because half his face was covered."

"Was he wearing a mask?"

"No. It was more like a big black handkerchief around his nose and mouth."

"Did you see his arms? Did he have an American and a Mexican flag tattooed on each arm?"

"I didn't. He covered my eyes right away, for my protection, he said. I couldn't see anything."

"Weren't you afraid?"

"No. Somehow I knew he wouldn't hurt me. He was very polite. He kissed my hands. He helped me into a van and drove me to a house. I don't know exactly where, but I could hear other women in the next room. The house smelled funny."

"What do you mean?"

"It smelled like new clothes, like a fabric store. I can't explain it."

"What happened there?"

"There were women in the room. They were touching me, calling me *mi santísima niña*, just like Hilda used to. They were praying and asked me to pray with them, and I did. I felt their terrible pain, their sadness, their helplessness. I touched their faces. Many of them were crying and clinging to me, asking me to ask the Virgin Mary to deliver them from evil. In my heart I knew they would be all right. I told them to have faith and wait."

"Did they speak to you in English or Spanish?"

"They spoke Spanish but the men English."

"Who were the men? I thought there was only the man who took you to the women."

"There was him and another man. The polite man asked the other to take me to Watsonville, but not to lay a hand on me or he would 'pay with his life.'"

"The other man, was he Moisés, the man who brought you here?"

"Yes. It was Moisés, but I didn't know his name then. His mother is a kind woman, a good woman."

Virginia stopped and closed her eyes. She began to recite "The Lord's Prayer."

I didn't doubt that Virginia was telling me the truth as she perceived it. But I still couldn't believe that she had just gone along with Hilda's plan, trusted her with her life so implicitly.

"Did you know that the women you saw at that house were prisoners and that they were exploited by those very polite men?" I asked, after she made the sign of the cross and sat next to me again.

"No, I didn't."

"It's hard to believe what you're saying . . ."

Virginia rested her elbows on her knees and her forehead on her laced hands.

I was being blunt and insensitive to the last person in the world who deserved it. In a softer tone, I rephrased what I had to say. "You have what I call a dark gift—a heightened intuition and empathy with others that borders on mind-reading. I don't know how else to explain it. But you can sense when people have good or bad intentions; you intuitively know what's in their hearts and minds. And if what I'm saying is true, why didn't you try to do something for those women? Why didn't you try to get away and phone your family, tell the Canteros, tell someone?"

Virginia put her hand on mine. I felt guilty for being so upset at her.

She looked at Jerry sleeping and said, "I trusted in God. He had sent those men to take me to my final destination. If that meant dying, I knew there was a good reason for it. But God did not want me to die. You see, the lake was my final destination. But it wasn't until I heard Jerry calling his mom from the car that I knew I was here for him and no one else. I had seen him in my dreams many times—the small dimpled hands, the black curls and his sweet face, his tiny voice. He was my reason for being here, to keep him from harm. I couldn't have done it without that nice man Moisés or without his mother. They took care of me. When the time came, you took care of baby Jerry and me as you were supposed to do. I knew you would come. I knew the Virgin would bring you to our aid."

"God and the Virgin sure have a very messy way to get things done," I snapped.

Virginia giggled. For the first time, she was just a young woman, laughing at my caustic comment.

At that moment, Molina came out of his office and signaled for Virginia to join him. My heart skipped a beat. Just before she went in, she said, "I'll be okay. Don't worry."

Hilda, Marshall, Fierro, Gallardo, Aster—all of them were victims of their own folly, their own disregard for life. The lovers had chosen death; the others faced incarceration perhaps for life. But what about Rosita who died at the edge of the creek? She couldn't be a victim of her own folly. Those were the cases that challenged my mind and spirit. A war always ensued between what I had been taught was divine justice and what I had witnessed and believed about human justice. I always ended up at the border between reason and faith, not knowing how to blend them into one. My reason won most of the time. But the scales remained slightly tipped.

Right then and there, I would have given anything to lie on someone's lap and sleep as peacefully as Jerry was on mine. Unbridled, my mind wandered from this to that milestone, to moments of great sadness or triumphs and new beginnings in my life. I thought about the cycles of my existence and about the moment I discovered I had a dark gift but also the talent and passion for investigative work.

I remembered another little boy thirty-five years earlier. His name was Michael David Cisneros—Little Michael as we all had called him *de cariño*. I had seen him only once, already lifeless, his body defiled and his life cut short by his father's hand. But the boy's presence had haunted my dreams throughout my life. Thinking about him, as my fingers traced the contour of Jerry's warm humid cheek, I realized that I had come to the end of one of my life's cycles. What a new start would bring I wasn't sure. But when all was said and done, I subscribed with heart, mind and soul to Virginia's notions that an innocent child's life had been saved that night. And perhaps that was all that mattered.

I was ready to answer Molina's questions when he finally called me in.

Paladin Valenzuela rushed into the station at five in the morning to collect his grandson.

"I'm sorry about your loss," I said when he approached. I did not volunteer my name nor did he ask for it. Virginia handed him the social worker's business card.

"May I impose on you a little longer? I must talk with her." Paladin handed me a blanket he'd brought with him.

He left to return an hour later, a sheaf of papers in his hand. He lifted his sleeping grandson.

"Thank you. Both of you are always welcome in my home. Will you two come to visit us at La Herradura, tomorrow or maybe Thursday?"

Virginia shook her head.

"I will, alone. But I'll call ahead to let you know," I said.

Valenzuela left, holding Jerry tight against his chest.

Much later, Julio, Estefanía and Lula Marie walked into the station as Molina was telling me that the medical examiner had issued his preliminary report. He had determined that Sal Gallardo did not die as the result of the shot I'd fired. Both Aster's and his death were unofficially a case of homicide and suicide. Moisés was alive but in critical condition; his doctors were cautiously optimistic.

"Miss Moreno, you're free to go. Mrs. Damasco, you can go, too. But I'll be in touch soon."

He handed me my ID wallet, my gun and a property release form. I signed it.

"Julio and I will take Virginia home. Lula Marie will drive you back to the ranch," Estefanía said.

She wrapped a navy blue throw blanket around Virginia's shoulders and a gray one around mine.

I was too emotionally and physically exhausted to utter even a yes, let alone a protest. Having been a passenger in Lula Marie's truck when I first arrived in the California Shenandoah Valley, I hesitated to put my life in her hands. But I was in no condition to drive. Resigned, I made the sign of the cross mentally. Virginia reached for my hand. I caught her sympathetic smile.

The marine layer was still dense when we headed out of Watsonville. Despite my efforts to remain awake and talk with Lula Marie, lulled by the hum of the engine, I fell into sound dreamless slumber. I did not stir until we arrived at the ranch three and a half hours later. Even then, my eyes closed again fast.

So as not to disturb my rest by helping me into the house, Lula Marie parked the Volvo under one of the oak trees by the house, rolled down the windows and left me there. Convinced that my life was in danger, an hour later I bolted into consciousness.

Everyone, except Virginia, who was still asleep, was gathered in celebration and cheered when I walked into the house. Judging by the heavenly aromas emanating from the kitchen, Emilia was already busy preparing a banquet.

"Come, come. Sit down. Would you like some gazpacho and a glass of champagne?" Cantero asked.

"What she needs right now is a soak in the tub and fresh clothes," Lula Marie said, already walking me down the hall to my room.

Soon I was undressing and wrapping myself in an oversized white towel that smelled of lavender. Lula Marie ran a bath for me with all kinds of aromatic salts. She sat outside the bathroom door while I soaked.

"Paladin called me this morning. He wants to see me and asked if I'd go with you to his house tomorrow," Lula Marie said.

I would have preferred not to talk about him at the moment. But it was useless and I decided just to listen.

"I told him it was over between us."

A fractured laugh followed an "oh, dear," and then a sniffle.

"Are you all right?" I asked.

"Yes, it's just that . . . how do you ever know you're making the right decision?"

"No one knows, really. The heart is a clinger and doesn't let go easily. But you might want to ask yourself if you'll regret your decision, let's say five years from now."

"How in hell can anyone answer that question! Grrr. I do love him, but I can't just give up my family. And I think you know what Estefanía and Cantero think of Paladin. And what if it doesn't work out between us? Darn! Either way it hurts like hell!"

"There've been many allegations made. But there's no proof that Paladin was involved in the cattle thefts or in all this, except to make sure that nothing happened to Virginia. You'll just have to convince Estefanía and Cantero."

"Easier said than done . . ."

I heard her long sigh, seconds later the door to my bedroom closed. A tepid shower rinse got rid of the remaining soil on my skin. I brushed my teeth and tongue and rinsed my mouth several times, to no avail. I couldn't so easily scour off the bitter taste of death still clinging to my tongue. I applied cream and makeup and combed my hair without looking at myself in the mirror.

I got dressed and repacked my suitcase. Then I joined the celebration. I had a glass of milk, cold slices of turkey, some grilled vegetables, iced mineral water and a generous dish of frozen vanilla yogurt.

About three in the afternoon, Finn joined us. He was on his way home and wanted to say good-bye.

"The sheriff would like to get your statement. He'd like to see you in his office about six this evening."

"I'd better start writing it then. I want to spend as little time at the sheriff's office as possible."

"You can use the computer in my office. I'll drive you to the sheriff's when you're ready," Estefanía offered, and I accepted.

"It's been a real pleasure working with you, Gloria," Finn said, and he pressed his lips to both my cheeks.

I typed away for two hours, trying to stick only to the pertinent facts and events in Amador County. I wrote about the morning Rosita was killed, both my visits to the house where the women were kept captive, and how when I was following a lead I had literally bumped into the spurious Deacon Renato Fierro. I had shared all pertinent information with Gerald "Finn" Finley. I omitted my talks with Diego Mendoza, information about Virginia Moreno's dark empathic gift and Estefanía Cantero's ghostly activities, which I felt were of no concern to either canonic or civil law enforcement institutions. For a brief instant, I wrestled with my conscience and then decided to omit Jerónimo Paladin Valenzuela's knowledge of his daughter Aster Cellier's crimes. Justice had already been served by her death. Little Jerry Cellier Gallardo deserved a new start.

While making a copy for myself and a second for the Canteros, I looked around Estefanía's office. The folding doors of a coat closet were slightly opened, and I snuck a peek. Two black outfits hung side by side in it, one larger than the other. Two sets of chaps and two black hats rested on a shelf above them.

We waited a while at the sheriff's office. Hank Thorpe finally came out. I handed him my statement. He called the same woman deputy I had met at St. Patrick's Church and handed it to her. Then he escorted us to his private office.

A gray-haired heavy-set man stood up slowly as we entered. The pupils of his dull blue eyes opened and narrowed again, his thick purple lips parted and he sucked spit in when he saw Estefanía. He pulled up his collar with both hands and pushed back his shoulders.

"This guy is bad news," Estefanía muttered.

"City Councilman Jasper, let me introduce you to Mrs. Gloria Damasco. I believe you and Mrs. Cantero have met before," the sheriff said.

The councilman totally ignored me, but he rushed to pull out a chair out for Estefanía.

"Councilman Jasper has been anxious to meet with you, Mrs. Damasco, and inform you of his plans for restitution to your community in this case." He pulled the chair next to Estefanía's out. I sat down.

Councilman Jasper cleared his throat before speaking, but Hank Thorpe enjoyed cutting him off. He told us that the feds had full confessions from Fierro and his cohorts.

"How long before the trial?" I asked.

"There won't be a trial. Fierro has confessed to extortion, fraud, kidnapping and transporting undocumented workers across the border, and pirating goods across state lines. The hearing took place this morning. So what I'm telling you is already a matter of public record. You understand your statement was necessary as part of that record. But the case is closed. He was granted immunity by the feds, who have bigger fish to fry. They're more interested in catching the *coyotes* helping people across the border, and Fierro also has knowledge of drug traffic routes into

California and can name names. DEA agents are arriving in the morning."

"What about the case against your deputy?"

Thorpe glanced at Jasper and said, "The feds want to make an example of John Marshall. His arrest and conviction will reflect positively on the FBI and the Homeland Security Agency. Of course they will use the women's testimony to strengthen their case. The fallout, no doubt, is going to hurt the department. I don't know if you are aware of it, but our department has enjoyed the reputation of being one of the best in California. But as far as I'm concerned, Marshall, like any other law enforcement officer, should uphold higher standards than everyone else."

Councilman Jasper smiled wide. His head bobbed in agreement.

With Sal Gallardo and Aster Cellier already out of the picture, I suspected the case against Fierro for disposing of Hilda's body was weak, but I asked about it anyway.

"The D.A. sees no need for prosecution. Fierro already confessed to having witnessed the murder and moving the body. According to him, Aster Cellier killed Mrs. Gallardo in a fit of jealousy. The Tuolomne Forensic Crime Scene team says that so far forensic evidence points that way as well."

"What about his participation in Virginia Moreno's abduction?"

"Fierro admits that, as a favor to his 'dear friend,' Mrs. Gallardo, he agreed to take Miss Virginia Moreno to a safe place. Apparently, the harebrained plan to kidnap young Miss Moreno was Marshall's, or so Mrs. Gallardo told Fierro. What Mrs. Gallardo didn't know is that her husband was also involved in this sordid affair. But smuggling people across the border is becoming more and more difficult, especially into California. And allegedly Sal Gallardo felt the risk for him personally was greater, so he was asking for more money to supply them with illegal workers for the sweatshops. But a few days later, Sal Gallardo went to Deputy Marshall with a different proposition. He agreed to continue supplying them with illegal workers. In return he expected Marshall to kidnap Virginia Moreno."

"Did he say why she was kidnapped?" I asked.

"Allegedly, Sal Gallardo wanted a divorce and hoped to trade Miss Moreno for his freedom. He was head over heels in love with Miss Cellier, and she was threatening to walk out for good unless he got a divorce. Gallardo wasn't going to make any more trips to the border unless they agreed to his request. The caveat being that Miss Moreno was to be kept from knowing who the kidnappers were so she could be returned to her family unharmed. Aster Cellier demanded that. "

"But if what Fierro told you is true, he himself wasn't doing it for the same reasons as Marshall."

"Right. When Mrs. Gallardo asked him to make sure Miss Moreno was taken to a safe place, he grabbed the opportunity to kill two birds with one stone. He would make sure nothing bad happened to Miss Moreno, and he and Marshall would get what they wanted from Sal Gallardo. So he arranged for a man by the name of Moisés, allegedly the bartender at the Golden Nugget Taverna, to take Miss Moreno to the home where he kept the captive women, before taking her to the bartender's home in Watsonville. He was to keep her there until they could find a way to let her go. You know the rest, Mrs. Damasco, since you provided us with essential information in this respect. We appreciate your collaboration."

"You're welcome. But how did Fierro happen to witness Mrs. Gallardo's murder?"

Sheriff Thorpe snuck a glance at the councilman, who gave his okay with a head nod.

"Fierro got a call from Mrs. Gallardo. He thought at first that she just wanted to make sure Miss Moreno was safe, but he soon found out that wasn't it. Mrs. Gallardo had found out about her husband's affair with Miss Cellier and was on her way to Sonora to catch her husband in the act. It was after three in the morning. Fierro panicked. His plan was about to backfire. So he tried to talk Mrs. Gallardo out of it. But she was just leaving Jackson. So he drove to Sonora.

"The Gallardos were arguing when he got there. Miss Cellier was coming out of a bedroom. It sounded like both husband and wife were trashing the kitchen. Fierro and Miss Cellier walked into the kitchen as Mrs. Gallardo lunged at her husband. She had an ice pick in her hand. Mr. Gallardo wrestled his wife to the floor and held both her hands above her head. Miss Cellier tried to grab the ice pick away but Mrs. Gallardo managed to stab her finger.

"Fierro said it all happened so quickly. He couldn't believe his eyes when an enraged Miss Cellier picked up the ice pick and drove it twice into each of Mrs. Gallardo's hands. She dropped the pick and ran out of the kitchen. Gallardo asked Fierro to take care of Hilda while he ran after Miss Cellier, who had locked herself in the bedroom. Gallardo showed up a few minutes later with gauze and bandages, and he cleaned and wrapped his wife's hands in them. But Mrs. Gallardo was going into shock. Gallardo slapped his wife's cheek, just hard enough to keep her from fainting. He kept saying, 'Stay with me, *corazón*,' or something like that.

"He didn't notice that Miss Cellier was back in the kitchen, clearly furious. Fierro grabbed her when she went for the ice pick, but she tried to stab him with it. She got free, dropped on Mrs. Gallardo's legs and drove the ice pick into her chest, only once. But once was enough."

"Do you believe him?" Estefanía asked.

"The evidence gathered at the house in Sonora by the Tuolomne County forensic team and by ours at Fierro's house in Jackson, together with the autopsy results, supports the facts as stated by him."

"How did Fierro end up with so much money, the ice pick and Carlota's Tears 'my emerald earring' in that paper bag?" she asked.

"Mrs. Gallardo was wearing only one earring. You might remember the other earring was found at your ranch the day of the murder. Gallardo removed the earring, of course, because Miss Cellier had stolen your earrings from your safe. I understand she was your sister's housekeeper. The money was payment from Gallardo for Fierro to dispose of the body, the earring and the ice pick. Fierro said that Miss Cellier was 'a wreck,' and Gallardo was afraid she would harm herself or their son, thankfully asleep in his room. Of course, given all we now know, Fierro kept the evidence just in case he needed it."

"So that's it?" Estefanía asked.

"Not much more we can do, Mrs. Cantero. No way to disprove his account of the events that led to Mrs. Gallardo's death since both Mr. Gallardo and Miss Cellier are dead. The prosecutor feels that a trial in this case would just be a waste of tax dollars.

Fierro is getting a suspended sentence for obstruction of justice.
I'm not happy about it, but yes, Mrs. Cantero, that's it."

The councilman cleared his throat again. We all looked at him.
He straightened in his chair.

"You see, Mrs. Cantero, we, in the sheriff's office, other
Amador County agencies and the Jackson City Council are not
only interested in bringing all these people to justice. I . . . we're
looking at a greater good to come out of these tragic events. So I
have convinced the D.A.'s office and the rest of the city council
that by obtaining a confession from Fierro and the others, we can
seize some of their ill-gotten profits to benefit the victims of their
crimes and make . . ."

"And in this case, the victims of their crimes are the women
they exploited," I interjected.

Hank Thorpe blinked a few times, and his upper lip curved up
at my unexpected query.

Jasper shook his head. "You already know the answer to that,
Mrs. Damasco. Illegal aliens are considered criminals. A criminal
cannot benefit from another criminal's illegal activities. No. The
only victims in this case are Mrs. Gallardo's young daughter and
perhaps Virginia Moreno. And I say perhaps because I hear that
she went with Fierro of her own accord. The D.A. is waiting to
depose Miss Moreno tomorrow and to corroborate Fierro's testimony. But I could work that out on her behalf, and she can also
be one of the beneficiaries."

"With all due respect, Councilman Jasper, this is a matter of
conscience not law," I said, trying to remain calm. But I felt as if
a torch burned inside my chest.

"I'm sorry. Not much I can do for the illegals. Please understand, they are criminals," Jasper replied.

Estefanía pounded on Hank Thorpe's desk with her fist. "This
is absolute nonsense, Hank, totally unacceptable!"

"You're preaching to the choir, Mrs. Cantero. Unfortunately,
my hands are tied," the sheriff said.

Jasper's nostrils flared, and his tone went up. "Mrs. Cantero
and Mrs. Damasco, the fact is that folks around here are also entitled to have this situation quickly and expeditiously dealt with.
And I couldn't agree with them more. Our constituents want justice, but they also want the media circus to end."

My rage reached critical point. I stood up and faced Jasper. Not knowing what to do, Hank Thorpe and Estefanía also rose to their feet. Jasper's legs jerked but he remained seated.

"Please understand, Mrs. Damasco. No one has anything against your people. We all just want to be done with this unfortunate situation."

"Oh yes, to get rid of this mess quietly, so all of you can go back to your bucolic existence as if nothing of consequence happened here. After all, these 'illegal aliens' serve your needs, grow and harvest your food, clean your homes, fluff your pillows, do your laundry, build your homes and take care of your children for next to nothing. But these dark-skinned people's inconsequential lives are not worth even the slightest discomfort on your parts. Not much has changed since the good ol' Gold Rush days, has it?"

"Mrs. Damasco, I know how you must feel. I sympathize. But you have to understand that . . . well, I'm not justifying Deputy Marshall's criminal behavior, but it was your own people who perpetrated these crimes. Our hands are tied," Jasper said.

So there it was, the "your own people" excuse. My rage reached melting-point intensity.

"I'll ignore your last remark, sir. Criminals come in all sizes and colors. Your own Deputy Marshall is proof of that. And I won't try to explain to you how social injustice promotes crime or that dispensing justice without a good dose of empathy and compassion is a futile enterprise at best. As an agent of justice, you should know that. But please don't insult my intelligence by pretending to know how the women or I feel."

I pushed my chair until it hit the desk. Jasper squinted and stood up. He glared at me and I at him. Estefanía's eyes glowed. I picked up my handbag.

Sheriff Thorpe gave me a wide smile. "Let me just say that I am personally grateful for all you've done for us, Mrs. Damasco. I hope your return to Oakland is uneventful."

Hank Thorpe escorted us to the door, stepped out and closed it behind him.

He held Estefanía's hand in both his hands. "It's been a pleasure seeing you again, Mrs. Cantero. My regards to your husband."

The sheriff went back into his office. We could hear Councilman Jasper's loud verbal whipping of Hank Thorpe all the way to the front door.

On our way to Highway 49, Estefanía said, "I guess I owe you an explanation."

"You don't. Based on what you've already told me, your night . . . activities began when you suspected that Paladin Valenzuela was behind the rustling and arson business."

"True. Cowards like him work their evil at night. We—Julio and I—started the rumor about the Ghost of Sonora. You know the rest."

"I figured as much. Did you ever get the proof you wanted?"

"Unfortunately, no. He's smart; he covered his tracks well. But there's no doubt in my mind he orchestrated Virginia's kidnapping."

"You heard the sheriff. Valenzuela's name didn't come up once." I took a deep breath and asked, "Did you and Julio ever suspect that the captive women were kept in that so-called haunted house?"

"Not really. Julio was almost sure that the place was used for illegal dog fights. We called the Animal Control hotline. Nothing happened. Now we know that Marshall made sure no one did anything about it."

"I gather you were the one who came to Rosita and Blanca's rescue. It would explain why your husband was so set on tracking the mountain lion that night. He feared for your safety. I'm assuming he knows about your nightly excursions."

"I'd never do anything like that behind his back. I told him when Virginia had her accident. I think she recognized Julio that night. I was out of town. Now you understand why we felt so guilty. And I couldn't tell Lula Marie about it then."

"I know she's very confused about your relationship with Julio. Perhaps it's time for the two of you to have a heart-to-heart. Maybe about Paladin, too."

"What makes you think there's a need for Lula Marie and me to talk about him? I'll never welcome Paladin into our family."

"I know that *you*, Estefanía, won't. But I hope you ask the Ghost of Sonora if *she* will. She seems to have a fairly good sense of what justice is all about."

"Hmm."

Back at the ranch, the mood was still festive. Virginia looked happy for awhile, but she left the party early. I followed her to the stables soon after. I found her with her eyes closed, lying on the hay beside Diablo. I sat on the other side.

I was feeling more confused than tired. I had to admit that the thought of taking a long break from the detective business was becoming very appealing. But what would I do with my dark gift? "That is the question," I said under my breath.

Virginia rolled to her side. "This isn't the right time to make serious decisions."

"Goodness! Can't I be alone with my thoughts anymore! Do you mind?"

Virginia laughed, and Diablo neighed softly.

"I guess we're both trying to decide what to do next," she said. "I don't know about you but I'm joining the Dominican order."

"Not the Carmelites, I see . . . Do you ever question yourself about your gift—doubt it?"

"Not since my accident. I accept it just the way it is, no more no less. But you do, don't you?"

"Always, especially because mine isn't a great gift. And more often than not it just gets me in trouble. I have this constant need to prove to myself that my dark gift is real. So I pursue leads, follow clues, question people, etc. until I solve the case."

"Maybe that is your real gift, and the dreams and visions are just the box, the package."

"Wow! You're too young to be so wise."

We heard snoring and looked at Diablo, who was lying on his side, asleep. We laughed and then strolled back to the cottage.

Virginia gave me a silver medal of the Virgin of Guadalupe attached to a chain.

"Tomorrow, when you see Jerry, please give this to him," she said and gave me a hug. "Drive home safely."

The door closed behind her. Sadness eddied in my chest, as when a dear lifelong friend parts company for good. I headed to my room.

"*En un rincón del alma/donde guardo la pena/que me dejó tu adiós. En un rincón del alma/se aburre aquel poema/que nuestro amor creó . . .*" Lula Marie sang softly in her room, a song about love that was no longer possible, its memory relegated to a corner of her soul, a soul filled already with longing and regret.

I pulled the covers over my head in an attempt not to listen. I tried hard to think of Justin waiting for me at home and swore that the hot stream unexpectedly running down my cheeks had been triggered by everything that had happened since I had arrived in the Gold Country. But it wasn't true. I loved Justin and he loved me. And the tears I shed were not even for the possibility that he and I would part before death did us part. They came from that *rincón,* that corner of my mind where my love for Darío Damasco, my late first husband, still lived.

Everyone was still asleep when I packed my few belongings. I got a plastic bag from the kitchen, put my holstered gun, still smelling of gunpowder, into it and buried it deep in my hardware bag. I loaded the Volvo's trunk. My eyes drank the dark misty blue of the mountains looming in the distance and the yellow of the waning oval moon, hanging high opposite the sunrise. In the kitchen, Lula Marie was making coffee. I noticed the bit of swelling under her eyes.

"You're getting an early start back to Oakland. I thought maybe you could stay, leave in the evening."

"I can't. I have another stop to make before I head home."

"At La Herradura?" she asked, taking her tired eyes away.

"Yes, I have an appointment at La Herradura."

We hugged tightly at the door. I drove out, but before I turned onto Highway 49 for the last time, I called Valenzuela and told him I was on my way.

Forty-five minutes later I arrived at La Herradura Ranch's gate. I braced my psyche in anticipation of the last emotional pounding. Paladin Valenzuela opened the front door himself.

Jerry was holding on to his grandfather's hand. I opened my arms, and Jerry walked into my embrace.

"Virginia sends this, all for you, little man," I said, as I kissed his small hand and slid the chain and medal over his head. "You can touch it anytime and remember Virginia and I love you very much. Okay?"

He looked at it and smiled, and then he hopped and skipped behind Gordo to the kitchen. Valenzuela guided me through the darkened living and dining rooms to a sunbathed deck. I put my dark glasses back on. A wide-rimmed black hat lay next to a tray that held a pitcher and two tall glasses of iced tea. He handed me a glass of tea, then reached for the hat and put it on.

I sat down. He remained standing, quiet, gazing up at the mountain stone tops crowning Yosemite Valley. In his black western slacks, pinstriped shirt and hat, he looked like a hacienda owner. He lacked the suave, urbane charm peculiar to Cantero. Not as strikingly handsome as Diego Mendoza or Julio Moreno, he, like them, however, moved with unfaltering step, as if he always knew where he was going and how to deal with whatever awaited him there. But it was in his eyes, as he greeted me at the door, that I saw that mix of angel and devil in him. It had won him Diego's admiration and Lula Marie's attention. He and Lula Marie were kindred. I was sure then that she would yearn for his embrace and passion till the day she died. Such a waste of heart, I thought.

Valenzuela turned around. "I'd like you to know I'm very grateful. All you have to do is ask and I'll see to it that you get what you wish for."

"Nothing material, thank you. But there are two or three things you can do for me," I said.

"I'm assuming you have questions for me about my daughter. I only ask that you keep all of what I say to yourself."

"Actually, that won't be necessary. I know what happened, and I'm very sorry that things turned out the way they did."

"So tell me. What can I do for you?"

"I'd like you to let Diego Mendoza off the hook. I'm sure you know what I'm talking about."

He laughed. "It doesn't surprise me that you're fond of him. I have the greatest affection for him, too. Rest assured. I destroyed the documents in question a long time ago. I just didn't tell him about it."

"I see. You were afraid he might not want to have anything to do with you once you told him. To the extent I know him, that's not likely to happen."

"I'm happy that's the case. Second wish?"

"I feel like Aladdin before the Genie," I said.

Valenzuela smiled widely, a spark of vanity in his eyes. Before he got too comfortable in his role, I continued. "I think you've already guessed that both Virginia and I are very concerned about Jerry's future. You don't have a very good track record. And with this dark cloud hanging over his young head, and if you spoil him, he might not learn to value life, his and others."

"No need to worry. I've given a great deal of thought to his future. He won't go without but I want him to know the value of honest hard work and to be a man of peace. I've had to do many things . . . *bueno*, those were my options and my choices. But my grandson and I have both had enough violence in our lives. With my daughter gone . . ."

Valenzuela raised a tight fist to his lips and repeatedly blew air through it, but even that didn't keep the tears from pouring out. Unashamedly, he let them run until he could control the outpour. He pulled out a white handkerchief from his back pocket and took care of both tears and sniffles.

"It was her sickness, bipolar disease, like her mother's, the specialists told us—my poor daughter. She was okay if she took her meds. But always so . . . mentally fragile. And Gallardo didn't help matters much. I wasn't really going to let her go to Watsonville. But I caved in, especially after Gallardo came here, looking for them. She believed . . . wanted to get La Santísima Niña's blessing and absolution. Aster wanted her to forgive her for all her sins. She was totally obsessed with that idea. And she was taking her medication, so I thought it was a good plan to get them to safety. She and Sal had been careful not to be seen together anywhere. Aster wanted it that way until he divorced his wife. She had Jerry at a hospital in San Francisco. She never told anyone who Jerry's father was. No one knew she was my daughter either. Just like my wife, she was always extremely secretive. But . . ."

His heart was heavy and mine went to him. I felt relieved when Jerry and Gordo were back. Jerry carried his own plate of food, Gordo a tray with our lunch, the best shredded beef tacos I'd ever had.

During our meal, Valenzuela talked to Jerry about all the things they would do together. I listened and laughed at Jerry's questions and Valenzuela's answers to swimming in the ocean, eating cookies like the Cookie Monster, taking Big Bird and Barney with them. And finally, the question that tied my soul in knots and brought tears to Valenzuela's eyes: Would they go in a rocket to the moon to see Mommy?

It was time to leave. I hugged Jerry and then Gordo took him to watch Barney and Friends before it was time for him to have his nap. Valenzuela walked me to my car. He opened the door for me and took my hand in his.

"If you ever need my help or want to check on Jerry, ask Diego to arrange a visit. He'll always know how to get in touch with us."

"I will. Thank you."

I got into my car. He pushed the door closed. I could still see him in the side mirror, standing by the front door when I finally went out the gate.

In two hours, I would be back in Oakland, perhaps beginning a new cycle in my life.

In time, my mind would select those memories worth preserving. The knowledge of death that had etched my conscience would not be so easily erased nor would the lessons of the heart be promptly forgotten.

But for now, like an aging gunslinger who had stared Death in the face, I was grateful that she had blinked first.

ACKNOWLEDGEMENTS

I am indeed blessed with dear friends, editors and fellow writers who have generously shared with me their knowledge, expertise and priceless feedback during the writing of this work.

My wonderful "sisters in crime research" María Herrera-Sobek, Gabriela Núñez and Susan Sotelo for providing me with essential research material on the Gold Rush Era; and Norma Alarcón, Gabriela Gutierrez Muhs and Mrs. Gutiérrez, her gracious mother, Monica Parle, and Marina Tristán, delightful and insightful companions on my research adventures in the California Shenandoah Valley, the Gold Country and Watsonville.

My husband Carlos Medina Gonzales for taking and organizing research photos and keeping me caffeinated and fed during intense, writing periods.

My friends and fellow writers Manuel Ramos and Mark Greenside for reading an earlier version of the novel and providing me with indispensable feedback.

My editors Nicolás Kanellos and Gabriela Baeza Ventura, not only for their invaluable editorial suggestions and final shaping of this book, but for their continued encouragement, support and unwavering belief in me and my work as well.

The Macondo Foundation, Sandra Cisneros and fellow Macondistas for welcoming and encouraging me, for helping my spirit to heal after one of the most disastrous and grueling years of my life.

Gloria Damasco and I thank all of you *de todo corazón*.